J. T. Edson

FEARLESS MASTER OF THE JUNGLE

CORGI BOOKS
A DIVISION OF TRANSWORLD PUBLISHERS LTD

FEARLESS MASTER OF THE JUNGLE

A CORGI BOOK 0 552 11405 7

First publication in Great Britain

PRINTING HISTORY
Corgi edition published 1980

Copyright © J T Edson 1980

Conditions of sale
1: This book is sold subject to the condition that it shall not, by way of trade *or otherwise,* be lent, re-sold, hired out or otherwise *circulated* without the publisher's prior consent in any form of binding or cover other than that in which it is published *and without a similar condition including this condition being imposed on the subsequent purchaser.*
2: This book is sold subject to the Standard Conditions of Sale of Net Books and may not be re-sold in the U.K. below the net price fixed by the publishers for the book.

This book is set in ten point Caledonia

Corgi Books are published by
Transworld Publishers Ltd.,
Century House, 61–63 Uxbridge Road,
Ealing, London, W5 5SA.

Printed and bound in Great Britain by
Cox & Wyman Ltd., Reading

*For Mike Ward of March, Cambs,
with apologies for the delay in
getting the dedication included.*

Author's note: As in the previous volumes of the Bunduki series, we are employing Earth's and not Zillikian's terms for distances, transport, measurements of time and animals, with the exception of the various types of domesticated zebras known as *'gatahs'*. We are also giving details of Dawn Drummond-Clayton's and James Allenvale 'Bunduki' Gunn's family background and upbringing in the form of appendices. J.T.E.

I would like to thank Philip José Farmer for the permission he has granted allowing me to make use of his characters, Lady Hazel and Sir Armond John Drummond-Clayton.

FEARLESS MASTER OF THE JUNGLE
IN EXPLANATION

The following is to help set the scene for new readers.
J.T.E.

When the Land Rover carrying them through the Ambagasali Wild Life Reserve in Africa had swerved and toppled over the edge of the Gambuti Gorge, it had appeared there was no escape for Dawn Drummond-Clayton and her adoptive cousin, James Allenvale Gunn; whose sobriquet 'Bunduki' was derived from the Swahili word meaning a hand-held firearm. Yet they had not been killed. Instead, Dawn had found herself alive and unharmed on open plains and Bunduki was in a jungle. Their original clothing had been changed for simple attire and certain weapons, which had not been on the vehicle, were now in their possession. Furthermore, while neither could imagine how the transfer had been made, each of them had a subconscious idea of where to find the other. In view of what had happened to them, it was fortunate that their family backgrounds and upbringings had been such as to equip them for survival under the conditions with which they found themselves faced.[1]

While searching for Dawn, Bunduki had come into contact with two members of the peace-loving, jungle-dwelling, Telonga nation. He had also met a family group

1. *Details of Dawn Drummond-Clayton's and Bunduki's family backgrounds and unconventional education are given in Appendices One and Two. J.T.E.*

of a species of giant *Australopithecus,* a pre-hominid race known to the Telongas as the 'Hairy People' who, in addition to possessing a rudimentary form of speech, used branches and roots as clubs or spears. In the course of the meetings, he had discovered that he was able to converse with both humans and *Australopithecus* in their own languages and duplicate the latter's various signalling calls.[2]

Before Dawn could locate Bunduki, she had fallen into the hands of the Mun-Gatahs; a warrior race who lived on the plains and rode various species of domesticated zebras known as *gatahs.*[3] During the time that Dawn was being held by the High Priest, Dryaka, Bunduki was captured by adherents of Charole, and the Protectress of the Quagga God. Taking advantage of the rivalry which had existed between their captors, the Earth couple had contrived to escape. Having done so, they had met one of the beings responsible for their rescue from the Land Rover, to be told where they were and why they had been saved.[4]

Dawn and Bunduki were rescued from what should have been certain death by the ultra sophisticated technology of a super-intelligent alien race which had turned Zillikian into a wild life preserve by transferring many kinds of animals, birds, reptiles, amphibians, fishes and insects from every continent on Earth. In addition, they had brought and settled various human and pre-hominid races. They continued to equip the people with homes,

2. *Like the gibbons, genus Hylobates, of Asia and the South American howler monkeys, genus Alouatta, the Australopithecus of Zillikian employed various cries and roars to warn of danger, ask for help, signify triumph, or issue a challenge which denoted a claim of ownership over a piece of territory. As some acoustic quality allowed these calls to be audible at distances far beyond the range of a normal human shout, Dawn and Bunduki used them for signalling purposes. J.T.E.*

3. *Information pertaining to the various types of* gatahs *and how they were used in the culture of the Mun-Gatah nation is given in Appendix Three. J.T.E.*

4. *Told in:* BUNDUKI. *J.T.E.*

tools, weapons, other necessities and even some luxury items, and they were known to the recipients as the 'Suppliers'. To ensure the survival of the various nations, they had also instilled cultural beliefs and customs to govern the people's behaviour and way of life. Dawn and Bunduki had been selected to act as game wardens on the planet, with the responsibility for the preservation of the human beings as well as the animals. Their appointment coincided with a threat to the existence of one nation.

As there were no harmful, disease-bearing insects, germs or bacteria on Zillikian, living conditions were so beneficial that some means of controlling the human population was essential. With one exception, warfare and raiding held the size of the various nations at an acceptable level. To prevent the numbers of the pacific Telongas increasing until their habitat could no longer support them, the 'Suppliers' had created a system of control between them and the Mun-Gatahs. Following a ritualized procedure, the former nation's 'People-Taker' and his escort made the rounds of the Telonga villages twice a year and removed a carefully proscribed number of young men and women. Morally wrong as the concept might be by Earth's standards, the system had worked successfully for generations. In return for their losses, the prolifically breeding Telongas had been granted protection from depredations by the other warrior races.

However, on his latest round of visits, the People-Taker had removed double the allowable quota. Then, on orders from the High Priest, he had returned to carry out an additional levy by abducting almost the entire population of the Jey-Mat Telgonga village in which the Earth couple were residing.

Circumstances had prevented Dawn and Bunduki from intervening. Every Telonga village had a small force of hunters to protect the otherwise unarmed and defenceless community from wild animals. To avoid the bloodshed which would have ensued if the hunters had tried to resist the levies, and to save such useful specialists from being claimed by the People-Taker, the 'Suppliers' had arranged that the hunters would always be

11

absent during the collections. Such effective cultural barriers had been established that the Mun-Gatahs had never even heard of the hunters' existence. Nor, despite realizing that some action must be taken to limit the People-Taker's activities before the Telonga nation was depopulated, had the Earth couple been able to pierce the wall of silence which surrounded the 'putting away' of the hunters. Before they could gain sufficient of their hosts' confidence to be admitted to the secret of the rite, they had discovered at first hand what was entailed. Learning that the People-Taker was coming, the Elders of the village had removed Bunduki along with the hunters. On his return, he was told that Dawn had been drugged so that she could not attempt to interfere with the 'putting away' and subsequent collection.

There had been even more terrible news for Bunduki!

While the Earth couple had been held prisoner by the Mun-Gatahs, the superlative quality of their weapons had aroused their respective captors' envy. As the People-Taker had learned of their presence in the village and knew of Dryaka's interest, he had had the Elders tortured in an attempt to find them. His victims had refused to disclose the secret of the 'putting away', but the wife of one of them had betrayed Dawn's hiding place in the hope of saving her husband's life. The unconscious girl had been carried off with the collected members of the community. Supported by the hunters, who were enraged by what they had found at the village, Bunduki had followed to wipe out the People-Taker's escort and liberate their prisoners. Unfortunately, Dawn had already been dispatched to the Mun-Gatahs' capital city, Bon Gatah. So, sending his companions back to Jey-Mat with orders that they make ready to defend themselves, he had set out alone to rescue her.[5]

Since Dawn and Bunduki had arrived on Zillikian, their attitudes towards each other had changed radically. They had grown up together on Earth, being almost as close as a brother and sister, but their feelings had

5. *Told in:* BUNDUKI AND DAWN. *J.T.E.*

changed from warm affection to real love. On the night prior to him being 'put away', she had dressed as a Telonga girl and performed the 'Dance Of The Maidens' in front of him while they were attending the wedding of their friends, Joar-Fane, 'The Loving One', and At-Vee the Hunter. By tradition, every Telonga spinster did this to signify she was willing to marry the man before whom she was dancing.

Bunduki's love would have been sufficient inducement for him to go after Dawn, but he had discovered that there was another very important reason why she must be set free. By a series of accidents, one of Dryaka's adherents had learned how to produce and make use of gun powder. With this potent substance at his disposal, the High Priest had contracted an alliance with the Protectress of the Quagga God. Using 'Terrifiers'[6] filled with the 'Thunder Powder', they had planned to gain control of their entire nation as a prelude to conquering every other race on Zillikain. However, before they could hope to achieve undisputed domination of the MunGatahs, they had been committed to presenting one of the 'Earths'[7] as a sacrifice for their nation's diety, the Quagga God. With Dawn in their power, this had seemed possible. Helped by a party of Amazons—one of whom, Beryl Snowhill,[8] was a friend from Earth who had also been transported to Zillikian by the 'Suppliers'[9]— Bunduki had effected a rescue.[10]

6. *The 'Terrifiers' were simple hand grenades made from hollowed out coconut shells filled with 'Thunder Powder'. Detonation was achieved by igniting a fuse made from an imflammable cord. J.T.E.*

7. *As there was no equivalent word in the linqua france of Zillikian, Dawn and Bunduki had said 'Earth' in English when speaking of their homeland. Being unaware of any other planets' existence, the people they met believed this to be the name of the couple's nation. J.T.E.*

8. *Some details of Beryl Snowhill's earlier career are given in:* 'CAP' FOG, TEXAS RANGER, MEET MR. J.G. REEDER. *J.T.E.*

9. *How this came about is told in:* THE AMAZONS OF ZILLIKIAN. *J.T.E.*

10. *Told in:* SACRIFICE FOR THE QUAGGA GOD. *J.T.E.*

Reunited, Dawn and Bunduki had left the Mun-Gatahs engrossed in a civil war and, parting company with the Amazons, were returning across the plains to the jungle so that they could help the Telongas to prepare for a new and more rugged way of life.

CHAPTER ONE

THEY'RE JUST WHAT WE NEED

Having carried out a successful approach through a clump of bushes, Dawn Drummond-Clayton and Bunduki came to a halt while still in concealment. Gazing at the animals which had caused them to break their journey, they decided that the delay and the trouble they had taken to reach their point of vantage was worthwhile. In fact, although there was plenty more for them to see, they had eyes for nothing else.

Rolling away to the distant horizon in every direction, the plains of Zillikian were a nature lover's paradise. The terrain was typical savannah of the kind which white settlers had jokingly and lovingly referred to as the M.M.B.A.A.; the Miles And Miles Of Bloody Awful Africa. Well watered, lush of vegetation, bespeckled at intervals by clumps of bushes and groves or individual trees, the area offered sustenance for a great variety of creatures. Some of them, such as nilgai or blackbuck from India, would not have been present in Africa; but they, along with whitetail deer and bison from America, mingled with zebra, gazelle and antelope of many kinds from various parts of that continent. They were preyed upon by carnivores other than those with which they would have had to contend in their native lands on Earth, but so carefully and wisely had the 'Suppliers' stocked the planet that the balance of nature was maintained.

Being knowledgeable about such matters, the very diversity of animal life had warned Dawn and Bunduki from the beginning that they could not be on Earth. If they had had any doubts on the matter, the animals at which they were now looking with such rapt attention would have been convincing proof that they could not be in any part of Twentieth Century Africa. There was nowhere on that continent, or any other, in which one could find a band of quagga. That particular sub-species of zebra—the name being onomatopoeic and derived from the animal's snort of alarm—had become extinct in the early 1870's.

Even if, by some miracle, a small breeding nucleus of the species *Equus Quagga Quagga* had contrived to survive undetected, they would hot have had the same appearance as the animals grazing close to the girl's and the blond giant's hiding place. The colouration was correct, variations of brown with the black and cream stripes confined to the head, neck and shoulders. However, the group of animals bore the same resemblance in conformation to wild zebras as a well bred riding horse would to the tarpan and Przewalski's horse which were the progenitors of the domestic breeds.

Two of the band stood out and it was at them that Dawn and Bunduki devoted the majority of attention. Each was suggestive of careful selective breeding for some other purpose than survival in the wild.

Standing a good seventeen hands,[1] the stallion being examined by Bunduki had a chestnut ground colour and its physical development showed that it was up to carrying a big rider.

Large in the shoe, with the concave soles open at the heels and provided with a big, flexible frog, the hooves narrowed only slightly to the coronets. Such feet were perfectly adapted to withstand the strains thrown upon them when running while bearing a rider's added weight. Above the coronets, the pasterns were at neither too straight nor too sloping an angle. Short in proportion to the forearms, the cannon-bones had an almost razor-

1. *'Hand': four inches, the height being measured to the highest point of the withers. J.T.E.*

like flatness. Long, not too horizontal forearms joined the sloping and powerful shoulders so as to cause the withers to lie farther to the rear than the elbows.

With the rib cage well sprung and offering plenty of room for the development of the vital organs, the short and sturdy back carried smoothly to long and slightly slipping hips. Being the most important portions of the animal's propulsive apparatus, the stifles had a muscular excellence indicative of tremendous power. Set high on the body, the long tail arched proudly as the stallion moved.

Of perfect proportions, the neck made a graceful curve, being fine and flexible at the junction with the head. Slightly large, but not donkey-like, the ears were carried upright upon a skull of an almost faultless diamond configuration that gave ample room for plenty of brain. Set well out on the sides of the head, the eyes glinted brightly and commanded a wide range of vision. Despite the face narrowing at the muzzle, the jaws were wide at the junction of the neck, giving ample space for the wind-pipe. The lips closed firmly over the teeth. Fine at the edges, the nostrils flared open for easy respiration. One major difference between the quagga and a horse showed in the forelock and mane. The latter rose in a crest instead of falling alongside the neck.

Perhaps four inches smaller than the stallion, the animal at which Dawn was looking was an equally fine isabelline coloured mare. Just as the pair stood out as magnificent examples of their kind, the watchers were superlative specimens of the genus *Homo Sapien*.

Kept cut short for convenience, Dawn's curly tawny hair formed a halo for a classically beautiful face which denoted breeding, strength of will, and intelligence above average in its lines. Tanned to a golden bronze, her five foot eight height was graced by a figure that would have turned many a 'sex symbol' movie actress on Earth green with envy. Its thirty-eight inch bust, twenty inch waist and thirty-six inch hips supplied contours which had no need of artificial aids. Her body was encased in a short, sleeveless, one piece dress made from the soft hide of a cow eland. Connected by leather thongs, the extremely low cut neck line left no doubt that what lay beneath was just as nature had formed it. Enhancing rather than detracting from her femininity, power packed muscles rippled under her smooth skin. Everything about her suggested that she could move with the fluid speed, grace and precision of a highly trained gymnast, or athlete, and she was both.

The simple garment, a pair of leopardskin briefs and a brown leather archer's armguard around her left wrist comprised the girl's entire raiment. About her waist was a belt on the left side of which hung a sheathed Randall Model 1 'All Purpose' fighting knife with an eight inches long blade and a 'fingergrip' hilt made from the horn of a sambur[2] stag. Nor did her armament end there. In her left hand, she grasped a recurved[3] Ben Pearson Marauder Take-Down hunting bow. It drew seventy pounds and there were eight fibreglass Micro-Flite arrows armed with Bear 4-Blade Razorhead points in the quiver attached to its right side. She had several more of the arrows in a shoulder quiver, but had left it with the *banar-gatahs* upon which she and Bunduki had been travelling since their departure from the Mun-Gatahs capital city. When taken with their surroundings and the primitive attire she was wearing, none of the weapons seemed out of place and she was highly skilled in their use.

In every detail, Bunduki's appearance was complimentary to that of the beautiful young woman at his side. However, while she conveyed the impression of a lioness's lithe and deadly grace, his was the imposing bulk and majesty of a lion.

Six foot three from his bare feet to the top of his head a curly golden blond hair, Bunduki's only garment—apart from his archer's armguard—was a leopardskin loincloth which left little to be imagined about his mag-

2. *Sambur:* Cervus Unicolour, *a species of deer originating in India.* J.T.E.
3. *Recurved bow: one with the ends of the limbs bent back from the straight line.* J.T.E.

nificent physical development. Exceptionally handsome, his face denoted similar qualities to those of the girl. He had a tremendous spread to his shoulders, with massive biceps and forearms to augment the strength they could put out when it was needed. Bronzed by long exposure to the elements, his torso slimmed down to a lean waist and a flat stomach ridged by cords of powerful muscles. His hips sat on legs so perfectly proportioned and puissant that they could carry his two hundred and twenty pounds' weight with effortless speed and agility. For all their bulk and quantity, due to the high tone and quality of his muscles, there was nothing slow, clumsy nor awkward about him.

Like Dawn, the blond giant was well—if primitively—armed. Hanging in its sheath down his left thigh he was equipped with a Randall Model 12 'Smithsonian' bowie knife. The concave ivory handle and brassed lugged hilt made Dawn's efficient weapon seem almost puny.[4] He too could indulge in archery. Custom built to his specifications, the recurved Fred Bear Super Kodiak bow had a draw weight of one hundred pounds and was fitted with an eight-capacity bow quiver. As in the case of his adoptive cousin—although he no longer thought of the girl in that relationship—he had left his back quiver with their off-saddled and hobbled mounts in order to make stalking and observing the quaggas less difficult. Nor had he brought the other piece of equipment with which he had been helped to effect Dawn's rescue.

Realizing that Bunduki's duties on Zillikian would call for him to be adequately armed, the 'Suppliers' had delivered his. m'kuki,—Masai throwing spear—and his shield. Although he had decided against encumbering himself with the m'kuki when setting out in search of Dawn, he had carried the shield hanging from the horn of his captured mount's saddle. The shield was of the same elliptical shape and size as those carried by Masai moran, warriors. However, beneath the convex outer

4. *The dimensions of the Randall Model 12 'Smithsonian' Bowie knife are given in APPENDIX ONE. J.T.E.*

cover—made from the shoulder hide of a Cape buffalo bull, with all the wrinkles smoothed out and decorated by a red and white paint heraldic device—the saucer shaped interior was formed of the kind of light weight, ultra strong fibreglass material used for the manufacture of bullet proof protective garments and it had a rim of the finest quality Swedish high carbon tool steel.

'Aren't they magnificent?' Dawn inquired, holding her voice to little more than a whisper and turning her gaze from the quaggas.

'They're the finest mounts I've seen on Zillikian,' Bunduki answered, just as quietly. 'Neither of the *banar-gatahs* you and I are riding comes anywhere near to matching them for quality.'

'*You* would insist on leaving the People-Taker's quagga gelding behind as a gesture of good will to whoever becomes High Priest,' Dawn pointed out, blatantly disregarding the fact that she had expressed complete agreement with the blond giant's decision. 'Not that it was as good as either of them, if it comes to that. I wonder how they come to be out here?"

'They must have escaped from the Mun-Gatahs,' Bunduki guessed. 'If not, they've been bred from a sire and dam that did.'

'My, how clever of you to work that out,' Dawn sniffed. 'And there was poor simple little me thinking they might be just ordinary, run-of-the-mill wild stock.' Then, becoming serious, she went on, 'As they're domesticated, or at least feral, they'll be able to survive in captivity and be trainable. If we can catch them, that is.'

'I'm all for trying,' Bunduki declared, duplicating the girl's line of reasoning. 'They're just what we need, provided we can catch and train them. Our work on Zillikian is far from finished and, if we're to do it properly in future, we'll need to be able to move around faster than we can on foot. That stallion looks as if he can carry my weight far better than the *banar-gatah* I'm riding.'

'And elephant would be better for doing *that*,' Dawn stated, starting to turn around cautiously. 'Come on, you oversize lump, let's go and see what we can do about catching them. It shouldn't be too difficult—providing that you leave all the brain work to me.'

'I'll give that a try first,' the blond giant promised, pivoting on his heel with an equal care to avoid making any unnecessary noise. 'Then, after you've made a fool of yourself as usual, I'll show you how to do it properly.'

While speaking, Bunduki was watching the beautiful young woman he intended to make his wife. She had only the previous day emerged from a very perilous situation that had brought her close to death. So, despite knowing her to be courageous, he had been wondering if the experience might have had an adverse effect upon her nerves. But her behaviour gave no sign that she had lost her usual high spirits.

'You can do that easily enough,' Dawn conceded, with the air of conferring a favour. 'Make a proper fool of yourself, I mean. But——'

The words were brought to a halt as the couple heard snorts of alarm from beyond the bushes in which they were hiding. Each of them recognized the sounds as those made by zebras which were being disturbed or frightened.

There were, Dawn and Bunduki knew, no *wild* zebras in the immediate vicinity!

'Something's troubling the *banar-gatahs!*' Dawn ejaculated, for they had left their borrowed mounts in the direction from which the snorts were originating.

'Come on!' Bunduki snapped, ignoring the possibility of making a noise that might scare away their potential quarry. 'If anything happens to them, we'll not be able to catch the quagga mare and stallion.'

CHAPTER TWO

I'D HATE TO GO THROUGH *THAT* AGAIN

When they had passed beyond the fringe of the clump of bushes, Dawn Drummond-Clayton and Bunduki needed only a single glance to know that their concern over the welfare of their borrowed mounts was well justified.

Because they had wished to make a closer examination of the band of quaggas and knowing that they could not ride near enough to do so without disturbing or frightening them, Dawn and Bunduki had left their *banar-gatahs* to graze on the banks of a small stream some fifty yards away from their place of concealment.

With a height slightly over fifteen hands, the two animals were marked by the numerous narrow black and white stripes peculiar to the Grevy's sub-species of zebra, *Equus Grevi*. However, like the quaggas, their physical conformation suggested that they had been deliberately bred for riding. Each had had its low horned, double girthed saddle—similar to those employed on Earth by Texas cowhands—and bridle removed, but the hobbles fastened to the pasterns of the front hooves were further evidence of their domestication. Such devices were useful in that they allowed the wearer to walk slowly and perform its bodily functions without too much hindrance, but not to travel far or move speedily.

Under the present circumstances, the hobbles were putting the lives of the *banar-gatahs* in jeopardy by restricting their movements. Wild eyed and snorting their distress, they reared on their hind legs to flail the air with their front limbs in a futile attempt to burst the restraints upon them. It was to no avail and they were unable to flee from the animal which was approaching.

What was more—and worse—the hobbles rendered the *banar-gatahs* incapable of acting in a normal manner. In the wild, any creature which behaved unusually would attract the attention of predators. This was happening in their case. Seeing that they did not dash away even though aware of its presence, the creature which was moving towards them and causing their alarm thought they would be easy prey.

'Oh lord!' Dawn ejaculated, staring with horror at the animal which was menacing their mounts. 'How can we stop it?'

There was, the blond giant silently conceded, good cause for the girl's consternation and question.

Supplying an answer was easy enough!

Carrying it out would be far harder!

The predator was not one which could have been encountered on the plains of Africa. In fact, if anything, it was far more dangerous than any kind of carnivore to be found roaming at liberty on that continent. Not even the largest lion could have matched it in size, weight and strength. Nor, unless conditions were favourable, could a good sized Nile crocodile have survived in a fight with it.

Almost eight feet in length—of which a mere three inches was tail—and a good half of that in height, the long, yellowish-brown hairs of the coat and various other physical features identified the predator as belonging to the California Coast sub-species of the North American grizzly bear which was designated *Ursus Horribilis Californicus*. The race's great size, truculent temperament and predilection for eating meat—particularly that of easily caught domestic animals—had caused its extinction on Earth. From all appearances, those which had been transported to Zillikian still retained their forebears'[1] feeding habits.

Slouching forward, the distinctive lump on its shoul-

1. *No pun intended, I assure you. J.T.E.*

ders giving it a decidely humpbacked appearance, the bear was clearly hungry and meant to make a meal from one, or both, of the *banar-gatahs*. Furthermore, it was superbly equipped to carry out its intentions. Supported on a short, thick neck, the skull—with its small, rounded ears placed well back and wide apart—had a bluntish muzzle and a forehead which was so strongly elevated above the line of the face as to produce a somewhat concave profile. Long and narrow though the mouth might be, it was operated by very powerful muscles and armed with sharp canine teeth to augment the broad-crowned crushing molars. While it lacked the ability to open its jaws as wide as could a member of the canine or feline species, relatively speaking, this did not render it any less capable of delivering a severely damaging bite. The great claws on the forefeet, driven by the propulsion of the sturdy legs and the enormous strength of its massively built seven hundred and fifty pounds' body made equally effective weapons.

Tackling such a formidable creature with only such primitive devices as the bows, arrows and knives—their excellent design and the superb quality of the materials from which they had been manufactured notwithstanding—was no task to be undertaken lightly.

There had been a growing tendency among certain professional naturalists and self-appointed authorities on conservation on Earth to try and foist on the public the belief that no animal was dangerous, or would think of attacking a human being without the most extreme provocation. According to the theories they propounded, the reputation of ferocity and aggression given to various animals was nothing but a tissue of lies created by sportsmen to justify hunting and killing.

Provided that Dawn and Bunduki had been willing to accept the 'discoveries' of some of the modern naturalists at face value, there was an absurdly simple and danger-free way for them to solve their dilemma. All they needed to do was advance boldly and shout at the grizzly bear who would be terrified of human beings and, anyway, would have no desire to harm them.

It was fortunate for the young couple that they appreciated the correct perspective of the naturalists' explanations. They conceded that such behaviour *might* happen on the planet of their birth, but realized it most certainly would not in the primitive world to which the 'Suppliers' had transported them. Their knowledge did not stem out of studies made from the safety of a motor vehicle in a national park where the creatures were accustomed to human beings, and where radically changed living conditions had necessitated alterations in patterns of behaviour. Furthermore, their instructors on Earth had been a family whose information had been gained by the practical experience of surviving for several decades among wild animals in completely natural, unaltered surroundings.

As Dawn and Bunduki were aware, the aggressive and dangerous animals which had been responsible for the sportsmen's stories on Earth were killed while attacking. The more cautious members of their species, who would not otherwise have been capable of winning mates and breeding before the demise of the more domineering animals, fled and survived to pass on similar passive traits to their offspring. These in turn produced young which also adopted and furthered the precept that discretion was the better part of valour.

Such a state of affairs did not prevail on Zillikian. While the dangerous creatures were hunted, it was done with such primitive weapons that they had a far greater chance of survival than when in contention against firearms. Certainly the major carnivores of the planet in particular had little need to fear human beings and considered them to be as much an acceptable source of food as any of the more conventional animal prey.

Being fully conversant with the situation, Dawn and Bunkuki reluctantly accepted that in all probability they would have to kill the grizzly bear if they wanted to save the *banar-gatahs* from injury. With that in mind, the blond giant darted a quick look to where he and the girl had left their shoulder quivers and other property, leaning against the animals' saddles. He decided against trying to reach the rigs before taking action.

Despite having had its excellent protective qualities demonstrated to him on more than one occasion recently, the blond giant realized that the Masai-style shield would not serve his purpose at that moment. Even if he could retrieve it in time, it would offer little or no defense against the grizzly's enormous weight and strength. Similar considerations ruled out an attempt to collect and don his shoulder quiver. Nor was it necessary, he was already carrying eight arrows instantly available.

Reaching up and across with his right hand, Bunduki plucked the nearest arrow from the clips of the quiver attached to the right side of his bow. So well trained was he that he did not need to look down as he started to nock the shaft to the string and settle it on the handle's arrow-rest. Instead, he glanced at Dawn. As he had expected, she did not need any advice upon the tactics they must employ to cope with their dangerous predicament. Instead of continuing to advance at his side, she was veering away, at the same time duplicating his actions in charging her bow. Moving to one side as she did so would warn their massive foe that it was facing two threats and *might* cause it to retire. Even if this did not happen, being some feet apart increased their own chances of survival.

Satisfied that Dawn was ready to play her part, Bunduki continued to advance and gave a very realistic impersonation of a lion's challenging roar. Hearing the sound, the grizzly bear's attention was diverted from the *banar-gatahs*. Because of its poor sight, it could make out little more than that two vague shapes were approaching. However, that they were doing so instead of standing back or fleeing was significant. So it reacted as it would against any other kind of carnivore which invaded its domain and showed an intention of contending with it for its selected prey.

Letting out a bawl that was just as menacing as the lion's roar it had heard, the bear swerved in the human beings' direction. It was moving fast for such a massive beast, employing a bounding gait that covered a lot of ground in a short time. With the long guard hairs of its coat bristling and seeming to increase its already impressive size, it made a terrifying sight.

Keeping Bunduki under observation from the corner of her eye, but giving the rest of her attention to the grizzly, Dawn needed no telling what to do when he caused it to turn upon them. Stepping out so as to keep pace with him, she increased the distance that was separating them and waited with bated breath to discover which of them the bear chose to attack. The answer was not long in coming.

Either because the bear considered the larger of the approaching shapes to be the greater threat, or through sheer chance, it made its way towards Bunduki. Although Dawn halted immediately, Bunduki advanced a few more steps with the intention of keeping the huge beast's attention on him.

Watching the blond giant come to a stop, the girl duplicated his next actions by starting to draw her bow. Their back and shoulder muscles, rather than those of the arms, took the majority of the strain as they pulled the strings to the full twenty-eight inches required to obtain the maximum propulsive power from the curving limbs of the bows. Even as they were reaching their 'anchor points'—with the second finger of the right hand just over the last tooth of the lower jaw—from whence they could pause and make sure of their aim, each appreciated the full peril of the course upon which they were now embarked. While confident they could kill the bear and probably would have no choice of doing otherwise, bringing this about quickly enough for safety was another matter.

Unlike the bullet from a modern medium to heavy calibre rifle, an arrow—even when propelled by the one hundred pounds' draw weight of Bunduki's Super Kodiak bow—lacked the velocity to create great shock and stopping power. Yet under the right conditions, particularly when a razor sharp four-bladed hunting point was affixed to the shaft, the actual killing potential of an arrow was greater than that of the heaviest calibre rifle bullet. Carving a cross-sectional swathe almost two inches in height and width through the recipient's flesh, the point would produce a greater volume of bleeding than any bullet. So a shaft which reached the heart or lungs would cause such extensive hæmorrhage that death would come swiftly.

On the other hand, as had happened when the blond giant had been compelled to shoot at an enraged stallion,[2] his bow was capable of sending an arrow through the bones of the grizzly's skull to its brain. That would stop it almost instantaneously. However, in the quagga's case he had been looking downwards at a target that was to all intents and purposes stationary during the draw, aim, loose and flight of the arrow. This time, he was practically horizontal to his mark and, in addition to its small size, the target area was in rapid motion. There was little margin for error. What was more, with the distance between him and the grizzly closing so rapidly, he would have time for only one shot.

Bunduki was fully cognizant of all the risks and accepted that they would almost certainly have to kill the bear, but he did not try to do so immediately he had completed the drawing of his bow. There was just a slender chance that the huge beast was only making a bluffing demonstration. If it had selected Dawn as its objective, he would not have hesitated to loose the arrow. As it was, despite the delay adding to the already great danger he was facing, more in hope than expectancy he decided to present it with an opportunity to withdraw.

The hope did not materialize!

Showing no indication that it intended to do other than press home its charge, the grizzly continued to rush nearer at a speed of close to thirty-five miles per hour. To make matters worse, as it was heading straight towards the blond giant, only a very small portion of its anatomy's most vulnerable area was exposed to his view and his aiming mark was greatly restricted.

2. *Told in:* SACRIFICE FOR THE QUAGGA GOD. J.T.E.

At last Bunduki conceded that he must yield to the inevitable!

In fact, despite understanding the blond giant's motives, to the watching Dawn it appeared that he was allowing the bear to pass beyond the limits of safety. For all her grave concern, she knew better than to say or do anything which might distract him. Instead, she concentrated her attention upon sighting her weapon at where she believed its arrow would have the most useful effect. Because of the bear's motions while moving at speed, she discarded the idea of a body shot. Only if she managed to strike an extremely limited vital area would her efforts supplement those of Bunduki, and achieving this would be far from easy. The placement of the grizzly's feet and its loose-fitting hide's seemingly rolling movements combined to create ever changing contours which rendered accurate sighting extremely difficult. Throughout its stride, the legs 'scissored' rapidly and added to the confusion. One moment the back legs would be close to the nose and the front feet under the rump, bunching the vital organs. Next the body appeared to have become extended out of all proportion, with the effect that the essential areas had changed positions in relation to the now extended frame. So she took aim accordingly.

Employing all of his skill in an attempt to maintain the correct alignment and allow for the speed at which the grizzly was approaching, Bunduki uncoiled his fingers from the bow's string. As the arrow was carried forward and he felt the slap of the string against his leather arm-guard, his instincts warned him that he had miscalculated. Not much, or through any fault of his own, but sufficient to place him in the gravest jeopardy.

Flying to meet the great beast, the blond giant's missile failed to reach its intended point of impact. He had hoped to strike the centre of the forehead just above the eyes. Instead, it passed over the top of the skull to bury almost to its fletching into the hump of the shoulders. A roar of pain, mingled with rage, burst from the grizzly's slavering jaws; but it never faltered in its stride.

Even as Bunduki was reaching for another arrow and

preparing to take what could easily prove to be futile evasive action, he heard a twang which informed him that Dawn had loosed her shaft.

Like her mate—as she now regarded the blond giant, although they had not yet gone through a formal marriage ceremony—the girl missed the mark at which she had been aiming. The error was not great, but would be enough to spoil the desired result. She too had hoped for a brain shot, seeking it at a point just below the bear's ear. Misled by the animal's speed, she saw her arrow was burying into the neck a good three inches behind where she had intended it to strike.

Finding itself being assailed from the right as well as ahead, the bear looked around. Then, to Bunduki's consternation, it began to swerve in Dawn's direction. Clearly, having discovered how painfully its challengers could strike, it had decided to tackle the smaller and, possibly, less dangerous of them.

By changing direction, the grizzly was threatening the life of the woman Bunduki loved.

In an instant, all semblance of civilization and thoughts of sympathy for the bear left the blond giant. He became a primeval savage whose mate was being endangered. For all that, the way in which he responded was far from as reckless and ill-advised as it might appear on the surface. Nor, in spite of his great anxiety, did he act without giving rapid thought to what he was doing.

Dropping the bow without liberating an arrow, but ensuring that it fell so that the quiver was uppermost, Bunduki sprang towards the great predatory beast. As he advanced, his right hand reached swiftly for the Randall Model 12 'Smithsonian' bowie knife. Flipping open the press-stud of the sheath's retainer strap in passing, his thumb and fingers enfolded the concave ivory handle.

Further evidence that the blond giant was behaving rationally and not out of a blindly impulsive rage was given by the manner in which he was arming himself. An exceptionally competent knife-fighter, he would have grasped the handle so that the blade extended below the thumb and forefinger if he had been up against a human adversary. Such a grip offered greater facility to cut, thrust and chop, but would not serve his purpose at that moment. Instead, he plucked the weapon from its sheath with the clip point[3] protruding below the heel of his clenched fist.

Just as startled as Bunduki had been at the sight of the infuriated grizzly turning upon her, Dawn duplicated his estimation of her dire straits. While her right hand was starting to pluck free a second arrow, she realized that the attacking beast would reach her before she could make use of it. What was more, despite the speed at which it was approaching, it still retained sufficient manoeuvrability to be able to counter any evasive attempt she made.

Striding out with all the speed he could muster, Bunduki converged with the grizzly. Thrusting ahead his left hand, he sank his fingers deep into and grasped the long hair on the back of the predator's neck. Giving it no chance to react to such treatment, he vaulted astride it as if making a flying mount on to a passing horse.

To Dawn, who was engrossed in trying to gauge the best moment for what would in all probability prove a pointless leap aside, it seemed as if the blond giant had suddenly materialized upon the grizzly's back out of thin air. Regardless of her surprise, she did not allow it to blind her to the fact that she was still far from being out of danger. She could guess what Bunduki was hoping to do; but she was equally aware that, even if he succeeded, it would not be swiftly enough to prevent the enraged animal from reaching her.

Massive though the bear might be, Bunduki's arrival on its back caused it to stagger a little. Retaining the grip with his left hand, he clamped his legs around the hairy ribs for added security. Seeing how close they were to the girl, he dare not waste a second. So he raised and brought around the huge knife in a semi-circular motion

3. *New readers can find an explanation of a 'clip' point in Footnote 4, Appendix One. J.T.E.*

that was powered by all the Herculean muscled force of his two hundred and twenty pounds' weight.

Made from the finest quality high carbon Swedish tool steel, the knife's blade had great strength. It was carefully tempered and designed so that it would hold an edge as sharp as a barber's razor. With the target its owner had selected, it needed all those sterling qualities. Coming around, the needle sharp tip of the clip point pierced the side of the grizzly's skull where Dawn had hoped to send in her arrow. Driven onwards, it punctured the brain for an instantaneous kill. Even so, the girl would still have been caught by its collapsing body if she had stood still.

Seeing what had happened when Bunduki jumped aboard the bear's back, Dawn had made the most of the opportunity with which she was presented. As it reeled slightly under the impact, she displayed her superb speed and agility by flinging herself in the opposite direction. Swiftly as she moved, it was only the marginal deviation in the animal's course which averted a collision. In fact, the blond giant's knee struck her a glancing blow in passing. Knocked off balance, she lost her hold of the bow and went sprawling to the ground.

Leaving his knife embedded in the bear's skull, Bunduki dived clear as it began to collapse beneath him. He landed rolling, as he had been taught to do when taking a fall. When his momentum ceased, he leapt to his feet and swung around to look at the huge beast he had killed. What he did next was a pure reflex action, stirred into being by some subconscious—or inborn—urging out of man's primeval past. Without any need for thought, he gave notice of his success in defeating such a savage and dangerous creature. Standing with his feet spread apart and fists clenched, he tossed back his head and thundered out an excellent reproduction of the *Australopithecus* male's victory roar.

Dawn had also regained her feet. Turning her head as she heard the triumphant sound which was bursting from the blond giant, she too could not hold back her pent up emotions. Running towards him, she threw herself into his arms. Oblivious of everything except each other for the moment, including the way in which the hobbled *banar-gatahs* were displaying alarm over the menacing roar Bunduki had uttered, they kissed long and passionately.

'Whew!' Bunduki ejaculated, after their emotional turmoil had been sated by the embrace. Separating, they began to take notice once more of their surroundings. 'I'd hate to go through *that* again.'

'Well, if you should have to,' Dawn replied, although she agreed with the sentiment, as she glanced pointedly at their snorting and rearing mounts, 'I hope that you remember how hearing a "Hairy Man" bellowing frightens *gatahs*. Those two are going to be too nervous to be any use to us for hunting the quaggas today. Not that it matters, though. Howling like you did has probably frightened them away.'

'It's too late for us to do anything about them today, anyway,' Bunduki called after the girl as she hurried towards their mounts. 'And another thing, the way you're nagging me now, I think I'll tell Tav-Han I want the tiger's skin back.'

'You just try it, my lad,' Dawn warned over her shoulder, the item in question having been given to Joar-Fane's father in lieu of her own parents as the traditional bride price from a Telonga hunter. 'I'm not letting you wriggle off the hook *that* easy.'

'I could always run away,' Bunduki pointed out, walking over to the bear with the intention of retrieiving his knife. 'I could always beat you in a foot ra——.'

The words trailed away as the blond giant saw two mounted figures coming over a ridge some distance to the south-east.

Apart from the party of Amazons under Beryl Snow-hill's command, no riders were likely to behave in a friendly manner!

In spite of the distance being too great for any positive identification, as one of the newcomers was clearly a man, Bunduki felt certain that they could not belong to the Earth woman's all female party!

CHAPTER THREE

DON'T COME BACK WHILE THEY LIVE

Although Charole's support for Dryaka in the abortive attempt to sacrifice Dawn of the 'Earths' had caused her to forfeit the title, 'Protectress of the Quagga God', she knew that she was fortunate not to be dead. What was more, staying alive in her present circumstances was anything but a sinecure. However, being a woman of spirit and resolution, she was determined not only to stay alive but also to regain her position of power in the Mun-Gatah nation. She realized that achieving her aims would be far from easy, which was why she was taking the chance of returning to her villa before attempting to escape from Bon-Gatah. Concealed at her private quarters were some items which she felt sure would help her attain her ambition.

When Charole and the High Priest had been knocked over the parapet of the temple's balcony at the unexpected conclusion of the sacrificial ceremony, they had fallen with him in the upper position. So his body had shielded her from the blast of the 'Terrifier' which had been thrown by one of the invaders and had exploded above them. By a piece of equally good fortune, another of the devices which she had been about to ignite had been knocked from her hand before she could do so. If it had not been, it would have gone off beneath her and she would have had no protection from its fury.

Charole had also benefited from having been clad in the attire prescribed for the Protectress when a sacrifice to the Quagga God was being made. Her magnificently endowed body was protected by a sturdy metal helmet with a crest made from the mane of a quagga, a thick oak brown breastplate of specially hardened leather, a brief kilt, greaves and sandals of the same material. So, despite having been stunned by the landing in the arena, she had not suffered any serious or incapacitating injuries.

With the High Priest's broken and obviously lifeless body draped over her as she had laid unconscious, the few people who had come close had assumed that Charole too must be dead. Nor, occupied as they were by the inter-factional fighting that had erupted following the failure to witness the promised sacrifice, did any of them find an opportunity to carry out an examination and correct the assumption.

On regaining consciousness, Charole had appreciated her very grave peril. She had made enemies even before becoming Dryaka's ally and they would want to see her pay the price of failure. After what had happened, she had not known whom she could still trust. Even her formerly loyal adherents could not be counted upon to remain staunch. So she had decided that, until she could form a better assessment of the situation, she must be wary of everybody. Also, although confident no bones had been broken, she had felt very weak and concluded it would be advisable to stay out of sight until her strength returned.

By the time she had reached her conclusions, the fighting was over in the arena and it was deserted. For all that, she had been aware that she might need to defend herself at any moment. Her ivory handled sword, shaped like the *gladius* of Ancient Rome, was still in its sheath at the left side of her gold disc belt. Yet, effectively as she could use it, there had been another and much more potent weapon readily available. The 'Terrifier' she had dropped still lay where it had fallen. None of the people who had entered the arena had touched it. They wanted nothing to do with such a—to them—inexplicable and dangerous device.

Having no such inhibitions, Charole had wriggled from beneath Dryaka's corpse and picked up the 'Terrifier'. Despite having lost the smouldering piece of cord from the perforated metal 'fire box' which was hanging from her left shoulder (thus being unable to ignite the device) she had been confident that she could use it to frighten away anybody who tried to molest her; but the need to do so had not arisen. Entering the room in which prisoners awaiting sacrifice were incarcerated, she had made her exit via one of the secret passages known to those Mun-Gatahs who held a sufficiently high office. From there, she had traversed some of the vast labyrinth of tunnels and caverns which spread beneath and even beyond the perimeter walls of the city.

Created by the 'Suppliers' as an aid to the Mun-Gatahs' inborn proclivity for intrigue, the subterranean area was ventilated and illuminated by a self-operating and maintaining power source. Attaining the status which gave access to the labyrinth was not hereditary, but came about by personal endeavour. So the 'Suppliers' were compelled to implant each who reached a specific rank with the requisite knowledge to open the secret doors and traverse the tunnels. In addition, the current six members of the ruling Council of Elders, the High Priest and the Protectress of the Quagga God each was allocated a private hiding place equipped for use in an emergency.

Charole did not relax her vigilance until she had entered and bolted the door of her hiding place. While she intended to rest, she realized that to remain in the small room for more than a short time would avail her nothing. Until she could acquire reliable and powerful support, Bon-Gatah would be an unhealthy location for her. So she would have to escape from the city and go in search of the necessary assistance.

Having removed her ceremonial clothing, which was too heavy to be comfortable, Charole settled down to rest. She took a drink of the clear, fresh water which flowed from a crack in one wall and out of a hole in the floor. There was food available, in the form of sun dried meat known as *fulsa*.[1] Having eaten, she lay on the comfortable couch and went to sleep.

On awakening, Charole had no idea of how long she had slept. However, she felt refreshed. Such was her excellent physical condition that she had completely recovered from the effects of the fall and she devoted her thoughts to the future. In her estimation, the first task was to leave Bon-Gatah until she could find out how badly public sentiment was against her and who would assume the posts of High Priest and Protectress. Secondly, she had to win over sufficient support to make it possible for her to return.

Always a realist, Charole had accepted that the time might one day come when she would have to flee for her life and she had made preparations against that day. With the exception of a mount, which was one of the reasons she had taken the risk of returning to her villa, she had everything she needed in the hiding place. She had no intention of trying to depart clad in her ceremonial attire. While it might offer protection if she should be recognized and attacked, it would also ruin her chances of slipping away unnoticed. No other woman dressed in such a fashion, so the garments would give her away even after night had fallen.

Leaving the helmet, breastplate and kilt where they had fallen when she undressed, Charole retained only the sandals. These had plain brown leather cross-straps extending to just below the knee and did not indicate that she belonged to any particular faction. She donned the silver lamé mesh halter and short skirt which formed the

1. On Earth, one name for fulsa is 'jerky'. The meat is cured by stripping an animal's hams in a manner that leaves a thin membrane covering on each of the approximately one inch thick segments. The portions are dipped in a strong solution of boiling brine, then smoked briefly before the curing process is completed by exposure to the sun. If done correctly, the result is a nourishing, palatable, long lasting, easily stored or transportable food. J.T.E.

everyday costume of a *banar-gatah* riding female warrior.[2] The uniform had sufficient status to allow her to adopt a high handed attitude if her identity was challenged.

Once dressed, using a pair of scissors and a mirror, Charole cropped at her black hair until it was short and boyish. As a disguise, it had its limitations. With the magnificent contours of her five foot nine inches' body—bust thirty-nine inches; waist, twenty-one; hips, thirty-seven—and her sensually beautiful, if arrogant, features, she could not hope to pass as other than a woman at close quarters. However, seen even at a distance, her shoulder long tresses might give her away. She was retaining the gold disc belt and, as it was her favourite weapon, the ivory handled sword which had helped to denote her rank. Until she was beyond the city's walls, it would be concealed beneath the long, hooded black 'cloak of mourning' she would be wearing.

Having completed the alterations to her appearance, Charole used the flint and steel from her 'fire box' to light another piece of the slow burning cord and coiled it inside. Realizing that to use the 'Terrifier' within the confines of the labyrinth would be as dangerous to her as to any assailant, she placed it in the leather pouch in which it was carried during the abortive sacrifice. However, she did not hang the pouch and 'fire box' across her shoulders. The cloak would have concealed them and was designed so that it could be discarded rapidly if necessary, but she did not want them to hamper her movements if there should be trouble. Instead, she carried them by their straps in her left hand and the sword was grasped in the right.

Leaving the hiding place, Charole made her way to the flight of stone steps which led to the secret entrance of her living quarters. The items she had come to recover were in a chest on the landing, but it would not be wise just to take them and then return through the labyrinth until safely outside the city. To make the only kind of

2. As Protectress of the Quagga God, Charole's garments had been made from gold lamé mesh and her female adherents wore sandals with silver coloured straps. J.T.E.

escape which would offer an adequate chance of salvation, she would need to be mounted. Provided that it had not been stolen, there was an animal ideally suited to her needs in the villa's stables.

Looking through the peephole in the wall alongside the sliding panel which gave access to her bedroom, Charole was puzzled by what she saw. She had hoped to satisfy herself that it was unoccupied before going in. It was already dark outside, but the lamps were lit and she should have been able to see what was happening. However, although the room seemed to be deserted, the drapes of her four poster bed had been drawn and it was large enough to offer concealment for more than one intruder. Furthermore, there was the matter to be considered of who had lit the lamps. She would not have expected her household staff to be attending still to such duties.

'Oh well,' Charole told herself silently. 'Standing here won't solve anything.'

With that, the woman laid down her belongings and raised the lid of the chest. Inside lay the means by which she hoped to pave the way for her reinstatement. Despite having allied herself to Dryaka, she had taken precautions in case he should try to turn against her after they had achieved their purpose. Without his knowledge, she had contrived to appropriate a small bag of the 'Thunder Powder' and one of the remarkable arrows belonging to Dawn of the 'Karths'. In addition, when it had been discovered that the latest batch of 'Terrifiers' to be delivered were filled with soil instead of 'Thunder Powder', she had collected the genuine articles which were in her adherents's possession. There were four of them and, added to the one she was already carrying, as nobody else had any—nor, since the death of Zongaffa the Herbalist, knew the secret of how they were manufactured—they formed a very potent source of power.

After Charole had transferred the bag of 'Thunder Powder' and the 'Terrifiers' to the leather pouch, she fixed the 'cloak of mourning' so it could be thrown off without an instant's delay and opened the panel. Carrying the arrow as well as the pouch and 'fire box', she stepped across the threshold with the sword ready for use. Once she was through, the entrance closed automatically.

The first thing to strike Charole as she walked forward was the lack of noise. She could not detect any sounds of activity in the building. Nor, although the windows were open, could she hear any disturbance outside. She would have expected the latter at least, considering that fighting had still been taking place elsewhere in the city when she fled from the arena.

Then Charole became aware of something which caused her to devote her full attention to her immediate surroundings.

Once before, not many weeks earlier, Charole's keen sense of smell had saved her life in that very room.[3] Her olfactory organs were now giving a similar warning that she might not be alone. However, on this occasion, the odour which was assailing her nostrils was not the fragrance of female perfume. Rather it was harsh, masculine and unpleasant, like perspiration mingling with the other emanations from a body that was rarely washed.

There was, Charole knew, only one kind of person in Bon-Gatah who invariably smelled in such a fashion.

Even as the realization was sending an alarm screeching through her mind, Charole noticed that the drapes of the bed were being violently agitated. Grasping a heavy wooden club, a figure erupted through them. With a snarl that sounded more bestial than human, it sprang towards her with the weapon raised to strike.

In spite of the way he was armed and the fact that he was clad in a white tunic emblazoned with a coloured illustration of a standing quagga, there was something brutishly inhuman about the woman's assailant. About five foot eight inches in height, the thickset and heavily muscled body was coated with shortish, curly brown hair. The somewhat stooped shoulders, disproportionately long arms and short, bowed legs seemed more suit-

3. *Told in:* BUNDUKI AND DAWN *by J.T. Edson.*

able to a chimpanzee than a man. Shaggy hair almost met the brows above the deep-set eyes, so narrow was the forehead. The snub nose, nostrils flaring like an animal's, topped a snarling mouth and a receding, bearded chin.

The attacker was, as Charole knew, a *Brelef*.[4] His sub-human race had been enslaved by the Mun-Gatahs to be employed as guards. There was no need for her to try and read the insignia on the brass 'collar of ownership' around his short, thick neck to learn where his allegiance lay. His tunic announced that he served the Council of Elders, being one of the contingent which were used to maintain order in the city.

Guessing why the *Brelef* had been concealed in the room, Charole knew that announcing her identity would not halt the attack. A trait which made the sub-humans so useful was their complete and unthinking loyalty to whoever owned them. Even as the Protectress of the Quagga God, she had had no control over the Council of Elders' *Brelefs* and would have even less authority now she had been deposed. Having been ordered to remain hidden and attack anybody who entered, he would carry out the duty regardless of who the arrival might be.

Accepting that verbal conciliation would avail her nothing and doubting whether she would have time to reach, much less open, the secret panel, Charole did not try to escape. Instead, she dropped the pouch, 'fire box' and arrow. Even as they were falling, she shrugged off the cloak and, to avoid stepping on them, took a long stride to the right. Although her rapid movement carried her clear of the club as it was driven downwards, it left her poorly placed to retaliate swiftly with her sword. Taking her weight on the right leg, as the *Brelef's* impetus carried him onwards, she snapped a side kick to the left. The sole of her foot caught him in the ribs with sufficient force to thrust him away from her, which proved fortunate.

4. *The* Brelefs *were an early type of Neanderthal Man,* Homo Neanderthalensis. *J.T.E.*

Showing surprising agility for one of his squat and heavy build, the *Brelef* changed the direction in which his club was moving. He swung it in a horizontal arc which would have caught the woman if her kick had not pushed him far enough for her to be clear of it. Nor, for all the haste in which it had been launched, would the blow have been a light one if it had landed. In fact, such was the vehemence he had used that he could not prevent himself from continuing to turn away from his objective when it missed.

Charole took advantage of her assailant's misfortune like a flash. While the majority of Mun-Gatahs tended to rely solely upon the edge of the blade when using a sword, Dryaka had taught her—without ever having heard it—the value of the Ancient Roman saying, *'Duas unicas in puncta mortalis est'*,[5] with regard to the point. Swivelling into a lunge and turning the twenty-four inches long, two inches wide blade so that it was parallel to the floor, she plunged it between his ribs and onwards until it reached his vital organs. A screech burst from him and the club left his hand. He jerked himself involuntarily away from the source of the agony that was being inflicted upon him and the action helped her to snatch the weapon free.

Liberating the sword was to be a matter of vital importance to Charole!

Even as the stricken sub-human's scream was dying out and he crashed to the floor, the connecting door to the dining-room was thrown open. Baring her teeth in a hiss of fury, the woman turned her attention to the three men who were entering. In the lead, also armed with clubs, were two more *Brelefs* of the Council's bodyguard. They were followed by a white haired Mun-Gatah of medium height whose formerly hard-fleshed, bulky body had grown soft and fat with good living. Holding a sword, he wore a white toga-like garment decorated by a rampant quagga. He was Elder Eokan and had never been

5. Duas unicas in puncta mortalis est: *advice given to Ancient Roman legionaries, roughly translated as, 'Two inches in the right spot is fatal.'* J.T.E.

friendly with Charole, so she decided that his presence could bode only evil.

For all her belief, Charole considered the elder Mun-Gatah was the least of her worries at that moment. She realized that she must defend herself against the two *Brelefs* before she could even start to think of dealing with him. However, she did not relish the prospect of a close quarters fight with the pair of brute-men.

On the face of it, Charole's solution to the predicament seemed at the least most ill-advised. Before either of the *Brelefs* could take more than three steps beyond the doorway, she flung her sword across the room. The result would have been completely satisfactory if only one assailant had been involved. Slightly in the lead, the brute-man at the right took the spear point[6] of the blade in the left breast. Dropping the club, he clutched at the hilt of the weapon which had buried deep into his vital organs. He wrenched it out with a spasmodic jerk and flung it aside. Spinning around, he staggered in front of his companion.

Employing the momentum she had gathered while throwing the sword, Charole turned and darted in the direction from which she had come. She picked up the pouch and 'fire box' in passing, leaving the arrow behind. Making for the wall through which she had entered, she had already extracted one of the 'Terrifiers' by the time she reached it. Turning to face the two men, she jabbed her elbow on to the disguised catch and the secret panel slid open. Then, dropping to her left knee in the opening, she set down the box and pouch. Raising the former's lid, she took out the smouldering cord. As she had anticipated, Eokan halted at the door, leaving the assault upon her to his remaining assistant.

Shoving aside his mortally wounded companion, with no more compunction than if he had been dealing with an inanimate object, the third *Brelef* lumbered forward. At the sight of the object in Charole's hand, a change

6. *Spear point: one where the double cutting edges of the blade come together in symmetrical convex arcs. J.T.E.*

came over him. He had been in the Council Chamber when Dryaka had demonstrated the potency of the 'Terrifiers' for the first time. While of limited intelligence, his retentive memory was sufficient for him to recall the shattering roar and the terrible devastation caused by the explosion. Letting out a howl of terror, he discarded his weapon and turned to scuttle from the room. Giving a snarl of rage as the brute-man approached, Eoken swung his sword and laid open the other's throat.

'You can put that down,' the Elder stated, as his stricken assistant stumbled onwards to collapse dying in the adjoining room. He remained by the door and continued, 'Since Dryaka failed to sacrifice Dawn of the "Earths", their power is gone.'

'Those you tried might have lost their power,' Charole replied, realizing that the Elders had been experimenting with the useless devices. 'Shall we see if this one has?'

'There's no need for that!' Eokan answered hurriedly, appreciating his peril. If the woman ignited the "Terrifier" and threw it, she could step back into the safety of the tunnel before it exploded. He dropped his sword and went on, 'I knew you were still alive—.'

'And intended to have me killed?' Charole interrupted, more as a statement than a question, nodding at the body of her first victim without relaxing her vigilance.

'To help you,' Eokan corrected. 'I only left him here to make sure nobody else could get in and wait for you. Once it was discovered that you hadn't been killed, they've been searching for you. You need a friend badly, Charole. And that's what I'm offering to be.'

In one respect, the Elder was sincere with his offer. Age had brought a greater wisdom and caution than when he had been a warrior of renown. Now he knew that it was safer to be the power behind the throne rather than the person who sat upon it. Even an opportunist, on learning that Charole was not dead, he had seen how he might attain such a position. She was not the kind to accept banishment. She would be determined to regain her lost eminence. That she had survived the explosion which killed Dryaka and had escaped from the

44

arena suggested that she had not entirely forfeited the Quagga God's favour. However, she would need help to re-establish herself. As her uncle, Elder Temnak, had turned against her when she had become the High Priest's ally, she could not obtain it from him.

Before deciding to commit himself, the ever-cautious Eokan had arranged a further test. He had left the *Brelef* hidden in the main bedroom while he was searching the rest of the villa. The way in which the woman had coped with the situation struck him as convincing proof that her fall from the Quagga God's grace was not too severe. So, providing that he could win her over, he could attain his ends.

'Has the fighting ended already?' Charole asked, wanting time to consider the offer.

'Things quietened down last night,' Eokan replied. 'They've been trying to find you all day, but I've spread the rumour that you've already fled the city. Your *banargatah* stallion is saddled and provisioned ready for you and it's safe for you to leave.'

'Why are you doing all this?' Charole inquired, realizing that she must have slept for almost thirty-six hours. She was impressed at the way the Elder had anticipated her plans.

'You're going to try and regain your lost status, if I know you,' Eokan explained. 'As I'm not averse to having the Protectress as a friend, I'll do what I can to help you. Have you any more of those hellish things?'

'Enough,' Charole answered evasively, glancing at the "Terrifier".

'Can you make more?' the Elder wanted to know.

'Yes,' Charole lied. 'But I'll need help to do it.'

'Go to Zeh-Gatah,' Eokan instructed. 'I've sent my nephew Abart there to take over as District Administrator and I'll give you a letter telling him to help you.'

'Very well,' Charole assented, although she would have preferred to receive aid from one of the larger and wealthier districts.

'There is one thing you must do before you can return to Bon-Gatah,' Eokan warned.

'What is that?' Charole challenged, although she could guess at the answer.

'Take revenge on the "Earths",' the Elder stated, as the woman had anticipated. 'Until you have, there's no hope of you ever becoming the Protectress again. Don't come back while they live, unless you bring them as your prisoners.'

'Don't worry,' Charole gritted, her face set in lines of hate-filled determination. 'I've no intention of returning until they're dead, or my captives.'

Despite Eokan having offered her the means to achieve her purpose, the woman did not tell him of her full intentions where the 'Earths' were concerned. She wanted to take them alive, not only for sacrifice to the Quagga God, but because she felt sure that they knew how to make the 'Thunder Powder' and she was determined to obtain that knowledge.

CHAPTER FOUR

THEY CAN'T BE AFTER US YET

'Forty yards at least,' Bunduki estimated *sotto voce*, studying the band of quaggas which were drinking at the stream in front of his and his companion's hiding place. 'This is as close as we can get without them seeing us, and we won't be able to get even this near once they've moved out on to the plains to graze.'

By the time the blond giant had withdrawn his knife from the grizzly bear's skull, and was on the point of collecting the rest of his armament, he had known there was no cause for alarm over the approaching figures. Although he had been somewhat puzzled by discovering that they were in the vicinity, he had recognized the two riders. In a short while, Joar-Fane and her husband At-Vee the Hunter had arrived. Their pleasure at having found Dawn Drummond-Clayton and Bunduki alive and unharmed was a tribute to the very warm relationship that had developed between the Telonga and Earth couples.

Following an exchange of delighted greetings, Dawn had suggested that all further conversation should be postponed until they had investigated the effects of the blond giant's proclamation of victory over the bear. Returning to the opposite side of the bushes, they had discovered that these were less serious than she had expected. The awesome bellow had caused the quaggas to flee, but they had not gone far and were still within visual distance. What was more, being animals with a strongly developed territorial instinct, they were unlikely to leave the vicinity unless continued harassment drove them from it.

However, as the day had been too far advanced to make any attempt to capture the mare and stallion, the quartet had sought for a safe place in which to spend the night. There had been no sign of pursuit from Bon-Gatah. Nor, considering the state of affairs in the city when they had taken their departure, did Dawn and Bunduki anticipate any at so early a date. In spite of that, they were disinclined to take chances. Anybody else who might come across them was almost certain to prove hostile and they had no desire to be compelled to leave the neighbourhood of the quaggas. So they had located a hollow not too far from the stream where a fire could be lit without the glow being visible beyond the rim. Leaving the men to take care of their mounts, the girls had gathered fuel and lit a blaze so they could cook a meal of meat taken from the dead bear. While they were eating, At-Vee had explained how he and his wife had come in search of the Earth couple.

Once the rescued population had been returned to the Jey-Mat Telonga village, Joar-Fane had insisted that she and At-Vee must follow Bunduki and help him rescue Dawn. Being equally concerned over their friends' welfare and conscious of the debt he owed to them, the Hunter had already been contemplating such a venture. It had not been his intention that his wife should accompany him, but she was adamant and he had yielded to her insistence. Leaving the rest of the hunters to organize any protection which might become necessary, they had set off on their mission. Although no member of the Telonga nation would even have considered using *gatahs* until the arrival of the Earth couple, Joar-Fane and At-Vee had now learned how to ride on the beasts which had come into their possession before the mass abduction. They had decided therefore to make use of two of the animals captured after the defeat of the People-Taker and his party so as to travel more quickly.

Following the tracks left by Dawn's abductors and Bunduki, which were becoming indistinct, the Telonga couple had heard the kind of triumphant roar given by a male *Australopithecus* at the moment of a victory. Although the sound had originated some distance to the east of the route they were following, they had decided to investigate. The 'Hairy People' were jungle-dwellers and hardly ever strayed so far onto the open plains. So they had concluded that, even if it was not Bunduki who had given the call, it might have been made by another member of the 'Earth' nation who could be of assistance in their quest.

Having described their own adventures, Dawn had left it to Bunduki to tell their friends why they were interested in the quaggas. Immediately Joar-Fane had announced that she and At-Vee would do all they could to help and her husband had seconded the assertion. Nor were they swayed from their determination when the blond giant had pointed out some of the difficulties involved in attempting to make the capture. The Earth couple were cognizant with the methods employed by the mustangers—professional wild horse catchers—who had operated throughout the 'Old West' days of the United States of America,[1] but they doubted whether any of these would be suitable under the circumstances. For one thing, they did not wish to be unduly delayed before returning to Jey-Mat and most of the old methods would have taken several days to prepare.

Remembering certain items which he had found in the saddlebags of the two *banar-gatahs* he and Dawn were using, Bunduki felt sure that he could produce a satisfactory solution to the problem. He had not mentioned it, having decided to wait until he had seen if it could be put into effect before raising the other three's hopes. Instead, he had proposed that they should take a good night's rest and this was done. On waking shortly before sunrise and ensuring that the fire was out, so there would be no smoke rising at daybreak to betray their

---

1. *A description of some of the methods employed by mustangers in the Old West can be read in:* .44 CALIBRE MAN *and* A HORSE CALLED MOGOLLON. *J.T.E.*

presence—a trick Dawn's father had taught to members of the British Army on anti-terrorist patrols in Kenya, although he had not originated the idea[2]—the blond giant had asked At-Vee to accompany him on a reconnaisance.

Leaving the girls to take care of the four *banar-gatahs*, the two young men had had no difficulty in locating their quarry. The band of quaggas were not more than three-quarters of a mile from the hollow and were in a location which would offer an opportunity for Bunduki to employ the method of capture which he had envisaged. However, as he had commented to his companion, their place of concealment was far from ideal and there were snags to be overcome.

'I've seen Dawn and you throwing ropes like those on your saddles,' At-Vee commented, referring to the coiled lariats strapped to the saddlehorns of the Earth couple's mounts and which had been one of the reasons why they had selected those particular animals. 'But you couldn't reach the quaggas from here with them, could you?'

'No,' Bunduki admitted. 'Thirty to forty feet is about as far as a lariat can be thrown, but I've something else in mind.'

'You wouldn't be able to hide behind this rock with your *banar-gatahs*,' the Hunter pointed out, as the quaggas finished drinking and began to make for the open plains. 'Of course, you could hide behind one of the clumps of bushes——.'

'They're too intelligent for us to go close enough to reach them with a lariat,' Bunduki answered. 'But there may be another way we can catch them. I'll tell you and the girls about it after we've taken a look around.'

'Whatever you say,' At-Vee assented. 'This's all new to me. I've never tried to catch any kind of animal alive.'

Six foot in height, although he did not slim down at the waist as well as the blond giant, At-Vee was broad shouldered and well muscled. His glossy black hair was

2. *In Texas during the mid-1870's, catering for outlaws and being fugitives from justice themselves, the citizens of the town called Hell had taken similar precautions against discovery. See:* HELL IN THE PALO DURO *and* GO BACK TO HELL. *J.T.E.*

cut after the fashion of Prince Valiant, but his brown and pleasantly good looking features were much like those of a Polynesian. Indicative of his profession, he was clad in a loincloth made from the hide of a jaguar. A sheathed, spear pointed knife hung sheathed on the left side of his belt. Suspended through a loop at the right was a *shilva*, which resembled a short handled pole-axe—or, more closely, a *czákan*[3]—its hammer-like head being backed by a long, slightly curved spike. In his right hand, he grasped the thick handle of a spear that matched his height and had a stout steel crossguard attached about two feet below its head. Although his arms had been designed as tools for hunting, he had learned that they could be turned into effective weapons for fighting against human beings.

'It looks like this is their regular drinking place,' At-Vee remarked, after he and Bunduki had carried out an examination along the bank of the stream. 'Will that help you?'

'It could,' the blond giant admitted, having drawn similar conclusions. 'Let's go back and tell the girls what we've learned.'

'I haven't learned *anything* worthwhile,' the Hunter objected with a grin. 'But I suppose I will one day.'

'Everything comes to him who waits, brother,' Bunduki stated and started to walk in the direction of the hollow.

'All right,' Dawn said, after the blond giant had given her and Joar-Fane a description of the situation. 'So there's a way we might be able to catch them. Now tell us the *bad* news.'

'The very earliest we can hope to try will be this evening,' Bunduki obliged. 'And perhaps not even then.'

'Hum!' At-Vee grunted thoughtfully, realizing what the blond giant was leading up to. 'If the Mun-Gatahs have settled their differences, they'll be coming looking for you to take revenge for all the trouble you've caused.'

3. Czákan: *a type of war-hammer used by Polish horsemen during the late Sixteenth and early Seventeenth Centuries. J.T.E.*

'They will,' Bunduki agreed, darting a concerned look at his companion's wife. 'Even the men we helped aren't going to overlook what I did.'

'You've had the most to do with them, Dawn,' Joar-Fane declared, appreciating why the blond giant was so perturbed and determined to prevent fears for her welfare interfering with her friends' plans to capture the quaggas. 'How much danger is there from them?'

'They won't be after us yet,' the Earth girl answered. 'From what you said, Bunduki, Charole and Dryaka must have been killed by the "Terrifier" Beryl threw after them when they fell from the balcony. It will be some time before anybody else can gain sufficient ascendancy to become the High Priest and Protectress.'

'What if they weren't killed?' At-Vee asked.

'In that case, having failed to sacrifice me as they promised,' Dawn replied, 'they will be too busy trying to save their own skins to start hunting for us.'

'All right then,' Joar-Fane said, placing her hands on her hips and eyeing the men defiantly. 'There's nothing to prevent us from staying here for a few days if necessary. Even if any of them do come after us, we'll be able to see them long before they get here. Once we're in the jungle, we should be able to cause them so much trouble that they'll turn back.'

Looking at the Telonga girl, Bunduki was amused and delighted by her attitude. At their first meeting, he had thought of her as having no interest other than that of making love at every opportunity and, to a certain degree, that had been true. However, later events had shown that she possessed intelligence, courage and fortitude. What was more, her association with Dawn had fostered a sturdy independence of will which the nature of her pacific nation had previously kept dormant. Prior to coming into contact with the Earth girl, she would never have thought of stating her opinion in such a forthright manner.

No more than five foot three inches in height, Joar-Fane had an exceptionally well developed and curvaceous figure which enhanced her pert, very attractive brown Polynesian features. Having anticipated the rigours of the quest upon which she and her husband were embarking, she had made changes to her appearance. She had cut her long black hair until it was more manageable. Instead of the usual feminine attire of her nation—a brief halter made from some kind of animal's skin and a grass skirt—she now wore a dress made from the hide of a bongo[4] which she had copied from Dawn's garment. A knife hung sheathed on the left side of her waist belt and she had carried along Bunduki's *m'kuki* in case he should need it.

'Very well,' Bunduki assented. 'We'll stay——.'

'I *knew* that you'd come round to *our* way of thinking eventually,' Dawn declared. 'Didn't you, Joar-Fane?'

'It was only a matter of time,' the Telonga girl agreed.

'We're going to have to make something before we can hope to do the catching,' the blond giant warned and told the others what he wanted them to do, finishing with, 'So let's make a start at it.'

'May I ask a question?' Dawn said, in tones redolent of suspicion.

'Please do,' Bunduki consented, his air that of one who was granting a favour.

'Thank you, *bwana mkuba*,' Dawn replied, using the Swahili term meaning "big master" but with none of the respect the honorific should have received. 'Why is it that Joar-Fane and I have to wade in the stream looking for the kind of stones you want?'

'I can't see anything wrong in that,' At-Vee commented with a grin.

'Or me,' Bunduki seconded.

'Well *we* can!' Dawn declared and Joar-Fane nodded agreement.

'Do you know something, brother?' At-Vee asked, in a tone pitched so that it was just loud enough for the distaff side of the quartet as well as Bunduki to hear what

4. *Bongo:* Boocercus Euryceros, *the largest of the African jungle-dwelling antelopes, a deep chestnut in colour, with numerous white stripes, a well developed spinal crest and large, smooth horns which form an open spiral. J.T.E.*

53

he was saying. 'I'd think twice before marrying into *that* family if I was you. The women talk too much and don't know their place.'

'I've noticed that,' Bunduki admitted, in a similar stage-whisper. Then, turning with a mock ingratiating smile to the girls, he went on in a louder voice, 'I asked you to do it because it's a little known fact that women are better than men at some——.'

'Tiger skin or not, sister,' Joar-Fane interrupted, looking at Dawn. 'I think you're marrying beneath yourself.'

'Well, dear, you've already done that,' the Earth girl replied, then directed a challenging look at her husband-to-be. 'And we still haven't had an answer that made sense. Not that either of us *expected* one.'

'If you *must* know,' Bunduki said, exuding an aura of patient martyrdom. 'Neither you nor Joar-Fane can splice a rope as well as we can, or At-Vee and I would be only too pleased to let you do it and keep the pleasure of finding the right kind of stones for ours——.'

'Come on, Joar-Fane, before I'm taken sick!' Dawn groaned, although she was willing to concede that at least part of the explanation was valid. '*They'd* never have the sense to make the right choice.'

'Oh I wouldn't say that,' the little Telonga girl protested. 'They each picked *one* thing correctly.'

'Nonsense, sister, *we* picked *them*,' Dawn corrected, before throwing a disgusted glare at the men and continuing, 'Which doesn't say much for *our* judgement, I suppose.'

With that, giving Bunduki and At-Vee no chance to reply, the girls went to the edge of the stream. Removing their dresses, which left them clad only in leopardskin briefs, they waded into the water and began to examine the small rocks and boulders which covered the bottom of the fairly swift flowing stretch near the hollow.

'That's what I like,' the blond giant remarked, watching the girls commencing the task he had set them. 'Loyal, obedient and hard-working women.'

'And that's what we Telongas had, before Dawn of the "Earths" got at them,' At-Vee pointed out, smiling. 'The trouble is I think they've changed for the better. Shall——?'

'All right!' Dawn yelled indignantly, throwing the boulder she had just picked up with sufficient accuracy to make the men jump out of its way. '*We're* working, so you two can make a start.'

Taking the hint, Bunduki led the way to where the saddles had been left. Opening his saddlebags, he took out a coiled length of cord. About half the diameter of the lariats, which had the hard-laid, triple strand texture of best quality five-eighths of an inch Manila rope, it was more pliant and was composed of half a dozen separate fibres. While he was doing this, At-Vee unpacked a ball of thin, very strong thread and several small leather pouches filled with *fulsa*, emptying the contents from six of them.

Drawing his bowie knife, Bunduki cut two lengths of about six foot six inches from the cord. Then he removed two further portions, each around thirty-nine inches long. Presenting one of each to At-Vee, he kept the others for himself. Sitting on the ground, although the Hunter was still unaware of exactly what they were producing, they set to work. Opening out the strands, each of them started to splice his shorter piece of cord into the centre of the longer segment. With this completed, they punctured holes around the mouths of the empty *fulsa* pouches and began to attach one to each tip of the connected cords.

By the time the men had performed that much of their task, the girls had dressed and returned with four round boulders about the size of billiard balls and two more, oval in shape, which were slightly smaller. Still puzzled, but receiving no enlightenment in spite of hinting that he would like information, At-Vee followed Bunduki's example by placing a round stone into the pouches on the ends of the longer piece of cord and one that was egg-shaped into that at the tip of the shorter. The pouches were then closed and held securely by having the stout thread whipped around the neck and the cord.

When the work was finished, Dawn and the blond giant each had in their possession a very reasonable facsimile of an Argentinian *bóleadora*, otherwise known as a *bola*. As neither of the Telonga couple had ever seen such a device, their interest was aroused and Joar-Fane requested an explanation of its purpose.

'I'd like to show you how they work on this pair,' Dawn replied, indicating the men with a derisive wave of her left hand. 'But, as we might need some heavy lifting done and they are *fairly* useful for that, I'd better find something I can't damage.'

'*Now* I get the idea!' At-Vee enthused, after the Earth couple had given an exhibition of the *boleadoras'* function. Then he frowned and went on, 'Will you be able to use them while you're riding?'

'They're meant to be thrown from the saddle as well as when on foot,' Bunduki answered. 'And, as the *banargatahs* have been trained for roping—which is why we chose them—teaching them to accept a *boleadora* instead of a lariat shouldn't be too difficult—.'

'You've still got to get close enough to the quaggas to make a throw,' Joar-Fane pointed out, before the blond giant could finish. 'And, from what you've told us, they're much finer animals than your *banar-gatahs*. Can you get near enough to use those things?'

'With practice you can make a catch with a *boleadora* as far away as forty to fifty yards, even from the saddle,' Dawn explained. 'That's their advantage over a lariat. And, all things being equal, a *gatah* carrying a rider can be persuaded to run faster than one which isn't.' She raised a prohibitive hand to her husband-to-be as he was on the verge of speaking and continued, 'But, before *anybody* tells me, all things *aren't* equal. Those two quaggas will be faster than our mounts, although we might be able to get close enough to make a throw.'

'Except for one thing,' Bunduki put in, knowing that Dawn was basing her judgement upon the behaviour of horses and sharing her belief that the same would apply where mounted and riderless *gatahs* were concerned. He also guessed that she had spotted the flaw in employing such tactics, but meant to beat her in delivering it. 'We can't use the *boleadoras* while we're riding after them.'

'But you said——!' Joar-Fane squealed indignantly and her husband also displayed surprise, if not vocally.

'I said we could teach the *banar-gatahs* to accept us throwing the *boleadoras* while we're riding them,' the blond giant elaborated. 'But doing that with the quaggas at a gallop, which they would be with us chasing them, could bring them down hard enough to cripple them.'

'Ooh!' Joar-Fane ejaculated, glaring in a threatening fashion at the big Earth man. 'I hope for your sake that, after you've had Dawn and me wading around in that cold water looking for the right kind of stones, you're not going to tell us you can't use those *bolea*—whatever you call them—after all?'

'We can use them all right,' Bunduki assured the little Telonga girl, amused by her truculence. 'But I'm only willing to chance it if there's no danger of them hurting the quaggas.'

'How do you intend to do that?' At-Vee inquired.

'Well now,' Bunduki said absently. 'It is something of a problem, I must admit.'

'Isn't it?' Dawn growled, studying the blond giant in a speculative fashion. 'And I hope for your sake that you can come up with the answer.'

'I think the best thing I can do is take a nap to help me consider the matter,' Bunduki suggested, turning away.

Which proved to be an error in tactics.

Dropping her *boleadora*, Dawn dived forward as if performing a tackle in a game of rugby football. She struck and wrapped her arms around the blond giant's knees to bring him down. Taken completely unawares, although he managed to break his fall with his hands, he could not save himself from her continuation of the attack. Giving him no chance to recover, she bent and crossed his legs. Sitting on the ankles, she leaned forward to cup her hands around the front of his head and pulled.

'All right, you exasperating over-sized lump!' Dawn hissed, retaining her hold while Joar-Fane whooped in delighted approval. 'There's no hurry as far as *I'm* concerned, I'm quite comfortable here. So, when *you're* ready, tell us what you have in mind.'

'It's like you told me, brother,' At-Vee grinned, moving to where Bunduki could see him and thinking of how he too had been irritated by the other's reticence. 'Everything comes to him who waits—and asks for it.'

CHAPTER FIVE

NOW ALL WE HAVE TO DO IS TAME THEM

To the accompaniment of the grating, almost metallic sounding songs of the barbets heralding the dawn, the sun was lifting slowly above the eastern horizon. Listening to the birds, as they had so often done in Africa, Dawn Drummond-Clayton and Bunduki were kneeling behind the same rock which he and At-Vee the Hunter had used while watching the band of quaggas slightly less than twenty-four hours earlier.

Having conceded defeat and being released by his wife-to-be, the blond giant had told the other three of how he hoped to catch the mare and stallion. Agreeing that the idea had merit, Dawn had suggested that they should spend some time in re-acquainting themselves with handling the *boleadoras*. As had been the case with the various other types of primitive weapons they had come across in the course of their adoptive family's extensive travels, they had been taught how to use the devices by acknowledged experts and had attained considerable skill. However, it was some time since either of them had found the need to employ the techniques they had learned. While they had not lost the knack of throwing a *boleadora*, each had felt it was advisable to practice, and there had also been something else to be made in case their efforts met with success.

In addition to refurbishing their skill with the *boleadoras*, Dawn and Bunduki had spent a most enjoyable day. While remaining alert in case her assessment of the situation at Bon-Gatah should prove at fault, they and the Telonga couple had taken the opportunity to study the vast variety of wild animals to be found on the open plains. They had kept up the same kind of happy banter which was the result of the pleasure they found in each other's company and the relief at their reunion. They had also held a serious discussion on the part each of them would be called upon to play in catching the quaggas.

During the late afternoon, having considered it was inadvisable to attempt to make the capture that day, the quartet had decided they might have a better chance in the morning if they could keep the quaggas away from the stream that evening. They had realized that doing so would not be easy if they were to achieve the desired effect. Care would have to be taken if the animals were merely to be prevented from quenching their thirsts that night and not frightened from the vicinity. So they had crossed the stream and made camp in plain view opposite the place where the band generally drank.

From all appearances, Bunduki concluded that the ploy had been successful. When the quaggas had approached the stream for their evening drink, the scent and sounds made by his party had combined with the glow of the camp fire—which had been lit, disregarding the possibility of its being seen by enemies—and brought them to a stop before they reached the water. Although they had milled nervously around, they had not bolted. Nor, even after night had fallen, had they advanced to drink nor sought for another place at which to quench their thirst.

Having spent an uneventful night, the quartet had been ready to put the next stage of the scheme into operation before sunrise. Working in the darkness, the fire having been allowed to die out, they had saddled the *banar-gatahs*. Then Joar-Fane and At-Vee had led the animals beyond a nearby ridge where they would be out of sight when the sun came up. With them had gone the Earth couple's bows and arrows. Wading the stream, Dawn and Bunduki had carried their *boleadoras*. The lariats were suspended across their shoulders. A set of Mun-Gatahs' hobbles were dangling over the hilt of each's knife. Above them were hanging two other devices which demonstrated the amount of thought that had been devoted to preparing for the endeavour.

The girl and the blond giant had appreciated that, in the event of the *boleadoras* justifying their confidence, some further means of control would be necessary to restrain their captives until the hobbles were fastened. Although they wanted to win over the animals with kindness, they had realized that in the early stages a certain amount of rough handling could not be avoided. The problem confronting them had been how this might be kept to a minimum.

After considering various methods, Dawn and Bunduki had concluded that there was only one satisfactory solution to their dilemma. They would use what, on Earth—where such implements were employed for influencing the behaviour of recalcitrant horses—was known as a 'twitch'. Producing the devices had entailed no greater effort than finding two straight and sturdy sticks about twenty-four inches in length, then attaching to one end of each a small loop of the cord from which the *boleadoras* had been made. Applying a 'twitch' was going to inflict some pain upon the recipients, but this would be less than by any other method the couple could envisage.

By the time the first glow of the breaking day was creeping into the sky, the girl and the blond giant were already settled in the shelter offered by the rock. While taking up their positions, they had neither seen nor heard anything to suggest that their presence had been detected and their quarry alarmed. So they had waited patiently and in silence to find out whether their efforts would bear the required fruit. Not that they had been kept in suspense for long. Daylight had come with the speed that was always the case on Zillikian and, after a very short period, the visibility was excellent.

'Here they come!' Dawn breathed, yet in tones redolent of anticipation. 'They've no idea that we're here and, provided our luck holds, they won't find out until it's too late to do anything about it.'

Glancing in the direction that his wife-to-be was peering, the blond giant nodded his agreement. As she had intimated, everything was going in their favour so far. Not only had their quarry remained in the vicinity and were coming to drink at the usual place, but there was another piece of good fortune. The angle at which the wind was blowing would carry their scent away from the animals.

The band of quaggas, with the big stallion and the isabelline mare in the lead, were making their way towards the stream. Although they were moving slowly and exercising a constant watchfulness, their behaviour was no more cautious than would ordinarily have been practised and it did not suggest that they suspected a trap. Their caution was only to be expected. No creature could survive in the wild unless it was wary and maintained great vigilance at all times.

Nearer and neared walked the quaggas!

Ahead of the band, the stallion kept its head held high. While its pricked ears sought to pick up the slightest threatening sound, the flaring nostrils constantly tested the breeze. Its vision was not so well developed as the other senses, but it was searching for any movements which might denote the presence of a lurking predator. As a sign of its intelligence, in addition to leading its band at a safe distance from the large rock which its instincts warned could conceal an enemy, it was devoting much of its attention to the other side of the stream. However, the human beings who had prevented them from taking their evening drink had already departed and were nowhere to be seen. So it continued to approach the edge of the water.

'Here come Joar-Fane and At-Vee!' Dawn whispered, glancing at the ridge beyond which their friends were concealed. 'I knew we could trust *her* to make sure *he* didn't do anything wrong.'

'Don't start the female chauvinist bit this early in the morning!' Bunduki begged, *sotto voce*, without taking his gaze from their quarry and, putting a note of warning into his next words, went on, 'As long as *you* don't do anything wrong, *my* idea's going to work.'

In accordance with their instructions, Joar-Fane and At-Vee had made their appearances from a point at which their scent would be carried to the quaggas. The girl was leading the Earth couple's *banar-gatahs*, with their archery equipment and Bunduki's shield hanging from the saddlehorns. Like the blond giant's *m'kuki*, the Hunter's spear was suspended in the loops on the left side skirt of his saddle. As they had been told, the Telongas were making no attempt to move in silence or unseen. Rather they were ensuring that they would be noticed and Joar-Fane was crooning one of their nation's love songs.

On hearing the sounds of hoof beats and the human voice, as well as catching the Telonga couple's aroma, the quaggas came to an immediate halt. All of them gazed across the stream, but as yet found nothing frightening. Joar-Fane and At-Vee were not approaching in a manner that could be construed as posing a threat. In fact, once they had attracted the animals' attention, they reined their mounts to a stop.

Satisfied that the situation was developing as the plan required, Dawn and Bunduki rose and emerged from behind the rock. They moved slowly, displaying no apparent interest in the quaggas. Although they did not speak and walked quietly, neither anticipated being able to close the distance between themselves and the animals to any great extent before they were discovered. Sauntering along with sufficient of a gap to allow each to throw the *boleadora* unimpeded, they held the egg-shaped weights of the shorter, *mañeque*, lengths of cord in their right hands and allowed the devices to dangle unobtrusively behind them.

Just as the Earth couple had anticipated, before they were taking their sixth steps, one of the quaggas noticed them. Giving a snort of alarm, it caused the rest of the band to look in their direction. Avoiding any sign of concern over having been detected, Dawn and Bunduki continued to stroll in a deliberately casual fashion at an angle which seemed to be taking them away from and past the animals.

The big young stallion who was the leader of the band devoted his full attention to the Earth couple. Tossing his head, he let out the kind of warning bark that had given his kind their onomatopoeic name and pawed restlessly at the ground. Powerful, strong, armed with rock hard hooves and efficient teeth, he was far from harmless or defenceless. Although his first inclination would be to lead the mares he had accumulated to safety in the event of danger threatening, he was also capable of defending them if the need should arise.

Appreciating his capabilities, Dawn and Bunduki kept a careful watch on the stallion. Studying his reactions, they decided that he was uncertain of their exact status. Whatever previous contact he might have had with human beings must have been restricted to avoiding mounted pursuers. In which case, as he had never seen a man and woman on foot, he saw nothing in their behaviour to cause concern any more than he would have if some kind of conventional carnivore was going by in a similarly open manner. If he had not been thirsty, he might have taken the precaution of moving away. Having spent a night without access to water, he was disinclined to depart before drinking unless there was some definite indication that the two strange creatures posed a threat to the safety of the band.

In spite of having attained the conditions they required, the girl and the blond giant were aware that their task was still anything but a sinecure. Not only did they know the dangers of attempting to make the capture with the quaggas in full flight, they had realized that the *boleadoras* could not be employed successfully if their quarry was standing still. So they had to produce the happy medium of causing sufficient movement to let the devices take the proper effect, but not such a rapid motion that being brought down unexpectedly could result in a serious injury. There was also, as they appreciated, the danger that one of the stone weights on the cords might strike the victim's legs and do damage. Such an eventuality was less likely to occur when the mare and stallion were walking, or at a slow trot, than if they were galloping. However, Bunduki had taken all these factors into consideration when giving his instructions.

'Come on, At-Vee!' the blond giant breathed, throwing a quick look across the river to find out whether the Telonga couple had fully understood what was wanted from them. He did not doubt their intelligence, but neither had ever been involved in such an activity and the way in which they played their parts could make all the difference in how it turned out. 'Now's the time!'

Almost as if he had heard Bunduki's barely audible words, the Hunter nodded at Joar-Fane. As they set their mounts into motion, it was obvious that they had not forgotten their orders. They induced the *banar-gatahs* to advance at a somewhat faster pace and the girl did not resume her singing. In spite of the latter omission, their actions were quickly noticed by the quaggas. One after another of the animals began to gaze around. Even the stallion turned his attention from the Earth couple.

As they watched to see how the quaggas were reacting, Dawn and Bunduki tensed ready to go into action. They came to a stop, conscious that everything now depended upon the way in which the stallion responded to the sight of the Telongas drawing nearer.

For a few seconds, while the rest of the band moved restlessly and awaited his guidance, the male quagga stood indecisive. Then, as the blond giant had hoped he would, he concluded that discretion was called for. He was not frightened, but considered it advisable to move away from the approaching human beings and also keep clear of the pair of strange creatures which had already caused him some perturbation. Letting out a commanding snort, he wheeled away from the stream.

Clearly having expected some such reaction, the isabelline mare threw up her head and started to lead the band away at a trot. The direction she was taking was such that they would go past Dawn and Bunduki at a distance of about forty yards. The rest of the band followed her, with the stallion bringing up the rear. Waiting until they were on the move, the Telongas gave yells intended to divert them from the real danger.

Everything was going exactly as Bunduki's plan needed, even to the formation of the band as it moved off. Having anticipated that the stallion would keep behind the rest and hoping the isabelline mare would take the lead, he and Dawn had positioned themselves accordingly. Furthermore, in spite of keeping an eye on the Telongas, the mare did not break into a gallop. Most important of all, neither she nor the stallion were looking at the Earth couple.

Satisfied that all was well, Bunduki knew there was no need to give the girl any further instructions. She was equally capable of assessing the situation. So, instead of wasting even a split second to make sure that she was ready, he devoted his full attention to the task upon which he was about to engage.

Forward and up rose the blond giant's right arm, swinging the *boleadora* vertically in a circle. Having done this, he carried it out and around horizontally above his head while taking aim. Waiting until the two round balls were directly behind him, he pitched the egg-shaped *mañeque* weight towards its objective. By his side, Dawn had done exactly the same with the mare as her target.

On leaving Bunduki's hand, the *boleadora* began to revolve slowly as it passed through the air. In doing so, it demonstrated another advantage in addition to having a greater effective range than a lariat. While a throw with the latter could be commenced employing a loop of more than half its length, because the other end of the rope was retained in the user's grasp, the honda[1] slid along the stem[2] and its size was continually being reduced during its flight. On the other hand, no matter how far a

1. *Honda: the 'business' end of a lariat. A knotted, or spliced, eyelet about two inches in diameter and usually lined with smooth leather, through which the 'end' of the rope is passed to form a 'running' noose. J.T.E.*

2. *Stem: in roping terminology, the portion of the lariat which is outside the honda and so does not form part of the 'noose'. J.T.E.*

boleadora was propelled, the spinning motion imparted by its weights held it fully extended so that—in the case of the pair Bunduki had had made—it covered an area six foot in diameter from the moment of its release until arriving at its destination.

Released so that it was directed at a gentle downwards angle, the blond giant's *boleadora* converged with the stallion. As it did, it exhibited yet a further example of its superiority over the lariat. Although the initial contact was made about six inches from the round stone at the left tip of the longer cord, the other two weights caused the remainder to whip around and trap its victim's legs just above the fetlocks. At the same instant, having been dispatched with an equal accuracy, Dawn's *boleadora* was ensnaring the mare's front legs just as efficiently. Both animals went down as if they had been pole-axed, but with only sufficient force to wind and daze them for a few seconds.

While they had attained the results they had hoped for, as far as the *boleadoras* were concerned, Dawn and Bunduki wasted no time in congratulations. They realized that their task was still incomplete. In fact, they were aware of the many difficulties which were still confronting them. Not the least of these was securing their captives, a task which must be carried out with the minimum of delay and before the animals could recover. So, even as the mare and stallion were falling, the Earth couple dashed forward to the accompaniment of loud whoops.

Despite their caution where the stallion was concerned, neither Dawn nor Bunduki expected any trouble from the rest of the band. In common with the other sub-species of the zebra family, the quaggas lived in a family group dominated by the most powerful male. It was his duty to provide any protection that might be required. By doing so, he ensured that the mares, subordinate stallions and foals had a better chance of escaping. Knowing what was expected of them and ignoring the isabelline mare's predicament, the others took their departure as fast as their legs would carry them.

Across the stream, bellowing with delight, At-Vee urged his *banar-gatah* forward at a gallop. The noise he was making helped to keep the remainder of the quaggas running away. However, his primary purpose was to join the Earth couple as quickly as possible and render any assistance that was required. Much to her annoyance, as she had been placed in charge of Dawn and Bunduki's mounts, Joar-Fane was unable to accompany her husband and take a more active part in the proceedings. Instead, she was compelled to follow at a more leisurely pace and watched what was happening with considerable interest. She had seen how successful her friends had been with the *boleadoras* and was waiting to find out whether all the other devices they had manufactured would prove equally effective.

Without waiting for At-Vee, who was only just approaching the opposite bank of the stream, Dawn and Bunduki lifted free the 'twitches' ready for use. Every second was now essential and none could be spared. On being tripped by the *boleadoras*, the quaggas had tumbled sideways with their feet towards their captors. Once they recovered their wits, for all that their front legs had been rendered inoperative, the hind hooves were at liberty and could still pose a serious threat. So the girl and the blond giant had concluded that it would be advisable for them to circle around and arrive from where they could not be kicked. They were equally alert to how dangerous a bite their captives could deliver if presented with an opportunity and they acted accordingly.

Once again Bunduki left Dawn to take care of the mare. Darting in rapidly, he used his knee to pin the stallion's neck to the ground. Before it could start to struggle or try to reach him with its hind legs, he hooked the loop of the 'twitch' around its top lip and twisted the stick until the cord was drawn tight. With that achieved, he rose and moved until he was standing in front of the quagga's head. When it showed signs of intending to resist, he applied a trifle more tension. Feeling the pain increasing, it displayed its intelligence by returning to immobility.

Not until he had established his control over the stallion could the blond giant spare a glance for Dawn. He found that she had been equally successful. However, lacking his size and weight, she had straddled and knelt astride the mare's neck while affixing the 'twitch'. As soon as it was securely in place, she had stood up and the female quagga was showing just as good sense as the stallion by refraining from pain-inducing struggles.

Spluttering out curses and trying to make the *banargatah* go faster as it churned through the water, At-Vee was hard put to restrain his impatience. Coming ashore, he reined the animal to a stop and almost tumbled from the saddle in his eagerness. However, he did not permit emotion to make him forget any part of his instructions. Allowing the reins to fall free and ground hitch his mount, he ran to Dawn's side. Although he had two more aids to the capture hanging over his knife and *shilva*, he left them there and removed the hobbles she was carrying.

As the Hunter knelt by the mare and touched its upper hoof, it snorted and tried to jerk the leg away. Instantly Dawn made use of the 'twitch' and its effort ended. Nor did it attempt further objections while he was buckling the cuffs of the hobbles into place. With that task completed, there was a further precaution he had to take before removing the *boleadora*.

The article At-Vee took from across his *shilva's* head was modelled upon the *hackamore* of the American Indians and cowhands. Made mainly from rope, it was shaped like a bridle. There was a loop known as a *bosal* at the lower end, which would encircle the quagga's head immediately above the mouth and serve as a bit. Higher, a three inch wide brow band made out of an opened up *fulsa* sack could be slid down the cheeks to act as a blindfold. While reins could be attached, as yet only a lead rope was fitted.

Working as quickly as possible, At-Vee clipped the *bosal* over the stick of the 'twitch' and, with the girl moving first one, then the other hand to let it pass, eased the hackamore into place as he had rehearsed the previous night. Having settled it firmly in position, he adjusted the brow band over the mare's eyes and set about untangling the cords around the forelegs. With that task completed, he went across and did the same for the blond giant.

Fifteen minutes later, the capture was complete.

Joar-Fane had joined her husband and friends to help put the finishing touches to their efforts. Wanting to give the quaggas an opportunity to recover from the fright and moderately rough handling they had received, the human beings had withdrawn a short distance. Having regained their feet, the combination of being blindfolded and hobbled was inducing the mare and stallion to refrain from trying to escape. They were further calmed by being able to smell and hear the *banar-gatahs*, which had been unsaddled, grazing close by.

'Well you've got them, brother!' At-Vee stated.

'We've got them,' Bunduki agreed, just as delightedly. 'Now all we have to do is tame them.'

'That won't be hard,' Dawn declared. 'All you pair will have to do is let *us* do all the thinking for you. Don't you agree, Joar——?'

As Bunduki had done the previous afternoon, the girl committed an error in tactics. Instead of keeping him under observation, she turned her head to look at Joar-Fane on starting the final sentence. A powerful hand caught her right wrist and, before she realized what was happening, the blond giant was sitting on a rock with her across his knee. Transferring his grip to the back of her neck and pinning her down, he applied the flat of his free palm to the seat of her leopardskin pants.

'Ow!' Dawn screeched and, the words being punctuated by further slaps and squeaks of pain, went on, 'Help me, Joar-Fane!'

'You try and you'll get the same,' At-Vee warned his wife.

For a moment, the little Telonga girl stood indecisive. Then she gave a shrug and, eyes bubbling with merriment, said, 'I'm sorry, sister. I don't *know* you. So it's not my place to interfere.'

'You should have listened to me last night, Dawn,' At-Vee commented, as the spanking ran its course. 'I said everything comes to those who wait——and ask for it.'

However, despite the levity, they all knew that their problems were not at an end. The capture had been successful, but they would have to wait until the quaggas would succumb to being led and that was certain to take a few more days.

CHAPTER SIX

DIE CHAROLE, YOU BITCH!

Despite the curses Charole had uttered over yielding to an impulse that had caused her some difficulties, when she looked back, she felt that her luck was still holding out.

Having made her escape from Bon-Gatah with nothing untoward occurring, Charole had decided against following the suggestions of Elder Eokan immediately. While she was satisfied that he had sufficient ulterior motives to be sincere in his offer of assistance, she considered that something else must take precedence over going directly to Zeh-Gatah. A shrewd strategist and born conspirator, she was aware of the value of negotiating from as strong a position as possible, and she hoped to gather the means to do just that.

When he had been preparing to betray his superior, Zongaffa the Herbalist had made a large quantity of 'Thunder Powder' and had, almost certainly, prepared a number of 'Terrifiers'. In which case, they must be hidden somewhere, and Charole had deduced that the hiding place would be in the vicinity of the late High Priest's country villa. So she had gone there with the intention of searching for what would be of the greatest help in her bid to return to power.

That had been five days ago.

Since then, the Protectress had had cause to regret having made the attempt!

While conducting the search, Charole had been seen

by the one person more than anybody else who had cause to hate her.

Not only had Elidor of Veet-Gatah been the High Priest's senior female adherent, she was the one he had hoped would supplant Charole as the Protectress of the Quagga God. However, having suffered defeat at the hands of Dawn of the 'Earths'—all the more humiliating because the foreigner's wrists had been manacled—she had fallen from grace. Before she could recover from the broken jaw she had sustained in the fight, Dryaka had formed his alliance with Charole and she was displaced permanently from his favour.

Obviously, on learning of the High Priest's death, Elidor had either decided to establish herself as owner of his estate, or had duplicated Charole's summation with regard to Zongaffa's treachery. Whatever the reason, she and six male companions had come on the scene while the Protectress was trying to locate the hoard of 'Thunder Powder'. Recognizing her from a distance, despite the changes she had made to her appearance, they had given chase.

If Charole had had her own quagga as a mount, she would have been able to leave her pursuers far behind during the early stages and lose them at her leisure. As it was, while the *banar-gatah* stallion circumstances had compelled her to use was an animal of excellent quality it could do no more than maintain roughly the same distance between her and her pursuers as she made for Zeh-Gatah. Naturally, after the original attempt failed to bring them together, neither she nor Elidor's party were riding at a gallop. Instead, the latter were following her with the aid of an exceptionally competent reader of tracks.

In spite of having been taught various methods of hiding signs of her passing, Charole did not offer to put any of them into practice.[1] They were all too time-consuming to carry out correctly and anything less, con-

1. *Examples of how tracks can be concealed are given in Part One, 'The Half Breed' of* THE HALF BREED. *J.T.E.*

sidering the obvious quality of the man doing the tracking, would be futile. Nor, as the advantages were outweighed by other factors, had she kept moving after night had fallen in order to increase her lead and, perhaps, lose her pursuers. In addition to having no wish to tire and possibly ride her stallion into the ground, she had known that the proliferation of carnivores with nocturnal hunting habits, and other dangerous animals, made travelling through the darkness an extremely hazardous undertaking. Sharing her appreciation of the difficulties, Elidor's party had also halted once the sun went down.

One worrying point for Charole was that she was prevented from taking the most direct route to her destination. She had been driven northwards by the original chase and was now making a semi-circular swing towards Zeh-Gatah. What was more, the area she had entered shortly before nightfall on the third afternoon was rolling, but not too dense, woodland that fringed the great 'Lake With Only One Shore' close to which—although she had estimated it was still some miles away—the city was situated.

For all Charole's misgivings, by noon on the fifth day of the pursuit, it seemed that her persistence had paid off. Since she had set out that morning, after breakfasting upon the *fulsa* and stream water which had been her only sustenance since fleeing from Bon-Gatah, she had seen nothing of Elidor's party. Of course, because of the woodland terrain she was traversing, her view to the rear was extremely limited. However, she was taking comfort from the thought that they would possibly be suffering even more than she was from the reduction of visibility. They would now be forced to rely entirely upon their tracker, which would compel them to move more slowly than she was.

Even as Charole was returning her gaze to the path ahead, her complacency was shattered in no uncertain fashion. She was going across a fair-sized clearing and, suddenly, found herself surrounded by riders who appeared from concealment all around it. There was even one to her rear, cutting off any slender chance of a retreat.

Facing the Protectress was Elidor!

Dressed and armed in the same style, except that she did not carry a lance, the woman almost matched Charole in height and dimensions. Although, in healing, the break had left her jaw slightly crooked, she was still sullenly beautiful and about the same age as the Protectress. Nearly as strong and fit, she had attained a well deserved reputation as a warrior. Lounging on the saddle of her *banar-gatah* stallion, which was showing just as much evidence of hard travelling as Charole's leg-weary mount, she had a sword dangling from her right hand.

'There, you see!' Elidor said, looking with triumphant exultation at the nearest man who was also mounted on a *banar-gatah* stallion. 'I told you that she was making for Zeh-Gatah and we could catch her by cutting across this way.'

'You did,' the warrior agreed.

'So you made a lucky guess for once,' Charole scoffed, turning the lance in her right hand and throwing it so that the point stuck in the ground by her mount. 'Now what?'

Before she started to speak, the Protectress's thoughts were racing. The bag containing the small sack of 'Thunder Powder' and the 'Terrifiers' was wrapped with her 'fire box' and other belongings in the cloak that was strapped on the cantle of her saddle. Even if they had been readily available, the latter's fuse cord was not lit. So she had no way of bringing the potent devices into operation. Nor did she consider that the lance, or the throwing spear hanging on the skirt of her saddle, would serve her needs. Her *banar-gatah* had been too hard pressed over the past few days to make a suitable mount on which to wield the former weapon, and she doubted whether she would be granted an opportunity to draw, much less throw, the latter. There was, she accepted, only one way open to her.

'You took an oath to sacrifice one of the "Earths" to the Quagga God,' Elidor replied. 'But we haven't seen it happen yet. So you have lost His favour and have forfeited your right to act as His Protectress.'

'I've yet to be deposed,' Charole pointed out.

'Your failure and flight from Bon-Gatah did that,' Elidor declared, after glancing around as if hoping one of her male companions would speak.

'I still have my robes of office,' Charole countered, indicating the bulky bundle wrapped in the cloak. Acting on Eokan's advice, she had collected the ceremonial garments before taking her departure. 'Without them, there can be no new Protectress.'

'Then they must be taken from you,' Elidor stated, falling into the trap that had been laid for her.

'By whom?' Charole challenged, swinging her right leg forward and over the saddlehorn to jump to the ground. 'Do you mean to have these six men do it for you?'

The words gave Elidor no choice over how she must respond. They were directed in a way which she could not ignore. In spite of having the men with her, she knew Mun-Gatah custom required that a dispute of such a nature must be settled between the main participants if they were of the same sex. Persons of the opposite gender were not allowed to interfere, no matter where their loyalties might lie. So a failure to respond to Charole's imputation of her courage would cause her a serious loss of face. It could even lead the warriors to desert her in the Protectress's favour.

For all that, Elidor hesitated instead of acting immediately. While Charole's failure to make the promised sacrifice had implied a fall from grace, the fact that she still lived, had escaped from the hostile capital city and was apparently going to Zeh-Gatah—which was not her home town—in search of assistance, suggested she had not entirely forfeited the Quagga God's favour. In which case, dealing with her was not a sinecure. She was too capable a fighter for that.

'Well?' Charole said derisively, wanting to make sure that the other's hesitancy did not go unnoticed by her companions. 'Why don't you tell *them* to do what you're obviously afraid to try.'

Any slight hope that Elidor might have nourished of evading the confrontation ended with the mocking words. One brief glance at the men informed her of their feelings on the matter. They expected her to accept the challenge. So, yielding to the inevitable, she wondered how she might fight with the best chance of survival.

Watching Charole stepping away from the *banar-gatah* and lance, Elidor drew her conclusions. While she was still mounted and her opponent on foot, she realized that the animal between her legs would be unable to respond with its best speed. Like the stallion the Protectress had been riding, it had covered many miles since leaving Dryaka's country estate. What was more, she had pushed it hard while making for the position between Charole and Zeh-Gatah. Taking all those factors into consideration, she felt that she would lose more than she gained by attacking while still in the saddle.

'All right!' the brunette ejaculated, making a rapid dismount. Raising her sword, she darted forward with a yell of, 'Die Charole, you bitch!'

Showing neither alarm nor any great concern over Elidor's threat and obvious eagerness to come to grips, the Protectress slid the ivory handled sword from its sheath and advanced to meet her.

Watching the way in which the women were moving towards each other, the male warriors dismounted. Leaving their *gatahs* ground hitched by the dangling reins, confident that their own numbers and the noise of the fighting would frighten away any predatory animals who might be lurking in the vicinity, they advanced on foot to obtain closer views of what promised to be a worthwhile engagement. Charole and Elidor were noted for their skill with swords. As there was so little to choose between them, unless something untoward happened, the contest was likely to be a long one.

Fully trained and competent swordsmen, the warriors were able to form their judgements even before the first blows had been struck. All of them considered that Elidor had one important factor in her favour. As a member of a hunting party whose quarry was aware of their presence, with others to share in keeping watch, and able to light a fire, her rest had been less disturbed than that of the Protectress. Travelling alone and of necessity being obliged to avoid anything that could guide her pursuers to her in the darkness, Charole could have had little sleep for the past four nights and so was much the tireder of the two.

Sharing her companions' summation, Elidor was determined to draw all she could from her advantage. So she made no attempt at performing the subtler aspects of sword-play. Although she too had learned from Dryaka the value of the blade's point and of thrusting rather than using the edge all the time, she concentrated upon merely slashing as rapidly and forcefully as she could. To the watchers, it seemed that she was dominating the action. Certainly she was compelling the Protectress to back away before her attack.

Equally conscious of the prevailing conditions, Charole had realized that she had never needed to use her feet and brain so much in order to take some of the strain from her right arm. Such was the fury of the brunette's onslaught that, at first, the Protectress could do nothing more than parry for her life. However, employing all her considerable skill to help ride out the storm, she was content to let her assailant expend most of the effort. The tactics being performed by Elidor would tire her sword hand and deplete the breath in her lungs.

When at last the brunette's whirlwind assault began to flag, Charole changed to the offensive. She feinted at the other's head and, as Elidor's sword went up for a parry, changed the apparent cut into a lunge. Showing her appreciation of the danger, the brunette sprang hurriedly backwards. Continuing to retire as Charole pressed after her, she made what fencers on Earth called a Maltese cross defensive pattern with her weapon. It was a style of guard which nothing could penetrate. However, particularly with the Protectress continually probing at it in a series of rapid and light feints, such a method was costly in breath and strength.

Suddenly, realizing the danger from the way she was behaving, Elidor carried her sword up and back for a cut at the top of the Protectress's skull. Judging that she had time for the manoeuvre, Charole did not attempt to parry. Instead, bounding rapidly to her left, she executed a swift *coup-de-flanc*. The blade passed beneath the brunette's raised right arm, slitting through the silver lamé material of her halter and biting across the flesh below. A little higher and the cut would have rendered her arm useless. As it was, the only result it achieved was to make a shallow gash. What was more, an instant after it was delivered, Elidor's sword descended to slice away a thin and small strip of skin from Charole's right thigh. This also failed to do any significant damage.

There was a rumble of excited comment from the watching men as the Protectress drew the first blood. However, she had inflicted only a minor wound and was repaid by an equally unimportant graze. Charole saw fear flicker momentarily across Elidor's face, but knew it was only caused by the worry that she might be too seriously injured to continue fighting. Then the brunette was withdrawing so quickly that she almost ran backwards for a few paces. As her opponent followed with an equal rapidity, she ducked below the ivory handled sword as it was directed sideways at her neck and lunged for its owner's bosom.

A lightning fast side step saved Charole, but only just! For all her speedy evasion, the Protectress felt the point and one edge of the brunette's weapon ploughing along her ribs and the other edge of the blade nicked the inside of her left bicep. However, she had always been famous for her ability to *riposte*.[2] Before Elidor could return her sword to the guard, Charole was bringing off a cut across her head. Fortunately for her, the blow was delivered backhand and it was almost the hilt that struck her. Otherwise, despite coming from such close quarters and in a comparatively clumsy fashion, had it been the

2. Riposte: *in fencing terminology, a return thrust or cut after an attack. J.T.E.*

79

middle of the cutting edge that made the contact, the fight would have been as good as over.

Even with the limitations imposed upon it, the blow put the brunette into difficulty. Blood gushed down the side of her face, but missed her eye and did not impede her vision. However, it caused her to change tactics once more. Grasping the sword in both hands, she began to swing it violently in a desperate gamble. One successful stroke could tear off a limb, sink the blade far into the head or torso, or—if they came together—batter the weapon from her antagonist's grasp.

Alert to the peril, Charole also realized it could be turned to her advantage. While the force of every blow was doubled, there was a corresponding decrease in the rapidity with which the blows could be repeated or a defence effected. So she had no intention of blindly following the other's lead. Instead of turning her sword into a hacking implement, she used it as what on Earth would have been called a 'foil' and relied upon the point. Where Elidor moved with slow and flat-footed steps, she kept up on her toes as if dancing while she dodged and feinted, awaiting an opportunity to thrust home the blade.

The onlookers' excitement and interest increased.

Would a slash or a thrust decide the issue?

A blow from Elidor would be death for Charole!

Just as surely, if a thrust from the ivory handled sword was successful, it would be fatal for the brunette!

As had happened in the opening moments of the fight, Elidor began to force the pace. However, where she attacked with a bull-like ferocity, Charole was bouncing and weaving in the manner of a *matador*.[3]

Everybody in the clearing, no matter whether protagonist or spectator, was growing increasingly aware that a climax could not be long in coming. It was a tribute to the skill and physical fitness of the women, as well as

3. Matador: *in the terminology of bullfighting, the man who dispatches the bull with a thrust of his sword. J.T.E.*

indicative of their bitter hatred for each other, that the fight had been so prolonged.

However, not one of the spectators even thought of intervening.

When two members of the Mun-Gatah nation took up arms against one another, regardless of their sex, the conventions dictated that it was they and they alone who could terminate the affair. So, despite having become Elidor's willing supporters in a bid to gain control of the late High Priest's country estate, the men intended to let her stand or fall by her own endeavours. To have done otherwise would offend the Quagga God and the outcome of the fight would be indicative of where His favour lay.

Nor, for all the pain and inconvenience caused by the cut on the side of her head, was it certain that the brunette would be the loser. In fact, the matter continued to hang in the balance for several more seconds.

Time after time, Elidor's sword swept with vicious power over or alongside Charole's head. On more than one occasion, it came sufficiently close to stir the short and sweat-soddened black hair in passing. However, the speed with which the brunette was still contriving to move prevented the Protectress from being able to find an opening and driving through it with her point to deliver a *coup-de-grace*.

By now, both of the women were beginning to show the severe strain caused by their exertions. Each was panting, her breath whistling through a parched throat and mouth. Replenishing their tormented lungs was growing increasingly difficult. Perspiration flowed copiously, making their skin glisten and diluting the blood that each was shedding. As their magnificent bosoms expanded and contracted like bellows in operation, their eyes glared glassily at each other and they were oblivious of all else.

'Quagga God strike her!' Elidor was croaking, using the words as a spur to drive her exhaustion-wrapped body to further efforts and went on, accompanying each

81

word with a terrific stroke of her sword, 'Curse you! Blast you! Stand! Fight!'

For her part, Charole was making no attempt to reply or comply with the demand to change her tactics. The night of broken sleep followed by days of almost continual travelling were beginning to have their effect, just as she, the brunette, and the male warriors had anticipated would happen. What was more, due to the perspiration restricting the blood's power to congeal, she was losing a fair amount from her injuries. In addition, her left arm felt as heavy and cumbersome as if it had been turned to lead. Through the accumulation of her sufferings, she was growing sick and faint.

The sensation caused the Protectress to slip and stagger slightly.

Instantly, with an expression of bitter hate and fury contorting her haggard features, Elidor prepared to make the most of the opportunity with which she was being presented. Gathering all her flagging reserves of strength, she carried the sword high above her head.

In her eagerness to strike, the exhausted brunette went a trifle too far!

Such was the vigour employed by Elidor that, before she could halt the sword, it was pointing downwards behind her. If the blow had been delivered, it could have cleaved the Protectress's skull open to the chin—but it was never struck.

In spite of all the torment she was enduring, Charole was not too far gone to see and recognize the chance she was being offered. Making a desperate effort to regain her equilibrium, she put all she had into an almost classic lunge. Her point went home beneath Elidor's left breast, passing onwards to emerge at the rear.

For a moment, the brunette's whole body went rigid. Then, releasing her weapon so it tumbled behind her, she went over backwards and wrenched the sword that had killed her from its user's grasp.

Disarmed and tottering, Charole saw her lance standing as she had left it. Pure instinct rather than conscious thought caused her to reel the few steps that separated her from it. Although she managed to take hold of the shaft with both hands, she knew that she did not have the strength or energy to use it. So she was at the mercy of Elidor's companions.

Keeping herself upright by leaning on the lance, the Protectress swung her gaze to the warrior who—by virtue of being the only male to ride a *banar-gatah*—was the leader of the party. Even as her gaze reached him, there was a hissing sound and, coming from somewhere beyond her now restricted range of vision, came an arrow that impaled itself in his throat.

CHAPTER SEVEN

I *HOPE* YOU KNOW WHAT YOU'RE DOING

'So you're going to ride *Shambulia* instead of just weighting his saddle, are you?' At-Vee the Hunter asked, watching Bunduki drawing tight the girths of the quagga stallion's saddle. He no longer fumbled with the pronunciation of the Swahili word meaning "attack" which had been selected as the animal's name.

'I am,' the blond giant agreed. 'And Dawn is going to do the same with Isabel.'

'She told me that *she* could have started riding Isabel the morning we captured them,' Joar-Fane put in, darting a mischievous smile at the other girl. 'But, for some reason or other, she found it was too painful to sit down.'

'With a *friend* like my little sister, you don't need *enemies*,' Dawn Drummond-Clayton informed the men, employing tones of mock acidity. Returning her gaze to the Telonga girl, she went on, 'In fact, I should have let those "Hairy People" have you.[1] But, knowing *you* as I do now, I don't think I disliked them *that* much.'

Although only five days had elapsed since the capture of the Quaggas, Bunduki's party were already back in the comparative safety of the jungle. However, the Earth couple were no longer to live in the Jey-Mat Telonga village. On their return, they had found that the 'Suppliers' had established a permanent home for them. It was about half a mile away, on the shores of a small, crystal

1. *The incident to which Dawn Drummond-Clayton was referring is recorded in:* BUNDUKI AND DAWN. *J.T.E.*

clear lake which was connected with a nearby large river.

Perched in the branches of an enormous and sturdy samaan tree, the well constructed house had all the comforts of home. There were three bedrooms, a large dining-cum-sitting-room, a store and a kitchen complete with a stove of what appeared to be dried mud but was actually made from some form of light weight and heat resistant metal. The latter was equipped with utensils and a small elevator manipulated by a rope and pulley by which supplies or fuel for the stove could be raised. All the furniture and fittings were made of materials which matched the primitive looking decor. Access was gained by a rope ladder, or a larger elevator.

At the rear of the tree, some ten yards away, a stream tumbled down a cliff. It not only offered a readily accessible shower, but an arrangement of what looked like bamboo pipes—they were actually tubes of the same metal which was used for the stove and other portions of the structure—diverted some of it for household purposes. The left side back corner of the verandah protruded over the stream and had on it a rudimentary, yet effective and hygienic, toilet. Extending above the lake, the rest of the wide verandah at that side made a fine position from which to dive into the deep and clear water of the lake.

Ever since their arrival on Zillikian—in fact, even before they had learned the truth about their transportation—Dawn and Bunduki had suspected that they were being kept under observation by somebody, or something, they could not locate. If they had required further evidence that the 'Suppliers' were still watching their activities, it was given by the predator-proof compound with which they were presented as a corral for their mounts. Large enough to house the two quaggas and up to half a dozen *gatahs* without crowding, along one side was a roofed over, open fronted shelter to protect the occupants from the elements. It was fitted with eight separate stalls, each having a manger and hay-rack. The surrounding fence also encompassed a small bay of the lake and solved the problem of watering the stock, but at the same time prevented the entrance of anything such as a crocodile which was large enough to harm the occupants.

When they considered the facilities that had been given to them, it strengthened a theory the Earth couple had formulated with regard to the quaggas. Neither had ever come across potentially dangerous animals which had settled down in captivity with so little distress or so few objections. In fact, despite the fact that Dawn and Bunduki both possessed a considerable affinity and empathy with wild creatures, they had been surprised at how quickly they had come to be on friendly terms with their captives.

Before nightfall on the day that the quaggas had fallen into their trap, Dawn and Bunduki were able to go close and remove the blindfolds. They had achieved this by having stayed near by throughout the entire period, allowing the animals to become accustomed to their respective body odours, voices and presence.

At daybreak on the following morning, the Earth couple had tested their captives' willingness to be led. After only a brief demonstration of dissent on the part of the stallion, which had allowed Dawn and Joar-Fane to exchange pungent comments on the subject of masculine obstinacy, they had been able to resume their homewards journey. Of necessity, neither the mare's nor her consort's hobbles had been removed at that stage. The omission had reduced the pace at which the party could travel, yet they had considered any distance they could put between themselves and Bon-Gatah was worthwhile. There had been no sign of pursuit, but every hour that went by increased the danger of a search being instituted.

Nightfall had found the four young people making camp within sight of the jungle. Once again, Dawn and Bunduki had slept in close proximity to the quaggas. When ready to move on the next day, they had made what proved to be a successful gamble by removing the restraints from their captives' front legs. Either because they were far from their original territory or through a growing trust of their captors, the mare and the stallion had behaved well and the party had been able to make much better time. There had been a slight reluctance on the quaggas' part when it came to entering the jungle, but this was smoothed over without causing any undue delay.

On making camp somewhat earlier in the afternoon than would otherwise have been the case, particularly with the Jey-Mat Telongas' village being so near, the Earth couple had commenced with the next stage of accustoming the quaggas to a new way of life. Securing them to sturdy bushes in a clearing, Dawn and Bunduki had started to place a blanket on the back of each. As was to be expected, this had caused some initial restlessness, but it was not prolonged. Nor had the girl and the blond giant attempted to take the training any further at that point.

Reaching the village shortly before noon on the third day, the party had been greeted by the whole of the population and the news of their arrival had been sent forth via the 'talking drums' by which the Telongas—and the other nations—communicated rapidly over considerable distances. So effective was the system that, within minutes, every other community had been notified of their return.

As on Joar-Fane's arrival following her first escape from the clutches of the Mun-Gatahs' People-Taker, the reception had been mixed. All of the hunters, whether from Jey-Mat or those who had gathered in response to the signal for defiance against their oppressors and were still present, had been delighted at seeing that Dawn and Bunduki were safe. They had regarded it as further evidence of the Mun-Gatahs' fallibility.

While pleased by the return of the four young people, the Council of Elders—who were the leaders of the community—and non-hunting citizens had had misgivings. However, these had struck Dawn and Bunduki as being less pronounced than on the earlier occasion. Not only had the people seen that the hitherto invincible Mun-

Gatahs could be defied and defeated, but they also remembered the needless brutality which had characterized the final and unprecedentedly large abduction. Loving their children and respecting the aged, not even the most pacific of them could forget or forgive what had happened. Mothers had been compelled to leave behind their babies as an unrequired encumbrance on the journey into slavery. Not only had the Elders been put to torture with the result that two had died, those too aged to travel had been deserted.

Bearing those facts in mind, the younger members of the community and the two men who had been elected to replace the dead Elders were now willing to consider the possibility of actively opposing further oppressions. The viewpoint was shared by the hunters from the other villages, but they had warned that their more passive populations might regard the suggestion with disfavour. It would, they had declared, all depend upon whether Bunduki of the 'Earths' could persuade their neighbours that the 'Suppliers' approved of resistance in the face of a convention that had been in existence for far longer than the oldest inhabitants could remember.

At the conclusion of the welcome, which had relieved Dawn and Bunduki from the necessity of starting to convert the Telonga nation from a pacifism that was no longer practical, Dawn and Bunduki had been told of their gift from the 'Suppliers'. Being accustomed to having their needs satisfied, the villagers had expressed neither surprise nor alarm at having found the tree-house where no such thing had previously existed. Although the lake was not far from the village, none of them had visited the region since the abduction. So they could not say when the construction had been commenced, how it had been carried out, nor how long it had taken to erect and equip the Earth couple's home.

Having no desire to look a gift horse too closely in the mouth, the girl and the blond giant had accepted the 'Suppliers' bounty without question. However, despite sharing Bunduki's eagerness to complete the quaggas' training and to set about the task of teaching the Telongas to defend their villages, Dawn was too much of a woman to do anything until she had ensured that all of the furniture and fittings were positioned to her satisfaction. In this, she had had the support and assistance of Joar-Fane and the rest of the female population of Jey-Mat.

Discovering that a number of weapons, tools and other devices which would be of use in the future had been delivered, Bunduki had conceded the wisdom of postponing any action until he and Dawn were settled in. Except for one detail, settling in would not have been a lengthy process. In fact, Dawn had announced herself satisfied by sundown. But here was one matter that prevented them from moving in immediately. As yet, she and Bunduki were not married.

Discussing the problem with Joar-Fane's father, who was still functioning in lieu of Dawn's actual parents, the blond giant had been told that the wedding could not be performed until all the arrangements had been completed. For all their proclivity towards lovemaking, the Telongas had strong views on marriage and were sticklers for conformation with ceremonial observances. The nuptials of two such prominent members of the community must be performed to the accompaniment of a celebration of great size. Knowing that their status would be enhanced and their work made easier if such a celebration took place, Bunduki had seen the wisdom of agreeing.

Tav-Han had promised he would do all in his power to speed things along, but his wife and daughter had been adamant that the preparations could not be completed for another seven days at least. They would, both had declared, even prefer that this was extended to ten days so that the best results could be attained. Much as Dawn had shared the blond giant's impatience, she had accepted the decision reached by her Telonga 'family' just as she would have done if it had been made by her mother on Earth. To conform with the local convention, she could not occupy her future home while she was unmarried and would have to stay at her adopted parents' house each night until after the ceremony.

Apart from short periods in the tree-house, the girl and Bunduki had spent the whole of the fourth day working with the quaggas. Wanting nothing to distract the animals, they had arranged to leave their borrowed *banargatahs* at the village with those which had been retained by the hunters following the annihilation of the People-Taker and his escort. What was more, at their request, only Joar-Fane and At-Vee had been present during the training periods. The Telonga couple had not entered the corral, but stayed on the porch of the house to watch what was being done.

In addition to continuing the blanket training, Dawn and Bunduki had worked at accustoming the quaggas to being caught by a thrown lariat. Judging from the way the animals had shown an understanding of the futility of fighting against the constriction of a running noose, the knowledge must have been inherited through experience gained during generations of domestication. Or, considering that they had progressed to the inclusion of a saddle by the early afternoon, there could have been another reason.

To have achieved so much in such short time was, as the girl and the blond giant had appreciated, remarkable. In fact, they realized that all of the quaggas' behaviour since capture was extraordinarily fortunate as far as their own needs were concerned. Not only had there been little sign of aggression, but the animals were already beginning to respond to the names, 'Isabel' and 'Shambulia'. Certainly the latter had never shown any inclination to carry out the instruction, 'attack'.

While the quaggas' acquiescence might have stemmed from a recent acquaintance with human beings, Dawn and Bunduki had grown increasingly convinced that it was more likely to be the result of mental conditioning by the 'Suppliers' who had already proved that they could influence the behaviour of wild elephants. In which case, having anticipated their protegés' need for reliable and superlative means of transport, they could have arranged the meeting. The Earth couple had been intended to see and capture the quaggas, which in turn had been prepared so as to make training them a less difficult and more speedy process than it would have been in their natural state.

For all their summations, Dawn and Bunduki had refused to be lulled into a state of over-confidence or complacency. They had felt sure that there must be a limit to the shortcuts their benefactors had made possible. So, instead of mounting personally when the quaggas had no longer shown any reluctance in bearing the saddles, they had contented themselves with placing sacks filled with soil on their backs. Watching the way in which the burdens were sent flying, they had considered their caution was well justified. So they had persevered with the same tactics until the disappearance of the sun had brought the day's work to an end. By that time, both animals had been growing tractable when carrying the loads.

Up until halfway through the fifth morning, Dawn and Bunduki had continued to implant the idea of accepting a weight on the saddle. When they had decided that the lesson had been absorbed, they had surprised Joar-Fane and At-Vee by leading the quaggas from the corral. Descending from the tree-house's porch, the Telonga couple had followed as they led the animals to the shore of the lake. Reaching a point where the bank was firm and level sand with no rocks or other obstructions to mar its surface as it sloped gently into the water, they had halted to commence the preparations which had provoked the Hunter's question and brief interplay of comments between the girls.

'I *hope* you know what you're doing,' Joar-Fane remarked, trying to conceal her concern by adopting a tone of an unspoken, "But I doubt it". Little as she knew about such things, she guessed that what was going to happen next could be dangerous. 'After I spent all that time wading in a cold stream and looking after your *banar-gatahs*, I'd hate to see those two get away.'

'I'll try my best to see it doesn't happen,' Bunduki

promised, fastening one end of the stout rope he had brought from the tree-house to the saddlehorn.

'Huh!' the little Telonga girl sniffed. 'If *you're* going to try *your* best, *Shambulia* is as good as on his way back to the Land-Without-Trees.'

'I'm beginning to think I shouldn't have stopped the "Hairy People" taking you *either* time,'[3] Bunduki replied, knotting the other end of the rope around his waist. Then he took out his knife and passed it to At-Vee continuing, 'Oh well, I may as well make a start and see what happens.'

'You'll make a fool of yourself as usual,' Dawn stated, but the words did not fool her friends. They knew she shared their anxiety. 'Go ahead. Then *I'll* show you how to do it properly.'

'I'll never know why you went to fetch her back, brother,' At-Vee commented, wondering what would happen when Bunduki mounted and drawing some comfort from the thought that the sand would be softer to land on than the ground in the corral.

Much to Joar-Fane's and At-Vee's surprise, although the latter had deduced one of the reasons why the location had been selected, the blond giant did not mount immediately. Instead, grasping the one-piece reins which were now attached securely to the *bosal* of the hackamore, he started to walk slowly into the lake. It said much for the confidence which had already developed between them that *Shambulia* began to follow him with little hesitation. What small reluctance was shown ended when Bunduki gave a softly spoken order in the simple language of the *Australopithecus*. Experience had taught him this could be understood better by the stallion than English or the *lingua franca* of Zillikian's human population. The wordsounds were accompanied by a gentle, yet commanding, tug on the reins. Stepping after him, *Shambulia* advanced until standing belly deep in the water.

3. *The first occasion when the blond giant had been compelled to intervene and defend Joar-Fane from a family of* Australopithecus *is told in:* BUNDUKI. *J.T.E.*

'Good luck, darling,' Dawn breathed, knowing why her husband-to-be had waded in so far.

Aware that he was almost certain to have a fight on his hands when he mounted the big stallion, Bunduki had accepted the need to take precautions. So he was employing two techniques practiced by, among others, the Comanche Indians of the United States. They were calculated to lessen the danger of injury to himself and the animal, as well as reducing the chance of *Shambulia's* escape if Bunduki was thrown.

Authorities in all matters equestrian, the *Nemenuh*[4] warriors had discovered that to submerge an unbroken horse until the water was lapping around its belly reduced its mobility and rendered it less capable of bucking. Even if it should succeed in pitching off the rider, his landing would be cushioned by the water no matter how awkwardly he fell. Furthermore, as they were connected by the rope, the animal's flight would be impeded by having to drag him along and it would be more readily recaptured.

There might be, the blond giant realized as he grasped the saddlehorn and found the near side wooden stirrup with his left foot, a chance that the same did not apply where a quagga was concerned. However, he had never been a man to be held back by vague doubts, possibilities, or uncertainties. So, throwing a grin at his wife-to-be and friends, he swung himself astride the saddle.

For a moment, nothing happened!

Having grown to accept a weight being placed upon the alien object which was attached to his body, at first *Shambulia* noticed only that this one was considerably heavier than its predecessors. Then the burden moved and he realized that it was alive.

4. Nemenuh: *the phonetic spelling of the Comanche Indians' name for their nation, meaning 'The People'. Most other Indian nations referred to them as the* Tshaoh, *the 'Enemy People', because of their propensity towards horse-stealing—called 'raiding' by the Comanches—and warfare. Some details of the* Nemenuh's *methods of horse catching and training are given in:* COMANCHE. J.T.E.

The realization provoked an immediate and instinctive reaction!

Letting out an explosive snort of mingled alarm and anger, the big stallion did not wait to try and discover what kind of creature was sitting on him. Instead, he set about making a determined effort to fling whatever it might be from its perch. Even though hampered by the depth of the water, the spine-arching bound he made was not to be despised. Rising until his hooves were inches clear of the surface, on his way down, he kicked upwards with his hind quarters. Known in rodeo circles on Earth as 'bucking straight away', such a tactic was, on occasion, exceptionally effective. However, for it to succeed, the rider's rump—having been lifted well above the saddle—had to descend upon the cantle rather than returning to the seat.[5]

Alert to the peril, Bunduki used the tremendous strength of his thighs to prevent his displacement. However, *Shambulia's* next attempt was to rear on his hind legs and, as the blond giant was still using a *bosal*, this was far more difficult to control than if a metal bit had been employed. Desperate measures called for just as desperate counter-measures. So, keeping the reins in his left hand as it also grabbed the saddlehorn, he delivered a slap to the top of the stallion's head with his right hand. Startled by the unexpected assault, *Shambulia* brought down his forelegs and took off again in another 'straight away' buck which proved no more effective than his first.

Refusing to be put off by his three failures to dislodge the blond giant, *Shambulia* continued to fight with unabated determination and vigour. Possessed of the ideal physique for such an effort—being large, very powerful and forceful in his actions—he concentrated upon the high-rising, plunging bounds of 'bucking straight away'

5. *Being caught in such a manner crippled General Jackson Baines 'Ole Devil' Hardin C.S.A. for life. Told in the 'The Paint' episode of* THE FASTEST GUN IN TEXAS. *J.T.E.*

with only an occasional variation of 'chinning the moon,'[6] to break the monotony. He was considerably hampered by being forced to fight in an unnatural element for one of his species and repeatedly sought to correct this.

In spite of the limitations imposed upon him by relying only upon the *bosal* as a means of control and guidance, Bunduki's skilful manipulation of the reins and his weight combined to prevent the stallion from regaining dry land. Nor, for all of *Shambulia's* dependence upon only two tactics, did he find the battle monotonous and easy. In fact, delighted as he was by his success in remaining astride the saddle, he was far from sorry when his expertise and bodily bulk contrived to exhaust and bring the stallion's struggles to an end.

'There you are, *Kichwa Mkubwa*,'[7] the blond giant said addressing Dawn triumphantly if breathlessly, as he guided *Shambulia* ashore and dismounted. The faces of the girl and the two Telongas were flushed with the vigour they had expended upon yelling encouragement that he had been too occupied to notice. 'That's how it *should* be done. Let's see if *you* can do anywhere near as well with Isabel.'

'*Kichwa Mkubwa* yourself!' Dawn replied, with a disdainful toss of her head, but unable to conceal her elation at her husband-to-be's victory. 'Stand back and watch an expert show you how it doesn't need all that splashing and fuss to win.'

For all her comment, the girl knew that she would need to call upon all the strength and equestrian ability she possessed if she was to be equally successful.

6. '*Chinning the moon*': in rodeo parlance, when a mount rears high on its hind legs and paws the air with its front hooves. A dangerous tactic because the animal might overbalance and fall backwards on to its rider. Some even learn to do this deliberately. J.T.E.

7. Kichwa Mkubwa: *Swahili for 'Big Head', literally 'Head Big'.* J.T.E.

CHAPTER EIGHT

TAKE THAT WOMAN ALIVE

Even as the stricken *banar-gatah* rider twirled on his heels and fell, his hands clawing ineffectually at the arrow piercing his throat, an understanding of what was happening began to seep into the exhausted thought processes of the Protectress of the Quagga God. She became aware that the killing of the warrior was not an isolated phenomenon. In fact, gazing back and forth as she clung to the lance as an aid to fending off the waves of dizziness which were threatening to engulf her, she found that a full scale and very effective attack was being launched almost simultaneously upon the rest of Elidor's unsuspecting supporters.

As was the almost invariable habit of male Mun-Gatah warriors when beyond the walls of their homes (the only exception being when they were dealing with the pacific jungle dwelling Telongas) the men were clad in round metal helmets, specially prepared rhinoceros-hide breastplates, thick leather kilts with slits at the front and rear for ease when mounted, stout greaves and sandals of the same material. All had swords for defensive purposes sheathed on their belts, which they supplemented by lances and war-axes. However, the former type of offensive weapon had been left either stuck into the ground alongside its owner's mount or was suspended by a loop at the point of balance being passed around the saddle-horn and the butt in a metal 'shoe' on the right stirrup iron. The axes were also hanging from their users' rigs and were unavailable for immediate use.

Not that any of the warriors was granted an opportunity to arm and defend himself!

Taking advantage of the fact that the men had been so completely absorbed in watching the fight between the two women, their assailants had approached as near as possible without alarming the *gatahs* which were trained to act as lookouts. At such close quarters, the otherwise effective protecting clothing offered little of the usual safeguards against the weapons of enemies.

While the breastplates could withstand the arrows from all bows except those of the mysterious "Earths",[1] and the helmets offered resistance to most weapons, long experience had taught the other warrior nations how to circumvent the advantages of the Mun-Gatahs' garments. One weak spot, although only practical from a short distance, was the gap between the bottom rim of the helmet and the collar of the breastplate. Small though it might be, as was demonstrated by the killing of the *banar-gatah* rider and two more of the men with arrows, the exposed area was vulnerable.

Hissing and twirling through the air at great speed, two curved pieces of wood felled the fourth and fifth warriors. One was struck at the rear of his helmet, which suffered a deep indentation. His head was slammed forward and there was a sharp pop as his neck was broken. Caught in the middle of the back, the breastplate—which

1. *The modern materials, excellent design and great strength of Dawn Drummond-Clayton's and Bunduki's sophisticated archery equipment provided the power required to penetrate the Mun-Gatahs' hitherto invulnerable breastplates. This was because even the seventy pounds draw weight of the girl's composite—fibreglass and wood—weapon was almost double that of the strongest all wood 'self' bows of the other archers on Zillikian. Another contributory factor was that the Earth couple employed the more efficient 'cheek' draw and not the 'chest' draw practised by the local bowmen. Full descriptions of the methods used by the girl and the blond giant are given in the earlier volumes of the 'BUNDUKI' series. For comparison, an explanation of one style of Japanese archery and its equipment can be read in the author's 'OLE DEVIL HARDIN' series of biographies. J.T.E.*

was thinner at the rear—proved no protection and the other went down with his spinal column snapped.

Nor did the last man fare any better. The cause of his death was a circular disc of metal shaped like two saucers stuck together, about six inches in diameter and with a hole through the middle. Skimming along at a gentle downwards angle, it struck the ground some feet to his rear. The convex curve caused it to ricochet and imparted an even more vicious spin as it rose. Brushing open the slit at the back of his kilt, its razor-sharp edge buried into the inside of his left thigh to sever the great femoral artery. Although he managed to draw his sword, the way in which the blood gushed and spurted from the wound prevented him from putting it to use. He was dying on his feet and collapsed just after the weapon had left its sheath.

If Charole had not been so debilitated, she could have drawn conclusions from the weapons that had been used. While the Amazons[2] and the Gruziak were archers, the former did not employ the simple but *very* effective throwing stick.[3] As the female warriors and the horse-riding Gruziak lived respectively to the east and north of the Mun-Gatahs' domain, this reduced the chances of members of either race being so far to the west of their home territories as they now were. Furthermore, there was only one race who carried the kind of metal disc which had killed the sixth warrior. The proximity to the salt-water 'Lake With Only One Shore' gave an added

2. *Details of the Amazon nation are given in* APPENDIX FOUR *of* SACRIFICE FOR THE QUAGGA GOD *by J.T. Edson.*

3. *The throwing stick used on Zillikian is similar to that employed by the Hopi and related Indian tribes of North America, or the war and hunting* boomerangs *of the Australian aborigines, but—unlike the latter—is not expected to return to the thrower if it should miss its target. This does not make it any less lethal or effective as a weapon. American author, Daniel Mannix, describes in Chapter Seven, 'The Boomerang, The Stick That Kills', of his book,* A SPORTING CHANCE—*which covers the the subject thoroughly—how he has thrown one a distance of* five hundred and forty feet *and it still retained sufficient momentum to crack an inch thick branch of a tree. J.T.E.*

clue to the attackers' identity. Unlike the land-based nations, the Cara-Bunte travelled to and from their raids in large boats propelled by oars and sails.

Charole was not kept for long before she received her first sight of the attackers and discovered to which nation they belonged. They left their places of concealment and darted forward, passing the *gatahs* whose snorts of alarm would have betrayed their presence if they had attempted to close in before dealing with the warriors. There were four men and two women, which had been the reason why they had struck from a distance instead of approaching and giving the enemy an opportunity to fight.

The male members of the party were all of medium height, but thickset and heavily muscled, with olive-coloured skin and the broad Mongoloid features of Earth's Oriental races. Apart from a black tuft growing from the center to dangle behind in a braid, their heads were devoid of hair. Barefooted, and moving with the somewhat rolling gait of sailors ashore, they had on voluminous knee-length pantaloons of various colours, broad silk sashes around their midriffs and short, sleeveless soft leather jerkins. For hand-to-hand combat, each carried thrust through his sash a sword shaped like a Sumatran *lading* in a colourful metal tipped wooden sheath. Its double-edged, spear shaped blade was twenty inches in length and had a breadth of two inches at its widest point, but the concave wood—with one exception's—handle had no guard. Two of them held short recurved bows which were supplied from the quivers of arrows swung across their shoulders. Empty-handed, another pair had flung the throwing sticks which had dispatched the fourth and fifth Mun-Gatah warriors.

Clearly the last man had not participated in the killing. Tallest, heaviest and oldest of the male Cara-Buntes, his jerkin was decorated on each breast by a silver filigree sailfish curving in the kind of leap which made the species *Istiophorus Albicans* so highly prized by big game anglers, and he had a portrait of a killer whale emblazoned across the back. As further proof of his superior status, the ivory hilt of his *lading* was inlaid with silver as was its sheath, and there was a broad golden bracelet embossed with a sailfish on each wrist. He was further armed with a short spear, the head of which was shaped like a crescent moon and sharpened all around its edge.

Having attractive Oriental features and colouration, with black hair taken back in what on Earth would be called a pony-tail, neither of the women was more than five foot four inches in height. The smaller, a girl in her late teens, was also the younger and she lacked two inches of that height. She had a curvaceous, if slender, build. For all that, armed with a bow only slightly less powerful than those of the men, it had been she whose arrow had killed the *banar-gatah* rider. The elder, who had attained her middle thirties, was buxom rather than lithe. However, there was no sign of fat on her firm body. It was she who had thrown the *halaka* as the razor-edged discs were known.

Each of the female Cara-Buntes wore a short, loose fitting, wide sleeved white smock and very little else. The smocks were not fastened in any way, their fronts being kept closed by a black cloth sash. Through the left side of this was tucked the sheath of a twenty inches long weapon resembling an Atjeh's *rentjong* in having a wavey single-edged blade and a hilt in the shape of a duck's head. Neither had any footwear. Like the tallest man, the older woman's smock bore the sailfish and killer whale patterns and the bracelets she wore sported the same motif. A second *halaka* hung on a hook attached to the right side of her sash.

'Take that woman alive!' shouted the eldest man, his voice sibilant.

'Leave her to me,' ordered the older woman, with a similar intonation which made some of the "l's" sound like "r's". 'Did you hear me, Muchkio?'

'I hear you, Shushi,' the girl answered sullenly, letting the bow she had been raising sink down, and relaxing its string.

Listening to what was being said, Charole made a desperate effort and drew free the head of the lance. Deprived of its support, she felt as if the ground was heaving beneath her feet. Desperately she spread her legs apart, lifting the weapon and wishing that she did not feel so helpless. She knew it would only take a short while for her excellent physical condition to throw off the worst of the exhaustion, but was equally and bitterly aware that the time would not be granted to her.

Advancing swiftly, the buxom woman did not trouble to draw her *rentjong*. Instead, she suddenly lunged and, as Charole made an ineffectual attempt to turn the lance on her, she caught hold of it with both hands. Giving a sharp and twisting heave, she wrenched it from its owner's grasp.

Staggering a few steps from the force with which she had been disarmed, Charole contrived to remain—albeit uncertainly—upright.

It proved to be of no benefit to the Protectress!

Throwing the lance aside with a contemptuous gesture, Shushi followed as Charole came to a halt and endeavoured to assume a defensive posture. It was to no avail. When close enough, the buxom woman pivoted on her left leg while snapping out the right in a fast yet power-packed kick.

The leather hard sole of the foot caught the Protectress in the *solar plexus* and, even if she had been in full possession of all her faculties, the impact would still have been more than her well developed stomach muscles could withstand. Giving a strangled croak of torment as what little breath she had was driven from her lungs, she folded over at the waist and her legs began to buckle like candles near a flame. Before they collapsed completely under her, Shushi struck again. Not with the foot this time, but just as effectively. Folding its thumb across the palm, but keeping the fingers extended and together, the woman chopped the heel of her right hand viciously against the back of Charole's neck. Everything went black for the already barely conscious Protectress and she fell face forward, as if she had been pole-axed, to sprawl motionless at her assailant's feet.

'Kill those *gatahs*,' commanded the oldest of the men, who was a senior war-lord of the Cara-Bunte nation. 'You'll stay here and start butchering them, Roshta, Muchkio. I'll send some of the others to help you bring in the meat and the loot. Keep your hands off *that* until the Lady Shushi and I have looked it over and taken what *we* want.'

'Yes, Lord Torisaki,' the younger of the male archers assented and the girl gave a surly nod of concurrence.

'Get something to lift her on so we can take her to the landing place, Goti!' Shushi ordered, indicating Charole's flaccid body, as Muchkio employed the arrow she had refrained from drawing to kill the Protectress's *banargatah*. Then she turned to her husband and went on, 'The Dragon God has smiled on us, Lord Torisaki, bringing this one to us so soon after we landed.'

'Yes,' the war-lord agreed, thinking of certain ambitions he and his wife had frequently discussed in the privacy of their living quarters. The raid upon which they were engaged had been organized with their future plans in mind. Having been making what they had expected to be an unproductive reconnaissance, they had seen Elidor's party taking up the ambush positions. While ordering his party to separate into two, each being able to deal with Mun-Gatahs, Charole had arrived and enabled them to approach with greater ease than if there had been no distraction. 'There will be much honour in taking such a one as her back to Tansha-Bunte. Take care of her and tend her wounds, my lady. She won't be able to walk for a while, but she's not too badly hurt and we want her in the best of health so that she can put up a good fight when we put her into the arena before the Emperor.'

* * *

As the unconscious body of the Protectress of the Quagga God—bound hand and foot and suspended from a sapling cut for that purpose—was being lifted ready to be carried to the Cara-Buntes' landing place, far to the south-west a struggle for domination between two magnificent looking females of different species was about to commence.

Having secured the isabelline mare to her in the *Nemenuh* fashion, Dawn Drummond-Clayton took hold of the reins. Starting to lead Isabel into the water, she experienced no greater reluctance than *Shambulia* had displayed over following Bunduki. Employing the *Australopithecus'* language as fluently and effectively as her husband-to-be had, she coaxed the mare to follow her. She expected a similar response on mounting. Nor was she disappointed. However, from Isabel's first reaction to the discovery that a living creature was sitting upon her, it was apparent that she intended to fight in a different fashion—though no less vigorously—to that of the big stallion. Being somewhat smaller and lighter than *Shambulia*, she did not place her reliance on the 'bucking straight away' which had formed his main line of defence. This in no way detracted from the spirited manner in which she carried out her efforts to dislodge the unwanted burden.

Commencing the proceedings by 'chinning the moon', and having it countered in the same manner as that of the stallion, the mare took off in a series of high and 'fence-cornering'[4] leaps. Despite entailing repeated changes of direction, to a rider of Dawn's experience these presented no difficulties—beyond making sure they did not allow her mount to reach the shallow water. However, on taking off for the eighth time, having found that she had not succeeded in removing her burden by such methods, Isabel elected to 'swap ends.' Curving her body in mid-flight, she turned a complete half circle while in the air. Taken unprepared, the girl gave a howl of distress and, sliding sideways from the saddle, went head first into the lake.

Seeing Dawn being unseated, Joar-Fane let out a frightened squeal and At-Vee the Hunter gave vent to a

4. *Fence cornering: rodeo terminology for bucking in a zigzag fashion. So called because it was said to resemble the meanderings of the kind of wooden rail fences sometimes erected during the Old West days of the United States of America. J.T.E.*

string of Telonga obscenities he only very rarely employed in the presence of a woman.

While equally alarmed, Bunduki wasted no time in verbally expressing his concern. Instead, having already made preparations to render assistance if it should be required, he shook loose the noose of the lariat which At-Vee had brought from the tree-house's corral and which Dawn had been holding during the conquest of *Shambulia*.

The blond giant appreciated that his wife-to-be was facing two major dangers. Even if her superbly tuned reflexes and rider's instincts had not had time to take over, the water would lessen the impact of her fall. Although she would doubtless alight without injury, Isabel might turn upon her. Or, if the mare should make a distress signal, *Shambulia's* feelings as a former *manadero*[5] might prompt him to dash to her rescue. So Bunduki was ready to deal with either, or both, threats to Dawn's well-being.

The need did not arise!

Feeling herself relieved of the insidious burden, Isabel's natural inclination was to put as much distance as possible between herself and whatever it had been. So, grunting with a mixture of alarm and relief, she went onwards for a couple more bounds.

Then the rope attached from Dawn's waist to the saddlehorn snapped tight!

Despite having been caught unawares, the girl justified Bunduki's faith in her ability to fall without injury—aided by the *Nemenuh* method of 'water breaking' which had proved equally efficacious on countless other occasions over the years—and was already starting to sit up when Isabel reached the end of the rope. Spitting out the liquid she had inadvertently swallowed, Dawn was jerked under again.

Although the girl's weight brought Isabel to a halt, she did not react as the blond giant had feared by either

5. Manadero: *the Spanish-Mexican term for the master stallion of a band of horses.* J.T.E.

returning to the attack or signalling to the stallion that she required help. Instead, she did no more than swing around until she was facing Dawn. *Shambulia* was still exhausted and having received no request for assistance, he remained passive and did not attempt to pull free the lead-rope by which he was tethered to a bush.

'Hey, expert!' Bunduki called, relief plain on his face, watching the soaking and bedraggled girl rising. 'That's a fancy way of doing it!'

'Yes,' agreed At-Vee, his concern alleviated by the discovery that Dawn was unharmed. 'But I thought you were supposed to be riding Isabel, not teaching her to swim.'

'Don't let those brutes mock you, sister,' Joar-Fane encouraged, sharing the men's sentiments, as the other girl glared towards the shore. 'She can't beat *us*.'

'All right, Isabel,' Dawn gritted, returning her attention to the mare. Taking the rope in both hands, but making sure she did not tug at it, she advanced slowly. As she moved, she continued to speak in a soft, soothing voice which was at odds with the content of the words she was uttering. 'All right, you tricky something-or-other, so-and-so, something-else. I'm going to get back on and stay there until you something-well give up.'[6]

As the language of the *Australopithecus* did not include obscenities, being limited to purposeful word-sounds, and sharing At-Vee's feelings on the subject of profanity—even though it was possibly justifiable under the circumstances—the girl conducted her, as it proved, effective method of calming the mare in English.

Coming alongside Isabel without having aroused a display of hostility, Dawn unhurriedly returned to the saddle. Pacific as the mare had been until that happened, she started to exhibit her objections almost as soon as the girl was settled on her back. Showing speed rather than strength, she intermingled 'swapping ends' with 'chin-

6. *While the author realizes that in this present 'permissive' society, he could record Dawn Drummond-Clayton's exact words, he sees no valid reason to do so. J.T.E.*

ning the moon', 'sunfishing',[7] 'crawfishing',[8] but without the murderously effective 'pinwheeling',[9] and *never* in the same order, and put her rider through a long and gruelling struggle. At last, however, hampered by the water—which she had been continually prevented from quitting—and countered by Dawn's superlative exhibition of equestrianism, she too was finally driven to a state of exhausted submission.

Even as the tired, but delighted, girl was returning to join them, the congratulations of her husband-to-be and friends were brought to an abrupt end.

Bunduki was the first of the party to notice that two boats filled with people and propelled by sails were turning from the river into the mouth of the lake. Long, narrow, carvel-built[10] and somewhat spoon-shaped, they reminded him of the *ghe ca vom* river craft he had seen in and around Saigon while on an expedition which his adoptive father had been carrying out for the International Union For Conservation And Natural Resources. The resemblance even extended to the fact that the single mast was stepped well forward and carried what looked like an oblong combination of an Oriental gaff[11] and lugsail.[12] There was a small bamboo deck-house to

7. *'Sunfishing': a bound during which the animal twists its body into crescents alternatively—at least, most of the time—to left or right, seeming to be trying to touch the ground with first one and then the other shoulder, as if wishing to let the sunlight hit its stomach in the process. J.T.E.*

8. *'Crawfishing': pitching backwards instead of to the front. J.T.E.*

9. *'Pinwheeling': undoubtedly the rarest and, arguably, most lethal kind of bucking. The animal leaps forward and upwards, turning with its feet in the air and alighting on its back. J.T.E.*

10. *Carvel-built: in shipbuilding terminology, where the planks of the hull are laid edge to edge and form a smooth surface; as opposed to 'clinker-built', where they are fitted so that they overlap one another. J.T.E.*

11. *A 'gaff' is a pole, or 'spar', extending from the after side of the mast to support a fore-and-aft sail. J.T.E.*

12. *A 'lug' is a four-sided sail without a boom, or lower yard, attached to an upper yard which hangs obliquely on the mast. J.T.E.*

shelter at least some of the dozen or so crew members; and the rudder, mounted on the stern-post, curved gracefully beneath the hull so as to offer a greater purchase, control and manoevrability on restricted water-ways. *Oculus*, eye-like, insignia decorated the bows, but the remainder was unpainted.

Not only had the blond giant never heard of the Telongas operating such boats, although he knew they used canoes on the rivers, but he found something else disconcerting. The occupants had the same skin pigmentation of facial characteristics as his jungle-dwelling hosts, but all but one of the men were completely hairless, and their clothing was made from animal skins of various kinds. Even the women amongst them carried weapons.

While the Telonga hunters went armed—although their weapons were more in the nature of tools for hunting—the same did not apply to the male non-hunting members of their communities. Nor, apart from Joar-Fane—who had recently adopted the practise—did any of the women carry weapons.

All of these details presented possibilities for which Bunduki did not care. Watching the boats approaching with all the facility for manoeuvring offered by the archaic-looking rigging, he sent his right hand flashing to the hilt of the bowie knife he had retrieved from At-Vee.

'Get back to the house, girls!' the blond giant ordered, wishing that he had thought to bring his bow and arrows as they would have been far more adequate than the knife for repelling what he believed to be an alien invasion. 'We'll try to stop them landing.'

CHAPTER NINE

I CAN MAKE THUNDER AND LIGHTNING

'Come on, you cowardly, cringing old Mun-Gatah bitch!' ordered the sullen Cara-Bunte girl called Mu-chkio, stirring the Protectress of the Quagga God's recumbent body with a bare foot. When this failed to elicit any response, she bent and, digging her fingers into the short black hair, went on in a mocking tone as she began to haul upwards, 'Stir yourself. The Lord Torisaki wants to question you.'

In spite of the fact that Charole had apparently been subdued for several hours, such treatment proved ill advised.

On regaining consciousness, which was not until she had been transported to the raiding party's camp, the Protectress's first thought—it was, in fact, produced by a subconscious reaction resulting from her last cohesive recollection—had been to try and struggle. Although she was no longer bound, having been released from the pole so that she could be revived and bathed in the stream upon the shores of which the Cara-Buntes had established their base, she had learned that this was not a wise move in her present weakened state.

Shushi having been supervising the cleansing and reviving, so as to administer treatment to the captive's wounds, had rammed a knee into her stomach and pinned her down. Then the buxom woman's right hand, which had a grip like the closing jaws of a bear-trap, took hold of and began to crush Charole's naked left breast. Such was the agony induced by the grinding fingers that she had almost fainted. So, realizing that resistance was futile until she had recovered at least some of her strength, she had laid passive and been released. Satisfied that she had cowed the Protectress, Shushi had applied an ointment to the abrasions acquired while fighting Elidor. From its stinging sensation, Charole had decided it was similar to the medication her nation used and hoped it had the same quick acting qualities.

After the Protectress's wounds had been tended, she was taken—dragged by the arms and legs as she was still in no state to walk—and dumped unceremoniously outside the sumptuous pavilion tent of War-Lord Torisaki. She had not been fastened in any way, but had known that the time was not ripe for an attempt to escape. Instead of expending energy in what she had known would be a pointless waste of it, she had devoted her attention to taking stock of the situation.

What Charole had seen warned her, although she had not really required the warning, that her position was very grave.

The first thing the Protectress had noticed, apart from the entirely expected fact that she was left without weapons, was that she was not allowed to dress. Instead, she was clad only in the brief black lace panties which were her underwear. The silver lamé halter, skirt, her greaves and sandals were nowhere to be seen.

Charole had not needed to ponder on the reason for the removal of her attire. It had not been done so that she could be assaulted sexually. Rape was carried out on *very* rare occasions, but the 'Suppliers' had implanted such a strong pride of race into the members of every nation that the thought of having sexual intercourse with a person of another race was generally considered abhorent and was infrequently practiced. She had been stripped because the lack of garments would make her escape increasingly difficult and her recapture more certain.

Continuing her surreptitious observations, while allowing her depleted energy to be restored by the inactivity, Charole had discovered that the Cara-Buntes' camp was in a valley between two sand dunes and within sight of the 'Lake With Only One Shore'. It was comprised of the War-Lord's pavilion encircled by twenty smaller tents. They were similar to the kind of temporary accommodation presented by the 'Suppliers' to the Mun-Gatah nation and gave shelter to the hundred or so male and female warriors who had accompanied Shushi and Torisaki on what was chiefly a food gathering expedition.

Down on the shore, drawn up above the high tide level, were a number of boats shaped like shallow oval baskets. Constructed on a framework of willow poles fastened together with rawhide lashings, they were covered with the hides of Defassa and Common waterbucks that were sewed together and whose natural water-resistant qualities were enhanced by a coating of melted fat from the species *Kobus Defassa* and *K. Ellipsiprymnus* mixed with earth and ashes. Like the so-called 'bullboats' made from the skins of bull bison and used by Indians and fur traders along the Missouri River, which they might have been patterned upon, they were very light and had a draught of less than ten inches. This and their exceptional carrying capacity[1] made it possible for each to transport a heavy load. So they were employed as a means of communicating between the sea-going vessels and the shore, or to carry back the loot when raiding along rivers.

For obvious reasons, the raiding party's four ships had been left out at sea almost beyond visual distance. Each was in the care of a small anchor watch and had had its sails furled and struck below to help make it even less noticeable. If they had been closer, Charole would have discovered that they were painted black and the leaping sailfish motif was reproduced in the natural colours on their extremely raked bows. Despite the need to prevent the vessels' presence being noticed, thus giving warning that they were in the vicinity, a flag bearing an equally

1. *A Missouri River 'bullboat' twenty-five feet in length, with a width of fifteen and a depth of three feet could carry up to six thousand pounds' burden. Although smaller, those of the Cara-Bunte were proportionately as effective. J.T.E.*

well depicted killer whale in all of *Orcinus Orca's* black and white majesty flew at each masthead to announce they were in the service of the War-Lord Torisaki and War-Lady Shushi of the Tansha clan.

In spite of the fact that the Cara-Buntes' physical characteristics and weapons were suggestive of the Orient, the ships showed a distinctly Arabian influence in their lines and rigging. Single-masted, lateen-rigged,[2] carvel built, they were of shallow draught and as sleekly sinister in appearance as any *zaruk* in which, until comparatively recent times, slavers, gun-runners and smugglers—of ivory in particular—had plied their nefarious trades across the length and breadth of the Red Sea.[3]

Operated by a system of blocks and tackles, with the tiller-lines hanging over the side in a completely exposed fashion, the rudder extended well below the keel and, while offering greater control when steering, added several inches to the overall draught. Not only did the bows rake forward sharply, but the lines of the stern were equally acute. This made the already weatherly vessels particularly suitable for handling in a high following sea, or through the heavy surf around much of the coastline of their homeland. Attached to the sides, which were pierced for the large, heavy oars known as 'sweeps', were the davits whereby two 'bullboats' could be carried while the ships were in passage.

Although the vessels were large enough to take a crew of forty, the complement was normally restricted to no more than thirty. This allowed prisoners, a good quantity of loot or—as in the case of Torisaki's party—meat to be transported. With the exception of the two berths situated beneath the short upper steering deck at the stern, supplied for the captain and his consort, there was no other shelter provided. However, this was only a slight

2. A 'lateen'—a European corruption of the word, 'Latin'—is a right-angled triangular sheet laced to a long, sloping yard and controlled by a system of blocks and tackles which allows the ship to sail against, as well as with, the wind. *J.T.E.*

3. When employed for legitimate purposes such as pearl-diving, the zaruk is sometimes called a 'garookuh'. *J.T.E.*

disadvantage and not a particularly severe hardship. The *zaruks* and the *badans*[4] preferred by some of the clans were only used when making the two hundred or so mile crossing between Cara-Bunte and the western side of the mainland, then raiding along that coast.[5]

As in the case between the Mun-Gatahs and the *Brelefs*, the Cara-Buntes had a subservient race at their disposal. Known as *Yung-Libs*,[6] they were tall, heavily built, hairy—although not so much as the *Brelefs*—unintelligent and inclined to be lazy. Their heads were long, large and narrow, while the features were short and broad with a tall nasal opening and eyes that appeared almost rectangular. Clad in animal skins, those in the camp were not armed and served as porters, or in other forms of menial capacity.

With the examination of her surroundings completed, Charole had turned her thoughts to survival and escape. She had realized that the former was entirely dependant upon her being able to achieve the latter. Various comments she had overheard led her to assume that the Cara-Bunte behaved in the same general fashion towards prisoners as her own people. Only those who were young enough to pose no threat were retained as slaves. Any of an age to be active warriors were either used for sacrifi-

---

4. *The principle difference between the* zaruk *and the* badan *is that the stem piece of the latter is almost perpendicular and lacks the extreme rake which is characteristic of the former. The author is unable to say which style of bow is most advantageous, as each kind of vessel is equally seaworthy. We suspect that the choice was made on the personal prejudices of the respective clans' warlords and dictated by past traditions. It is noticeable that none of the Tansha clan's rivals used the* zaruk. *J.T.E.*

5. *Although it has no bearing on the present volume, the Cara-Buntes made their voyages to raid the northern, southern and western shores of the mainland in replicas of Arabian sambuks. Graceful, carvel-built, lateen-rigged, square-sterned and weatherly, these large vessels have two forward raking masts, a built-up poop deck and offer far more adequate accommodation for the crews than either a* zaruk *or a* badan. *More details of the sambuks are given in the author's* THE AMAZONS OF ZILLIKIAN. *J.T.E.*

6. *The* Yung-Libs *are a very early type of Cro-Magnons. J.T.E.*

cial purposes or to fight in gladiatorial combats. So, unless she could find some means of attaining her liberty before she was carried off in the *zaruks*, she was doomed to certain death.

It was not a prospect with which the Protectress was enamoured.

Accepting these unpalatable facts, Charole had no intention of submitting mildly to her fate. It was not that she feared death. For all her faults, she had great personal courage. Apart from her driving desire to regain her power as the Protectress of the Quagga God, she was also motivated by a disinclination to be killed for the entertainment of her captors.

Having yielded to the inevitable, Charole had succumbed to the waves of exhaustion that were assailing her and fallen into a deep sleep. Nor had she been disturbed by any of the raiding party. They were all occupied with guard duties and setting up the racks upon which the meat they would be gathering was to be sundried and turned into *fulsa*, or otherwise prepared for being shipped to Cara-Bunte. When she had awakened, the sun was almost touching the horizon. Although she had felt much refreshed, she had not shown it. Instead, she had concentrated upon conveying the impression that she was still asleep.

Muchkio had returned as the light was fading accompanied by the party Torisaki had sent out to assist with the butchering of the slaughtered *gatahs*. These were regarded as a delicacy by the Cara-Bunte because they were acquired as trophies of war. The party were laden down with the meat and with their victims' property. It had been apparent that the girl was not enamoured of the task she had been given, nor by having to turn over the loot to the war-lord. However, apart from looking sulky, she had said and done nothing to make her sentiments known. She and the rest of the party had gone to wash the blood and other signs of their labour from them in the stream.

Waiting until night had fallen, the Cara-Buntes had lit fires. While food was being prepared by their *Yung-Lib* slaves, Shushi and Torisaki had started to examine the loot. When they had searched the bundle which was strapped to Charole's saddle, they had clearly been impressed by the sight of her ceremonial garments. However, before they had opened the bag containing the 'Thunder Powder' and 'Terrifiers', the war-lady had told Muchkio—who was standing close by in a way which suggested she belonged to an influential family—to fetch the Protectress.

As any member of the Mun-Gatah nation could have warned the girl, she was not carrying out her task in the most prudent fashion.

Propelling herself upwards with great rapidity, Charole thrust her left arm between the girl's thighs. Catching Muchkio by the throat with her right hand, she lifted the girl from the ground. Then, as the fingers untangled from her hair, she swung around and hurled Muchkio from her.

Startled exclamations arose and everybody in the camp looked to see what was happening. Holding their crescent-shaped *galaki* spears in positions of readiness, two of the men who were standing guard began to hurry forward. So did Shushi and some of the other women, but none of them offered to draw a weapon.

Even as her victim alighted supine on the soft sandy ground Charole darted after her ignoring the approaching male and female warriors. Straddling the girl's weakly moving recumbent body, she delivered a vicious and power-packed punch with first the right and then the left fist. Already winded and dazed by the landing, Muchkio was unable to resist. Her head was snapped back and forth by the blows, but she did not feel the second land and went limp.

Leaping to her feet, Charole looked around to find out which of the men and women who were closing in upon her posed the greatest threat. She knew there was no hope of fighting her way through them, but she meant to defend herself. However, it soon became apparent that they merely intended to prevent her from trying to escape and did not mean to take any punitive action for what she had done to the girl.

'Nice work. I couldn't have done much better myself,' Shushi remarked calmly. 'Come with me.'

'Very well,' Charole assented, knowing that although the war-lady was no longer carrying either the *rentjong* nor *halakas*, she had no other choice but to obey.

'Who did these belong to?' Torisaki asked, indicating the ceremonial garments as his wife walked up with Charole.

'They're mine,' the Mun-Gatah woman replied, standing erect and speaking proudly. 'I am Charole, the Protectress of the Quagga God.'

'Are *you!*' Torisaki ejaculated, sounding both pleased and impressed. Glancing at his wife, he continued, 'Then she's an even better catch than we imagined, my lady.'

'She is, lord,' Shushi agreed, studying Charole in a speculative fashion. Then, picking up the sack, she tipped out its contents. 'Huh! You must like coconuts, Protectress of the Quagga God.'

'They're not just ordinary coconuts,' Charole corrected, seeing at last that a chance was being offered. 'In fact, using one of them, I can make thunder and lightning.'

'*That* I would like to see!' Stated in tones redolent of disbelief.

'Very well,' Charole replied, trying to conceal her eagerness. 'Give one to me and you will see.'

'All right,' Shushi said, picking up a "Terrifier" and looking it over without seeing anything significant in the little piece of "burning cord" that protruded from one of the "eyes". Holding it forward, she went on, 'Here.'

'Wait!' Torisaki barked, before Charole could take the proffered device. He dropped his hand to the *lading's* hilt ready to enforce his command. Sensibly, she refrained and he growled, 'While I've never seen *anybody* who can make it happen, I know how dangerous lightning is when it strikes. So give the coconut to that *Yung-Lib* there and tell him what to do with it.'

'It won't work that way,' Charole protested.

'It won't work in *any* way, you lying Mun-Gatah

115

bitch!' Shushi scoffed and, tossing the "Terrifier" down, she lashed a slap across the Protectress's face.

Rocking on her heels, Charole emitted a squeal of rage and pain, then brought her right fist across in a punch to the war-lady's jaw. Spun around and sent staggering a few steps, Shushi managed to avoid going down. What was more, as Charole darted forward, she tried to snap home the kind of kick which had served her so well earlier. This time, the results were far less satisfactory. Refreshed by the hours of sleep, the Protectress was able to react with her usual speed. Catching the rising ankle, she gave a twisting heave which flipped the other woman over in a half somersault. Then, as Shushi landed on her back, Charole bounded into the air and bent her legs so as to land with her knees on Shushi's breasts.

Once again, exclamations arose all round and the Cara-Buntes started to gather. However, as when the Protectress had thrown and leapt on to Muchkio, none of them—not even the war-lord—showed any sign of intervening. In fact, he stood with folded arms and displayed nothing other than interest.

Timing the move perfectly and in a way that showed she might have been shaken, but was far from incapacitated, Shushi rolled clear of her descending assailant. A screech of rage burst from Charole as she saw her intended prey avoiding her. It turned to a wail of distress as she came down and, despite the sand being soft, felt some of the skin being peeled from her knees. However, she could have thought herself fortunate to have suffered no worse an injury; but she was not granted an opportunity to do so. Twisting back in the direction from which she had come, the war-lady coiled her body and folded her legs on to her chest. Straightening them out quickly, she smashed both feet full into the Protectress's imposing bosom. A flood of agony rushed through Charole and she went over backwards with her hands clutching at the stricken area.

If Shushi had been less roughly handled, she could have brought the fight to an end there and then. As it was, sensing that there was an arduous struggle ahead, both she and Charole stayed down and let several seconds go by while they recouped. Each was watching the other and they regained their feet, a couple of yards apart, at almost the same instant.

Circling one another warily and like two primeval jungle cats, the women paid not the slightest attention to the exhortations of the crowd. As her sash had come unfastened, Shushi shed her tunic to leave her clad only in a pair of scarlet silk panties as brief as the Protectess's solitary garment. Long experience had taught the Cara-Bunte women warriors the danger of fighting bare handed with the hair in the traditional ponytail. So the war-lady knew what to do to alleviate the risk. Reaching behind her head with her left hand, she jerked off the semicircular silver band and shook her long black tresses free.

Quick though Shushi's move had been, Charole acted even more swiftly. Darting forward, she bounded up in a dropkick. Although the war-lady tried to leap rearwards, the feet reached her breasts with sufficient force to repay the treatment she had given to Charole. Crying in pain, the buxom woman tumbled on to her back. However, remembering what had happened the last time she made the attempt, the Protectress did not essay another knee-drop. Instead, she flung herself bodily on to her supine but far from helpless rival.

Both of the women were trained warriors, skilled in unarmed combat, but pure feminine instinct elicited exactly the same response from each as their bodies came into contact. Even as Charole's fingers were burying into and wrenching at Shushi's hair, pain burst like a raging fire through her own head. She felt as if her short locks were in danger of being torn out by the roots as they were savaged just as vigorously.

Over and over the embattled women churned, alternating between pulling at hair and swinging wild, yet hard, punches or slaps indiscriminately. Snapping forward at one stage, Charole's forehead pulped Shushi's nose to bring blood gushing out. Not long after, a butt from the war-lady split the Protectress's top lip. During the rolling, squirming mill, Charole found herself kneeling behind Shushi. Her left arm was across the buxom woman's face and the right was drawing upwards on a hank of hair. Just as she was deciding to put the right hand to some more useful purpose, she felt a set of firm white teeth sinking into flesh. Not in a gentle nip either and the blood on the limb was soon no longer all from Shushi's nostrils.

After one piercing shriek, the Protectress replied in kind and just as effectively. Bringing her head forward, she closed her mouth on Shushi's shoulder and tore at it like a wild animal. Wailing like a soul in torment, the war-lady reached over her shoulder to catch her assailant by the hair. Then, forcing herself and Charole from the kneeling position to their feet, she bent at the waist and, taking advantage of the leverage offered by being shorter, catapulted the other woman over. Although Shushi also went down, the impact separated them. They were up in an instant, both breathing hard through the exertions of almost ten minutes' hair-tearing, rolling-around brawling. Each had now a blackened eye, bloody nostrils and lips, grazes on elbows, knees and shoulders. Blood also trickled down Charole's left arm and along Shushi's neck to flow through the valley between her heaving breasts.

Oblivious of the audience, who were still encouraging them to better efforts, Charole and Shushi came to grips again. This time, however, it was like trained warriors. There was little to choose between them in skill, or strength. What was more, each had seen sufficient members of the other's nation fighting in the arena to possess a fair idea of what to expect. So Charole countered the war-lady's chops and open handed jabs by punching, while each was conversant in using the feet and knees as weapons. Nor did either have any ascendancy when they used wrestling throws, locks and grips.

For almost an hour longer the battle raged. It went through the camp, up and back down the nearest sand dune. About half way through, having recovered, Muchkio tried to interfere. Turning on her, Charole and

Shushi battered her unconscious and trampled on her as they resumed their briefly interrupted hostilities. There was only one other intervention. Locked in a clinch, they had been in danger of falling into a fire. Leaping forward, Torisaki grabbed each one by the hair and threw them clear of the danger.

Stumbling in exhaustion, barely able to see through her right eye and with the left swollen closed, Shushi launched a swing at Charole's head. In only a little better shape, the Protectress sidestepped and, as the warlady staggered by, turned to jump on to her from behind. Desperately trying to counter the move, Shushi made the mistake of falling backwards. While she landed upon her opponent, she found her waist trapped between the other's sweat-soddened thighs.

Because of the time they spent riding, the Mun-Gatahs' leg muscles were so developed that the scissors was a deadly tactic for them. Crossing her ankles to help crush on Shushi's midriff, she began to apply an—even in her present condition—murderous constriction. Nor did she restrict herself just to that. Rocking her body on to its shoulders, she raised her victim into the air. What little breath Shushi had was leaving her in a pitiful moan. Never had she experienced such strength, nor an equal pressure. It was as if her body was being pulped into two pieces. Then she felt herself descending sideways. The landing made the legs tighten until it seemed that the lower was on the verge of caving in her ribs. However, it also had the effect of breaking the grip. As the limbs opened, she rolled free and managed to continue moving away.

A good minute went by before either woman could rise. When they did, it was obvious that they were both on their last legs. Tottering towards each other, they weakly grabbed for hair and wobbled in a circle tugging as hard as they could. After almost thirty seconds of such ineffectual behaviour, Charole summoned every dreg of energy she could muster. Suddenly she slipped backwards, dragging Shushi after her. Placing both feet against the war-lady's barely resisting body, she brought off a stomach throw.

By some miracle, Shushi managed to at least partially break her fall. Hardly aware of what she was doing, driven only by an indomitable fighting instinct and courage, she turned on to her stomach and forced herself up until reaching her knees. Charole was already up. Sobbing for breath, she reeled in to smash a kick between the bare olive-skinned shoulders which pitched its recipient face down once more. Falling to her knees beside Shushi, the Protectress turned her over and, drawing her into a sitting position by the hair, delivered a *coup-de-grace* with a punch to the jaw. As the defeated war-lady flopped supine, the victress toppled forward across her. Charole made one desperate, unavailing attempt to get up, then she too subsided into loss of consciousness.

'What a fight!' Torisaki enthused, his face alight with a mixture of excitement and lust as he studied the two battered, motionless figures at his feet. "Take them both into the pavilion and tend to their injuries. By the Dragon God, I'm going to enjoy tonight.'

While the war-lord's orders were being attended to, he noticed the 'Terrifier' lying where his wife had dropped it. Going over, he picked it up and stood looking at it for a few seconds. Then, giving a shrug as he decided the Protectress had been bluffing for some reason, he tossed it across into the fire. Turning, he strolled towards the pavilion in the wake of the women carrying the unconscious fighters. Before he had taken three steps, the device exploded.

CHAPTER TEN

WE ALL DON'T JUST *TALK!*

'Here you, foreign woman!' the visitor named Deneb-Ginwe called to Dawn Drummond-Clayton. 'Bring me some of that food and be quick about it.'

'Yes, noble master,' the Earth girl responded, sounding humble and walking forward with a bowl of the succulent stew for which Joar-Fane's mother was famous.

There had been no need for Bunduki's instructions to be carried out earlier in the day. Even as Dawn had been on the point of obeying and making for the tree-house to collect weapons, At-Vee the Hunter had declared there was no cause for alarm. The newcomers in the boats were members of the Wurka-Telonga village. Joar-Fane had replied to the blond giant's comment that he had not heard of such a village by stating, 'We don't talk about *them.*' She had sounded prim and spoke in a way which reminded the Earth couple of an elderly Victorian maiden aunt commenting about a disreputable branch of her family to whom she would prefer not to be related.

Before either Dawn or Bunduki could try to discover what had caused the reticence among all the Telonga people with regard to the Wurkas, the boats swung around in a wide reach. Displaying skill that told of long practice, the crew had dropped the sails. Then, as one anchor was let down in each *ghe ca vom,* two of the men had leapt from each boat to carry a second anchor ashore and buried its head in the sand to act as a kedge. By the time this had been done, the boats were secured bows to the wind and, in not more than a couple of feet of water, some thirty feet from the beach. It had been, the Earth couple considered, a masterly exhibition of boat handling. Whatever else the new arrivals might be, they were exceptionally competent in such matters.

Having brought the two *ghe ca voms* to a stop, the kedge anchor handlers stood in silence. They were all youngish, with what should have been friendly faces and yet they seemed both shy and ill-at-ease. None of them offered to speak. Instead, they had looked to where three men out of the second boat had started to wade ashore. Nobody else had followed the quintet.

In the lead of the delegation had been the only man whose skull was not completely bald. Clad in the flowing white robes of a village Elder, he had a veritable mane of white hair and an unpleasantly sour cast of features which had exuded a self-righteous and sanctimonious aura. Unlike every other Telonga of the Earth couple's acquaintance, who always endeavoured to keep their attire clean, his garment was grubby beyond what might have been expected from a journey in a boat. He alone had been unarmed, and he announced that he was Tik-Felum, the senior Elder, in tones that implied he considered nothing further need be said to establish his superior status. Then, without waiting for any acknowledgement, he had presented the men who had followed him ashore. Two of them were his sons. All had on loincloths made from the beautiful dark brown hides of sea otters (which none of the other occupants of the *ghe ca voms* had been wearing) encircled by leather belts. From these, at the left side, hung wooden handled swords which had proved to have the undulating blades with the hook-like *bĕlalaigaja* of the Javanese *dapur bener kris*.

Deneb-Ginwe, the elder of the sons, had a skull which bulged over a face that tapered to a thin and weak chin. His expression was modelled upon that of his father. Nor was his sibling, Han-Ateep, any more prepossessing: Something under six foot in height and like the rest of his family having a far from impressive physique, he had also shared their attitude of arrogant self importance.

Not quite as tall, the other two were more thickset and heavily built. Clean shaven and domineering looking, Sraat-Challig had the air of a truculent bully and was slightly the larger of the two. Exceeding the other in weight, Jomus-Takn had a massive moustache which made him look pompous without relieving the glint of real cruelty in his close-set and piggy little eyes. Hanging from the right side of his belt was a carefully folded fishing net made of slender and weighted cords.

'So these are the famous "Earths" who have come to change our way of life, are they?' Tik-Felum had asked, making no attempt to address Dawn and Bunduki.

'They are our friends,' At-Vee had replied coldly.

'The Telonga nation have never had the need to make outsiders their friends,' Tik-Felum had stated pompously. '*We* see no need for it to start happening now.'

'That's because the People-Taker never reached the Wurka-Telonga village,' Joar-Fane had put in hotly. 'If he had, and had done what he did to the people in *our* village, you would have welcomed the friendship of Dawn and Bunduki of the "Earths".'

'It seems that other things have changed for the worse among the Jey-Mat Telongas,' Tik-Felum had growled, taking in the girl's hostile attitude and the way in which she was dressed. No other woman of their people had ever dared to speak so forthrightly to him. 'I shall have much to say to the Elders of your village, Hunter.'

'Talk is what the Elders always do best,' At-Vee had answered off-handedly.

'We all don't just *talk!*' Jomus-Takn had injected, with a threatening scowl which had warned that he was looking for trouble.

'Look there!' Han-Ateep had almost yelped, before any more could be said, pointing to the tree-house. 'I've never seen anything like that before!'

'The "Suppliers" have built it for our home,' Bunduki had explained, seeing that the other four were equally impressed by the sight. 'We "Earths" are well favoured by them.'

The quintet had exchanged worried glances and the truculence had left the burly pair to be replaced by a lack of ease. They had regarded the tree-house as a sign that the 'Suppliers' were not averse to the changes proposed by the 'Earths'. Saying that his party would continue their journey to Jey-Mat, Tik-Felum had turned and strode rapidly away. Nor had his sons been dilatory in following his lead, but had almost scuttled along on his heels. Although Jomus-Takn and Sraat-Challig had tried to comport themselves with indifference, they too had departed with more haste than they had come ashore. Once they were all aboard, the anchors were taken in. Then the *ghe ca voms* had been taken across the lake under the propulsion of their oars until they could pick up the wind.

After their unpleasant visitors had departed, the four young people had returned to the tree-house. The Earth couple had attended to the welfare of the quaggas, then they had climbed up to eat a belated lunch. Over the meal, they had learned why the rest of the villages' populations did not care for the Wurkas. It went beyond their swampland territory having granted them complete immunity from the attentions of the Mun-Gatahs' People-Taker. Because of their comparative isolation, they had developed a number of behaviour patterns and habits which their less favoured fellows found distasteful in the extreme. For one thing, although they had never offered to take up arms on behalf of the rest of their nation—the 'Suppliers' having conditioned them to avoid the other villages at times when the abductions were taking place—their aggressive ways and a proclivity for picking fights had not endeared them to the non-hunting fraternity. Nor had the hunters developed any greater liking for them.

Dawn and Bunduki had learned something about the quintet who had come ashore from Joar-Fane and At-Vee. The only son of a rich Wurka family, Tik-Felum had been too idle to adopt the hard working habits by which his parents had acquired their wealth. Instead, he had applied all his intelligence and low cunning to persuade the rest of the population that it would greatly benefit them all if everybody shared the results of their labours with one another. Such an idea had proved particularly attractive to other idlers and loafers. They had done all they could to propagate the scheme and ensure its acceptance.

By the time that those of the Wurkas who were willing to work had started to realize how their efforts were supporting the bone idle coterie, Tik-Felum had been in a position to keep them under his domination. By a further display of his cunning, he had contrived to restrict the ownership of the very effective *dapur bener kris* to his supporters. So he, Jomus-Takn and Sraat-Challig had been better armed than the rest of the villagers and could enforce their will upon anybody who tried to oppose it. By such means, they had achieved the ability to wield power without being answerable to anyone other than themselves and, according to the Hunter, were said to make the most of it.

Even before they had heard the Telonga couple's story, the girl and the blond giant had not been enamoured of the five Wurkas. Being aware of the effect men with similar philosophies had had on Earth, they had seen no reason to revise their points of view. All in all, they had come to regard Tik-Felum and the other four with anything but favour. While the aggressive spirit of the other Wurkas could have been turned to the Telonga nation's benefit, they had known the quintet would be opposed to it being utilized for such a purpose.

Putting the matter of the Wurkas from their thoughts at the end of the meal, the two young couples had descended from the tree-house. Collecting and saddling the quaggas, Dawn and Bunduki had returned with them to the sandy beach. After another session of 'water breaking' apiece, in which the animals' struggles had been somewhat less protracted than on the first occasions, they had decided to call it a day as far as the training was concerned. So, leading Isabel and *Shambulia* back to the corral, they had made all secure for the night. Setting off for the village, they had arrived shortly after sundown to find the visitors were being entertained with typical Telonga hospitality.

It had soon become apparent to the blond giant that Tik-Felum's coterie had spread a warning to the other Wurkas that he was to be considered *non persona grata*. According to Tav-Han, before Tik-Felum had arrived, the rest of the newcomers had been expressing interest in his ideas for defending their nation's territory; but would change the subject if any of the quintet had come near. What was more, when Bunduki had approached a group, the Wurkas who were present had showed they were ill-at-ease and had stopped talking until he left. So, when the food was ready to be served, all he had learned about them was that they used bows and *shilvas* as adjuncts to the fishing which brought in the majority of their sustenance and that, while they had light, barbed throwing spears, they did not employ the heavy variety with which the hunters of the jungle villages tackled leopards, jaguars and even, on rare occasions, tigers.

The blond giant had gone into Tav-Han's house to pay his compliments to his future 'mother-in-law' shortly before Deneb-Ginwe made the demand for service. If he had been present, he could have warned the Wurka that such conduct where Dawn was concerned was most ill-advised. Of course, if Bunduki had been in the vicinity, the surly and far from courageous Deneb-Ginwe would have thought twice before addressing the 'Earths' girl in the manner he always employed when dealing with the distaff side of his own race.

Even if Dawn had liked the surly Wurka, she would have objected to the manner in which he had addressed her. As she did not like him, she felt disinclined to accept his bad manners. Looking as if butter would not melt in her mouth, she deliberately poured the bowl of stew into his lap.

'You clumsy bitch!' Deneb-Ginwe shrieked, bounding to his feet with rage suffusing his unpleasant features. Not only was the food very hot, but the laughter which arose from the onlookers added to his humiliation. A quick glance around informed him that the big white haired "Earth" was nowhere to be seen. So he whipped his arm around, meaning to slap the girl across the face, continuing, 'I'll teach you——.'

At which point, the Wurka learned that there was a major difference between Dawn of the 'Earths' and a Telonga woman. The latter would either have mildly accepted the blow, or dodged it and fled. Not so the spirited foreign girl.

While Dawn ducked so that the man's hand passed harmlessly over her head, she made no attempt to flee. Instead, she thrust forward her left arm to ram its clenched fist with some force just below his breast bone. The blow was hard enough to drive him back a few steps and fold him at the waist. Breathless obscenities bubbled from him as he came to a halt. On the point of returning and attacking her, he became aware that the girl was showing no fear. He also noticed the extremely competent way in which she was facing him with her hands still folded into hard little fists—and observed something else!

Ready, willing and very capable of defending herself further, Dawn suddenly felt her arms being encircled at the biceps and pinned to her sides from behind.

It was not loyalty that prompted Han-Ateep to go to his brother's aid but his own bullying nature. Usually he was far too self-centred to help anybody, but he was also just intelligent enough to appreciate the danger of letting disrespect for one of his family go unpunished. However, having for once acted without being told, in what—from the family's point of view—was a laudable fashion, he found himself in the same position as the man who caught a tiger by the tail and found that it would not let him go.

At her first indication of what was happening, Dawn's reaction was instantaneous and effective. Her training in the Japanese fighting art of *karate* in which—as in *jujitsu*—she was a third *dan* black belt, supplied the answer to the entrapment from the rear.

Almost without the need for conscious thought, the girl allowed herself to go limp as if in fear. However, while she convinced Han-Ateep that she was afraid, he failed to oblige by relaxing his grip. So she revised her original intention in a split second. A quick glance downwards allowed her to locate what she wanted. Up and down whipped her left leg, so that her heel landed on top of his right foot with all the force of her shapely, but steel hard calf and thigh muscles impelling it. A yell of pain burst from him and, this time, his arms loosened although without opening completely and releasing her.

Still moving with the same rapidity, Dawn bent her knees a little and flung up both arms with a force that caused those encircling her to rise until they were over her shoulders. Having done so, she slipped her hips slightly to the left and, reversing the direction sharply, she slammed the heel of her clenched fist into his groin. That produced the desired effect. Letting out a croaking moan, Han-Ateep stumbled away from her with his hands clasping at that portion of the male anatomy most vulnerable to such an attack.

Liberated, Dawn took in the sight of Deneb-Ginwe approaching. His expression gave her all the inducement she needed to continue her defence. Springing to meet him, she rose into the air with an almost balletic grace and delivered a *yoko tobi geri*, leaping side kick, which sent the ball of her right foot into the centre of his chest. He was pitched away from her by the impact, landing winded and helpless flat on his back.

Naturally the altercation had attracted considerable attention among both villagers and visitors. Seeing what was happening to his sons, Tik-Felum came to the same conclusion as Han-Ateep about how allowing such treatment to go unavenged might have an adverse effect on their future position in the tribe. So he threw a meaningful glance at the burly man on either side of him. Sharing his sentiments and not averse to the prospect of manhandling such an attractive girl, Jomus-Takn and Sraat-Challig started to lumber towards her.

Before the moustached Wurka had taken three paces,

he heard the rapid patter of bare feet and a snarl as savage as that of a 'Hairy Man' from close behind him. Two huge hands closed upon his shoulders in a vastly more powerful grip than he had ever previously encountered. So severe was the crushing force they exerted that his arms went numb. He found himself swung and thrown aside as if he weighed no more than a newly born baby and, as he spun around with no control over his limbs, he saw the white-haired male 'Earth' rushing at his companion.

Becoming equally aware of Bunduki's intervention, Sraat-Challig did not care for what it portended. He had seen how Jomus-Takn was being treated and he considered that a man who was capable of such strength and violence should not be met in bare-handed combat. However, massive though the ivory handled knife hanging from the 'Earth's' belt might be, the blade of his *kris* was almost twice its length and offered him the kind of edge he liked when in a fight.

Among the Wurkas was one of the lesser lights of Tik-Felum coterie, Fiant-Wlip by name. About five foot ten inches tall, lean and with a sharp, viciously miserable face, he was ever an opportunist. Seeing a chance to earn the Senior Elder's approbation, he dashed forward as Dawn was alighting from the kick. It was his intention to grab hold of her before she was able to regain her balance.

Unfortunately for Sraat-Challig, before he could make use of the *kris's* advantages, it had to be drawn. Nor, for all that he had carried the weapon for many years, had he ever taken the trouble and *work* required to attain anything like the speed with which a competent member of a warrior race could whip a sword from its sheath. Although he did succeed in extracting the weapon, it was nowhere near a position to pose a threat when Bunduki reached him.

Disdaining to soil the blade of his big bowie knife with the blood of such an obviously incompetent person, the blond giant caught Sraat-Challig's right wrist in both his hands with a grasp no less painful than that he had applied to Jomus-Takn's shoulders. It proved just as effi-cacious. The Wurka let out a howl of pain and released the *kris* as his trapped limb was raised with an irresisti-ble force. Ducking under the arm and swivelling around, he snapped it sharply downwards. Sraat-Challig found his feet were leaving the ground. However, his wrist was released and he contrived to return to earth in an upright position, even though his impetus caused him to stagger several paces away from his big assailant.

Much to Flant-Wlip's annoyance, Dawn not only alighted before he could reach her, but showed no suggestion of being off balance. To his dismay, neither could he halt his impetuous rush. Catching his out-stretched left arm just above the hand in both her power-ful little fists, she twirled until her back was towards him. Sinking to her right knee, she propelled him over aided by his own impetus. Letting go, so that he sailed onwards to come down even more heavily than Deneb-Ginwe had, she rose and gazed about her.

'Look out behind you, Bunduki!' Tav-Han bellowed, as the blond giant was about to turn and find out if his wife-to-be needed any help.

Even as the warning was delivered, Bunduki discov-ered that Jomus-Takn had not been incapacitated.

On coming to a halt without falling, although his shoulders were still hurting, the moustached Wurka snatched the fishing net free from his belt and shook it. Specially folded for the purpose, it spread out to its full extent as he cast it in the blond giant's direction. Falling over Bunduki's head, shoulders and arms, the thin strands began to ensnare him. Giving a howl of delight, for every other victim of his skill had been easy meat once caught in the meshes, Jomus-Takn ran back in the direction from which he had been propelled. What was more, spurred into activity by what he saw, Sraat-Challig lurched erect and started to close in on the blond giant. With his arms pinioned as effectively as if they had been bound, Bunduki glanced from left to right. There was cause to worry, he decided, apart from the fact that his legs were unimpeded. Already Jomus-Takn was grasping and pulling at his left arm. Still a few feet away, Sraat-Challig was lumbering at him from the right. Nor could he count upon Dawn for assistance.

Although still obviously in pain, Han-Ateep had taken advantage of the respite given to him by Flant-Wlip and was making for the girl again. Having been in another part of the village, At-Vee was running towards the scene of the altercation; but he would not arrive in time to save his friend. None of the other Jey-Mat hunters were offering to intervene, either, for they still lacked the instincts of fighting men.

Not that Bunduki intended to rely upon anybody else for succour. His training in *ju-jitsu* and *karate*, reaching a fifth *dan* grade, had taken into consideration the possibility of an attack being launched upon him when his arms were indisposed. He had already decided what action was called for by his present situation.

Instead of struggling against Jomus-Takn's tugging net, the blond giant blended his own response into it. Pivoting swiftly on his left foot until his toes were pointing at his assailant, he swung his right leg so that its bent knee met the other's groin with great force. Turning an ashy grey-green colour and letting out a moan of torment, Jomus-Takn let go of Bunduki's arm. Twisting away, he collapsed, retching piteously, to his hands and knees.

To Han-Ateep, flinging himself at Dawn, it seemed at first as if he was going to knock her over. However, as he discovered an instant later, this was not the case. She had already commenced dropping backwards just before he reached her, bringing off a stomach throw every bit as effective as the one that had been performed by Charole far to the north-west a little earlier in the evening. More effective in fact, as the force with which her would-be attacker landed rendered him *hors-de-combat* without the need for any further attention on her part.

Satisfied that he need devote no more time and attention to Jomus-Takn, Bunduki turned upon his second assailant. In spite of what he had just witnessed, Sraat-Challig was over-confident. He too had never seen anybody who had been netted capable of raising more than a minimal defence. So, believing the blond giant to be almost helpless, he was charging recklessly forward.

Looking over his shoulder and measuring the distance with his eye, Bunduki suddenly whipped his right leg backwards in an arc which caused his torso to incline beneath the blow that the Wurka was swinging at him. Although his kick landed slightly higher than on Jomus-Takn, he had no reason to consider it less effective. Struck in the pit of the stomach, Sraat-Challig was put into an involuntary retreat and was bent almost double by the pain and nausea which was assailing him.

Using the ball of his other foot as a swivel, Bunduki turned and, changing legs deftly, landed a kick with the left to his victim's descending face. Lifted erect, Sraat-Challig over-compensated through no fault of his own. Tumbling over backwards, he met the ground with a thud that sounded like music to a number of the other Wurka guests' ears and lost all interest in the proceedings for several minutes.

'My apologies, Tav-Han and Elders of the Jet-Mat village,' the blond giant said, saying the words in a way which emphasized that he was not including Tik-Felum in the sentiment, as he gripped and began to tear the net apart with his powerful hands.

'None are needed, Bunduki of the "Earths",' Tav-Han stated, eyeing the Wurkas' Senior Elder defiantly. 'The fault was not yours.'

'I'll say one thing, though,' At-Vee commented, grinning broadly and glancing at the moaning Jomus-Takn. 'This is one time when an Elder should have stuck to talking.'

CHAPTER ELEVEN

HOW CAN WE FIND THE "EARTHS"

'Very well, Lady Charole,' War-Lord Torisaki said almost amiably, indicating the three "Terrifiers" which remained after the accidental explosion, and a deliberate experiment he had carried out later the previous night. They, the small bag of "Thunder Powder", the Protectress of the Quagga God's ceremonial garments and weapons had been brought into his quarters after the fight. So had the "Earth's" arrow, overlooked until then because of the more obviously unusual and impressive nature of the other items. 'How do those things do what they do?'

Bruised, only able to focus through her left eye as the right was still swollen shut and both were blackened, Charole was stiff in every muscle and joint in spite of the ministrations she had received. So she lay back and relaxed upon the comfortable floor-cushions which furnished the dining-room portion of the Cara-Buntes' large pavilion.

On recovering consciousness the previous evening, Charole had found herself in a soft bed. As always happened when she had emerged victorious from a hand-to-hand conflict with another woman, she had felt sexually stimulated. Nor, despite a general disinclination among the people of Zillikian to have intercourse with members of another race, had her passion been left unsatiated. Although more than an hour had elapsed since her collapse across the defeated body of War-Lady Shushi, Torisaki was still experiencing the erotic stimulus caused by watching two all but naked and shapely women fighting.

Not even the narrow escape he had had when the 'Terrifier' detonated was enough to have cooled his ardour. As his wife was still indisposed, he had joined her defeatress in bed and all thoughts of racial antipathy were forgotten. Charole was thoroughly satisfied with the service she had received.

When the Protectress had woken up that morning, she had accepted that she had no hope of escaping in her present condition. The soothing oils and capable manipulations at the hands of Shushi's personal maid, a skilled masseuse, had done no more than somewhat alleviate her sufferings. It would be several days before she would throw off the effect of the sword and fist fights in which she had participated. Yielding to the inevitable, she was trying to think of a way to liberate herself from captivity once she had recovered.

Relaxing by her husband's side, Shushi was watching Charole as well as she could with her left eye closed and the right a mere puffy slit. She was not troubled by the knowledge that her husband had spent the night making love to the foreign woman. What rankled was that he had seen her go down in defeat. However, having studied the Protectress's badly mauled condition and knowing herself to be in even worse shape, she conceded that the time was not ripe for her to seek revenge. Instead, as convention demanded, she had ensured that Charole's injuries received the same care and attention as her own. With that done, she had settled down and listened to Torisaki's story of the mysterious devices the other woman had been carrying. She was now waiting eagerly to hear the answer to his question.

'I don't know,' Charole admitted truthfully and, seeing the angry glances exchanged by her captors, she continued hurriedly, 'I really *don't* know. I know what they will do and how to make them do it. But I haven't the slightest idea, apart from that they are filled with "Thunder Powder", of how it happens.'

' "Thunder Powder"?' Shushi repeated interrogatively.

'The black dust in the bag there,' Charole elaborated, then told of the discoveries made by Zongaffa the Herbalist and of the devastation caused when the "Terri-fiers" were used. She finished by saying, 'Whoever has them can be the greatest of all in his, or *her*, nation.'

'Do you know how to make the "Thunder Powder"?' Torisaki inquired, concluding that manufacturing the containers would be simple enough.

'Do *I* look like a damned herbalist?' the Protectress de-manded haughtily.

'You looked like a woman with many enemies and few friends when we first saw you,' Shushi put in. 'Why were you riding alone?'

'There had been serious troubles in Bon-Gatah,' Char-ole replied, her thoughts mingling with recollections that finally made her decide that speaking the truth might be to her advantage. 'I considered it was advisable for me to leave until I could gather some support and I was on my way to fetch it when they found me.'

'What kind of trouble?' Shushi asked.

'So those so-called "Terrifiers" didn't do any good for you after all,' Torisaki growled, his disappointment plain, after the Protectress had briefly explained how she had supported the High Priest in a bid for power that failed. She made no mention at this stage of the part Dawn and Bunduki of the "Earths" had played in the debacle.

'They would have made all the difference,' Charole said and could not prevent bitterness creeping into her voice. 'But that damned Zongaffa and my maid brought us coconuts filled with soil and hid those holding the "Thunder Powder", except for the few we had already, to be used by themselves.'

'Are there many of them?' the war-lady wanted to know, when her husband did not speak.

'A lot,' Charole guessed, but so convincingly she might have been certain.

'Where are they?' inquired Shushi, showing more ea-gerness than the war-lord.

Unlike Torisaki, the buxom woman could sense that the Protectress might be concealing some facts, but was neither lying nor exaggerating. So, in spite of suspecting that the other was speaking the truth for her personal

135

ends, Shushi meant to encourage her to continue in the hope of learning something worthwhile.

'Too far on the plains for *you* to reach them,' Charole warned. 'You don't have enough warriors to smash your way through and there are too many of you to slip through, especially on foot.' Striving to hold her tone with a timbre of no more than making a casual request for information, she went on, 'Are you the leaders of your nation?'

'No!' Shushi spat the denial out as if it had a bad taste.

The one word reply confirmed the Protectress's suspicions with regard to Torisaki and his wife. While making love with him, she had been struck by how closely his behaviour and manner resembled that of the late High Priest of the Mun-Gatah nation. Keeping him under observation since waking up, she had been even more convinced of the likeness. So she had felt sure that the warlord was a man of high ambition and craved an even greater position of power than was his present lot. In which case, she had had an inkling of how she might turn his desire for aggrandisement to her advantage. Such a person would see the possibilities offered by the 'Thunder Powder' and the 'Terrifiers', particularly as he had-according to various comments she had overheard—already been granted a demonstration of what the latter could do. He would certainly want to learn more about them, either with regard to their manufacture, or from whence he might obtain a supply.

While Charole could not help him with the former wish, she felt that she could turn his second aim to her own use. If so, she would be increasing her chances of effecting an escape.

'Then you could call upon your leader to give you a sufficiently large force to fight your way through,' the Protectress suggested, almost disinterestedly it seemed, doubting whether such a proposal would be considered acceptable by the Cara-Bunte couple and having no desire that it should be.

Charole's scheme did not include taking part in an invasion of her homeland, although loyalty to the Mun-

Gatah nation had no part in her unwillingness. She was confident that such a venture would be doomed to failure when carried out in the only way Torisaki would regard as suitable for his purposes.

With those thoughts in mind, the Protectress was determined to guide the war-lord's thoughts away from the possible source of supply left by the dead Zongaffa. If she succeeded in steering him as she wanted, her hopes of regaining her liberty would be greatly improved.

'The trouble is that with a large force, there are too many people in it for *anything* to be kept a secret,' Charole remarked, sounding pensive, when neither the man nor the woman made a comment. 'And one's leaders *always* want to take anything new and useful for themselves.'

'Is there anybody else who knows how to make the "Thunder Powder"?' Shushi asked, having been told of Zongaffa's demise.

'Not among my people,' Charole admitted, struggling to conceal her delight at the way in which the conversation was developing. 'Have you heard of, or met, the "Earths"?'

'"Earths"?' Shushi repeated, fumbling with the unfamiliar word. 'What are they?'

'Not "What", "who",' Charole corrected. 'I've only seen two of them, a man and a woman, but those two have weapons the like of which I've never seen equalled. They have bows which can drive an arrow so far through one of our breastplates that its head came out at the back. And that is something neither the Cara-Buntes, nor any other people we've fought against *ever* managed to do. That is one of their arrows there.'

'Huh!' Shushi grunted, unimpressed, after picking up and giving the missile a cursory examination. 'I don't see anything special about it, except that its head has four cutting edges instead of two.'

'And is made from a far better steel than any of us are given' the Protectress pointed out. 'What's more, you've never seen a tree with "wood" like that from which the shaft it made. I had a broken one in my bundle. If it's still lying around out there and you have it fetched, you'll see what I mean.'

'I'll take a look at the "wood" in this arrow,' Shushi stated.

Gripping the ends of the shaft in her hands, as Charole had done on first making contact with a similar missile, the war-lady began to bend it. She soon learned, again as the Protectress had, that the 'wood' had exceptional strength and resisted a pressure that would have snapped any Cara-Bunte arrow.

'Here, you!' Torisaki barked, paying more attention and addressing a male *Yung-Lib* who had been squatting on his heels in the corner showing not the slightest interest in what was going on. Telling what was wanted, the war-lord concluded, 'Go and fetch it here. And don't take all day about it, damn you!'

'Tell us more about these "Earths", or whatever you call them,' Shushi requested, as the *Yung-Lib* slouched out of the pavilion. 'Nobody has ever brought any of them back to Cara-Bunte and our people have raided all around the mainland.'

'We've not had many of them ourselves,' Charole answered, trying not to grit out the words as she remembered how much of her present misfortune was attributable to Dawn Drummond-Clayton and Bunduki. 'In fact, I personally have only seen two of them.'

'What did they look like?' the war-lady demanded with a touch of impatience, and her one-eyed gaze kept returning to the arrow, studying its points of difference fom those to which she was accustomed.

'The man was the biggest, strongest, most handsome male I've ever seen,' Charole began, 'for all of his white hair.'

'*White* hair?' echoed Shushi, who had the habit of repetition when puzzled or disbelieving some statement. 'How old was he?'

'Not out of his twenties,' the Protectress estimated. 'His hair wasn't the white of an old man's, but more golden in colour. The woman was about the same age and——.' On the point of describing Dawn in unflattering terms, she saw how doing so would not help her to achieve her purpose. 'Well, not *bad* looking and fairly well formed. In fact, the Lord Dryaka found her all too attractive the first time w—he had her as his prisoner. That was how she came to escape.' Again she paused just in time to avoid a possible indiscretion and decided to distort the next facts. 'We've never had the man, but he followed us to our hunting camp. It was he who prevented us from chasing her after she'd escaped.'

'How?' asked Shushi.

'According to our warriors who started after her, they have magic powers,' Charole explained, speaking slowly and trying to avoid any emotion as she approached one of the vital portions of her scheme. 'She and the man changed themselves into a couple of those "Hairy People" that live in the jungle.'

'Rubbish!' the war-lady snorted, having seen a few of the very occasional *Australopithecus* who had fallen into raiding parties' hands and reached Cara-Bunte.

'That's what the warriors told us,' Charole insisted, her brows knitting in annoyance at the buxom woman's curt interjection. 'All *I* know personally is that I heard first a female and then a male of the "Hairy People" give one of those damned cries, or bellows in his case, that you hear them making in the jungle. Only these sounded close to the camp and we were miles from the nearest woodland, much less the real jungle.'

'I don't believe it!' Shushi stated, before she could stop herself.

'Have a care, damn you!' Charole warned, forcing herself into a sitting position and glaring as best she could with her features so battered. 'Have you forgotten already what happened the last time you called me a liar?'

'Stop that, damn you, or I'll crack your heads together and knock some sense into you!' Torisaki thundered, as his wife spat out a Cara-Bunte obscenity and grasped the arrow in the manner of a knife. In the face of his obvious determination to prevent a resumption of hostilities and also appreciating how little either of them was capable of fighting, the women relaxed. Satisfied that he had kept the peace, he continued, 'Are the Mun-Gatahs so frightened of the dark, or the "Hairy People", that hearing what might have been no more than somebody making noises would prevent you from chasing an escaped prisoner?'

'We are *not* afraid!' the Protectress contradicted indignantly, still having pride in her nation for all that she would have been willing to help plan and participate in any invasion that might prove successful, providing it offered her the means to return to power. 'We'd have gone after them, but that blasted "Hairy Man's" bellow terrified our mounts so much they stampeded through the camp. By the time we'd rounded them up, the "Earths" had disappeared.'

'Never to be seen ag——?' Shushi commenced in a mocking voice, but subsided into silence as her husband directed a furious and prohibitive glare at her.

'We saw them again all right,' Charole corrected, appreciating the futility of allowing herself to be provoked and promising herself that she would have a reckoning with the war-lady if a more suitable opportunity was presented. '*Both* of them.'

With that, delighted by the way in which the two Cara-Buntes were taking in every word, the Protectress told the story of Dawn's recapture and its aftermath. She noticed how they exchanged glances on hearing of the People-Taker's fate, which suggested that they were aware of the Telonga population's normally pacific and cowardly nature, but not even Shushi showed scepticism. Basing her story on what she had seen, learned from Elder Eokan on the night of her flight from Bon-Gatah and deduced during the lonely hours that had followed, she went on to describe what Bunduki had achieved.

'Not only did he bring together three of our District Administrators who had always hated each others' guts, but he formed an alliance with the captain of the Amazon's Black Panther Regiment to help rescue his woman. Have you ever known anybody else who could do so much, or of any *man* who could make friends with those hell-cats?'

'I haven't,' Torisaki conceded without hesitation, but the return of the *Yung-Lib* with the two segments of the broken arrow brought the conversation to a temporary halt.

While the war-lord was examining the pieces, paying particular attention to the point at which Charole had cut through them with her sword after trying to break the shaft by hand, the *Yung-Lib* bent and whispered something to Shushi. Darting a glance at the left side wall, which was on the outside of the pavilion, she made an equally quiet reply. Alert for any kind of hostility or treachery on the war-lady's part, Charole was watching the by-play. She felt a surge of alarm as the servant went to collect one of the disc-like *halakas* which lay with the other's weapons. However, Shushi did no more than accept and place the deadly device on the pillow beside her without making any reference to why she was doing so. Instead, she gave a jerk of her head and the *Yung-Lib* turned to go into the kitchen at the rear of the pavilion.

'You're right, Charole,' Torisaki admitted, too engrossed to have noticed what his wife was doing and passing the arrow to her. 'I've never come across wood of that kind.' He paused for a few seconds, then asked the question that the Protectress was hoping to hear, 'How can we find the "Earths"?'

'They can ride very well,' Charole replied, thinking of the occasion when her life had depended upon the blond giant's ability while riding a fast-moving *gatah*.[1] 'But, in spite of that, I believe they are jungle dwellers.'

'Huh!' Shushi put in, turning her gaze briefly from the left side wall. 'Much that tells us. The jungle covers all the southern end of the mainland.'

'Yes,' Charole conceded, knowing that she was approaching the crux of her efforts and controlling her asperity over the war-lady's comment. 'But, vast though it might be, is it large enough to hide a complete nation, which we were told had five cities, so completely that

1. *The occasion is recorded in:* BUNDUKI. *J.T.E.*

nobody has ever come across *any* of its people until these two appeared?'

'It doesn't seem likely, or even possible,' Torisaki admitted, so interested now—as was his wife—that neither of them noticed a slight inconsistency between the Protectress's last comment and an earlier statement with regard to the "Earths".

'Either way, it doesn't make things any easier,' Shushi declared, without looking away from the left side wall. 'Finding just two people in the jungle would be even more impossible than locating a whole nation. Even if we had any reason for wanting to find them.'

'Would you say that the "Earths" knowing how to make the "Thunder Powder" is reason enough?' Charole challenged.

'Do *they* know *that?*' Torisaki demanded, and his wife was so impressed with the possibility that she turned her attention from the wall.

'They do,' the Protectress bluffed, having no concrete evidence upon which to base the statement. She explained why she believed that the "Earths" possessed the requisite knowledge, concluding with, 'Bunduki certainly recognized it as soon as he saw it——.'

'*You've* had him as your prisoner?' Shushi asked.

'I did!'

'And let him escape?'

'Yes!'

'You never mentioned *that* before,' the war-lady reminded the Protectress.

'Would *you* have?' Charole countered, showing annoyance.

'That doesn't matter,' Torisaki put in, before his wife could make any reply. 'If they know how to make it, we'll have to try and find them.'

Which was exactly what Charole had been leading up to.

If the theory which the Protectress had been formulating was correct and accepted by the Cara-Buntes, it could prove beneficial to her in three ways. Firstly, it would prolong the time before her captors set off for their island home; from which she would have not the remotest chance of escaping. Secondly, if she achieved all she wanted, she had the means by which she could avenge herself upon Dawn and Bunduki of the 'Earths' as well as being given the opportunity to try and extract whatever knowledge they possessed with regards to the 'Thunder Powder'. Thirdly, and not the least imoprtant of the considerations, even if the search of the jungle should prove abortive, there would be a far greater chance of her regaining her liberty there than here, on the banks of, or while being taken across, the 'Lake With Only One Shore'.

'Then I may be able to help you,' Charole said, sounding more casual than she felt.

'You?' Shushi snorted. 'Why should you?'

'To gain my liberty,' Charole answered. 'I would have to be given your sacred oath to the Dragon God that, if you find the "Earths" with my help, you will set me free and let me share the secret of how to make the "Thunder Powder".'

'We can make you talk without needing to give any promises,' Shushi warned.

'You could *try*,' the Protectress corrected. 'But you wouldn't know for sure whether I'd told you the truth—— And you daren't take too much time in making sure, or your ruler will get suspicious and start trying to find out what's delaying you. I'm sure that you *don't* want that to happen, Lord Torisaki.'

'You can have what you wish,' the Cara-Bunte promised, standing up and raising his right hand. He recited an oath sufficiently like the one used by the Mun-Gatahs, with a dragon instead of a quagga as the deity to whom it was directed, for Charole to be both satisfied that it was genuine, and confident that it would be equally binding once uttered. At the end, sitting again, he asked impatiently, 'Well, where are they?'

'At the Jey-Mat Telonga village,' the Protectress guessed and elaborated with, although she did not realize it, valid reasons for the assumption. She finished, 'So

I think the "Suppliers" have sent them to look after those cowards.'

'That could be correct,' Torisaki agreed. 'If the rest of their weapons are as fine and different as their arrows, the "Earths" must be well favoured by the "Suppliers".'

'Or they might even be "Suppliers" themselves,' Charole suggested, in a voice that throbbed with excitement.

'They might at that!' Torisaki ejaculated, sounding equally thrilled by the possibility of being able to lay hands on one or more of their mysterious benefactors. It had always been his ambition to do so. He yearned to attain the position of Emperor of the Cara-Bunte nation and, without being aware of them, he shared the late High Priest of the Mun-Gatahs' dreams of conquerring the other races with whom his people had come into contact.

'How soon can we march to Jey-Mat?' Charole inquired, deciding that she had been correct in comparing the war-lord with Dryaka.

'*March*?' Torisaki barked. 'You mean go across country?'

'Yes,' Charole confirmed. 'It's a pity that you can't ride——'

'We can ride,' Shushi protested. As their homeland was roughly the size and shape of Madagascar, the "Suppliers" had allocated small ponies as a means of transport around it. 'But we never bring our mounts on raids. What we'll do is go by sea and, although we've never bothered to try it before,[2] we'll find a way through the swamplands to a village. Even if it isn't Jey-Mat, we can make the people there take us to it.'

While she was speaking, the war-lady picked up the *halaka*. At the end of her words, she propelled it across the pavilion. Slicing through the left wall, its disappearance was followed almost instantaneously by the scream of a woman in mortal agony.

2. *In addition to the entire coastline of the Telongas' territory being fringed by swampland after the fashion of the Florida Everglades, the Cara-Buntes' failure to penetrate the region was induced by the 'Suppliers'. J.T.E.*

'That was Muchio,' Shushi announced, as Charole and her husband stared from the wall to her and back. 'The *Yung-Lib* told me she was eavesdropping and I've been watching to find out where she was standing.'

'If you've killed her——!' Torisaki began.

'Not even the second cousin of the Empress is allowed to spy on a war-lord and war-lady,' Shushi pointed out. 'But I know what you mean, my husband. If I've killed her—and, from the way she screamed, I probably have—we've *got* to know how to make "Thunder Powder" and "Terrifiers" before we go back to Tansha-Bunte.'

'Only the "Earths" can tell you,' Charole warned. 'That means you'll have to find them to learn how to do it.'

CHAPTER TWELVE

I DON'T WANT YOUR CHILDREN

'Darling!' gasped Dawn Gunn, née Drummond-Clayton, resting her back against the pillows of her nuptial bed and staring in delight at the well-laid tray of food her husband of only a few hours was placing on her lap. 'This is wonderful. Oh thank you!'

'Don't mention it,' Bunduki replied, sitting alongside the girl who was now his wife. Wondering if he had ever seen her looking so radiantly beautiful, he grinned and went on, 'Just remember, this's how I want it brought to *me* every morning from now on.'

All through the days preceding that on which their marriage ceremony had taken place, in addition to the various preparations for the event, the girl and the blond giant had had much to keep them occupied.

One of the main problems that had demanded Dawn's and Bunduki's attention had been to continue the training of the quaggas. However, as soon as Isabel and *Shambulia* had come to accept being saddled and ridden—which had been attained after only one more spell of abortive resistance apiece—the progress had been rapid. While there was much for them still to learn, both would answer to their names and come in response to their respective owner's whistle. So successful had this aspect proved that the Earth couple had already started to teach the animals to obey certain *Australopithecus'* signal calls as an aid to communication over even longer distances. Noticing how little fear was shown by their mounts to sounds which usually induced panic among *gatahs*, Dawn and Bunduki had been even more sure that they were gifts from the 'Suppliers'.

During the evenings, when time had permitted, Bunduki had set about instructing the Jey-Mat Telonga hunters in armed and bare-handed self defense. As in the case of the quaggas, he had wondered how much of the rapidity with which At-Vee was attaining competence was due to mental conditioning by the 'Suppliers'. Keen and intelligent as the Hunter undoubtedly was, the way in which his ability with weapons and unarmed combat improved was exceptional. None of the others could keep pace with him in either accomplishment. Nor did they approach the skill displayed by Joar-Fane and At-Vee in all matters pertaining to the care and riding of the captured *gatahs*. There was, the Earth couple had realized, much still to be done before they had established a reliable fighting force. They had also felt that they had no cause to be ashamed of what had already been achieved along those lines.

While riding their quaggas in the jungle, Dawn and Bunduki had renewed their acquaintance with a band of forest elephants they had befriended and which had later proved of the greatest service to them.[1] What was more, ranging further than would have been possible on foot, they had discovered that—as they had been promised by the 'Supplier' they had met—they apparently possessed a similar empathy with all members of the subspecies *Loxodonta Africana Cyclotis*.[2] They had had no difficulty in establishing equally cordial relations with two other bands they had met in their travels.

With the willing agreement of Tav-Han and other members of Dawn's Telonga 'family', granted out of consideration for all he was striving to do on behalf of their

1. *The occasions are described in:* BUNDUKI AND DAWN. J.T.E.
2. *The larger 'plains' sub-species of African elephant is classified* Loxodonta Africana Africana. *Up to twenty-four inches taller than* L.A. Cyclotis, *their ears are less rounded and the tusks which are bulkier and longer, curl upwards instead of being straight and parallel; an adaptation making it easier for the 'forest' elephants to move through thick undergrowth.* J.T.E.

people, Bunduki had been relieved of much of a task that would otherwise have fallen upon him. They had taken it upon themselves to carry out most of the work, including the production of the majority of the food, required to make a resounding success of the premarital feasting and dancing demanded by convention. It said much for their efforts that everybody who attended had claimed the festivities had never been bettered.

However, to establish his position as a leading member of the hunting fraternity, there was one thing that the blond giant could not leave to others. So on three occasions he had gone into the jungle alone at night. Armed with his bow and a selection of the specialized hunting points—which he had found at the tree-house and surmised were presented by the 'Suppliers' in response to his almost subconscious wishes—to supplement the utilitarian Razorheads on the first and third expeditions, he had restricted himself to the *m'kuki* and shield for the second. His yield for archery had been a large bull gaur and a five hundred pound giant forest hog. Combined with *very* careful stalking, his skill at throwing the Masai spear had brought him an exceptionally fine male bongo.

When the heads and hides of Bunduki's trophies had been exhibited at the Telongas' equivalent of his bachelor party on the night before the wedding, which had been attended by hunters from several other villages and four young men who had made the journey from Wurka by boat, all had been the source of admiration and acclaim. The means by which he had acquired them had increased his prestige enormously.

No other herbivorous animals in the jungle, not even the forest elephants, were so highly regarded and respected by the Telonga hunters as the gaur or the—to be strictly accurate—omnivorous giant forest hog. Both had characteristics which made it a most dangerous adversary. Each was tough, aggressive and hard to stop when launching an attack, particularly when opposed by the primitive weapons owned by the human beings.

Largest of all the Asiatic wild cattle, *Bos (Bibos) Gau-*

rus was, on Zillikian, matched in size only by the great Cape buffalo, and the plains-dwelling habits of *Cyncerus Caffer*[3] precluded the Telonga hunters from making its acquaintance. Knowing both species, Bunduki was in full agreement with those sportsmen on Earth who had claimed the gaur was the equal to the Cape buffalo on all the points by which they set their standards.

Most massive of all the *Suidae*, wild pigs, and possessing its full measure of that genus's courageously pugnacious tendencies when roused, the giant forest hog was a creature that was not generally sought after by the Telonga hunters. While they had a liking for its meat, they preferred to give the sub-species *Hylochoerus Meinerzhageni* a wide berth in its jungle habitat and go after the smaller, less dangerous red river hog.

The bongo was not regarded as being particularly dangerous, although it could be on certain occasions and in some conditions. Yet it too was held in high esteem. As on Earth, the hunting fraternity were aware that no animal was more wary, alert and adequately protected by its senses than the species *Boocercus Euryceros*. Those qualities had made its flesh highly prized. That the blond giant should have taken his specimen with the comparatively short ranged *m'kuki* and, instead of waiting in ambush near a watering place for the prey to come to him, had adopted the vastly more difficult task of going in search of it, had added to the credit he was given for his success.

Such had been the high regard for all Budnuki had achieved since he had come among them, which each man had admitted he could not have himself performed, that before the party had broken up, they had conferred upon him the greatest honour and title their fraternity could bestow. In future, Tav-Han had announced—and the information was relayed across the entire Telonga

3. *The smaller sub-species of African buffalo*, Syncerus Caffer Namus, *known as the 'dwarf forest buffalo' was also very aggressive and dangerous, but it did not inhabit the jungle in the Telongas' territory.* J.T.E.

nation by the 'talking drums'—the blond giant was to be known as the *Dapan-Dankara*.

Translated into English, the words meant, 'Fearless Master Of The Jungle'.

During the evening, Bunduki had had an opportunity to meet the men from Wurka. They had proved to be a vastly more likeable group than the Senior Elder, Tik-Felum, and his coterie. Free from the quintet's supervision and the presence of toadies who would have informed upon them, they had not hesitated to discuss their village's affairs.

Despite Tik-Felum and his companions' attempts to prevent it, the story of their defeat had passed around the population. It had given added strength to such of them, the four visitors in particular, who were resentful of working hard to support those who were too idle to do so. However, although desirous of bringing about a change in policy, they had not yet been able to raise sufficient support from their neighbours. No hints or suggestions had been passed on either side, but Bunduki had sensed that the men from Wurka might want to solicit his assistance in the not too distant future.

Thanks to the organizing abilities of Tav-Han, his wife, Joar-Fane and At-Vee, the Earth couple's wedding day had passed most enjoyably and without a hitch. Thinking of how close they had grown recently, Bunduki and Dawn were relieved when they were finally united in matrimony. Both had felt sure that, in the absence of a minister ordained in a Christian Church, their adoptive and, in the girl's case, actual families would consider the union completely honourable, legal and binding.

So it had been with a clear conscience that the blond giant had carried his bride to the tree-house and, having made the ascent on the elevator with her in his arms (several hunters supplying the motive power) across the threshold. Left alone, they had entered the comfortable double bed to consummate the marriage.

Now, in the light of early morning, Bunduki had brought a meal which Joar-Fane had prepared earlier for them. Much as he loved the beautiful girl before him, he had been unable to resist pulling a hoary old joke on her.

'And that's *not* how you're going to get it every morning from now on!' Dawn stated, with her eyes sparkling. 'Hurry up and eat, then go out and do some work—or something.'

'*Something?*' Bunduki hinted.

'*Something*,' Dawn replied, her expression showing what she was really meaning.

'I'm damned if I feel like going out to work now I've eaten,' the blond giant declared, after they had finished the meal and he was setting the tray on the floor.

'Then it looks like—*something*,' Dawn answered, tossing back the sheet which was her only covering.

'*Something* it is,' Bunduki said firmly and climbed back into bed.

'Darling,' Dawn breathed, as she and her husband lay relaxed in each other's arms about an hour later. 'You *really* don't mind if I continue to use the contraceptive tablets now we're married, do you?"

"Of course not, dear,' the blond giant assured her.

'It isn't that I don't want your children, or that I feel they would be illegitimate,' Dawn went on, repeating a point they had discussed at length on the day preceding their wedding. When she and Bunduki had felt a growing need for each other's love, Joar-Fane had presented her with the means to avoid offending their host nation's conventions.[4] 'But there's still so much work to be done. And for some time yet, it will need *both* of us. What's more, I want to make sure everything is comparatively peaceful, or at least until you have some support you can count on, before I start bringing children into the world.'

'You won't get any arguments from me about that,' Bunduki promised, agreeing whole-heartedly with every word his wife had said. Until he could rely upon the other Telonga hunters as well as At-Vee, he might need

---

4. *Although the Telongas had a predilection for making love, they also held strong views regarding babies being born out of wedlock. So, to allow the former and avoid the latter, they had obtained very effective oral contraceptive tablets for use by the maidens from the 'Suppliers'. J.T.E.*

the kind of assistance she would be unable to render if pregnant or with children demanding her attention. 'Now, what about it, my girl. Shall we get up or—*something*?'

'I can't see the slightest thing against doing—*something*,' Dawn breathed and gave herself freely to her husband.

* * *

'Hey there, brother,' At-Vee greeted, strolling up shortly after lunch and grinning broadly as he watched Bunduki reaching for *Shambulia's* double-girthed saddle. 'Can you manage to lift that all by yourself?'

'Why shouldn't I be able to?' the blond giant inquired, with assumed innocence.

'I thought *everybody* knew *it's* weakening unless it's had in moderation,' the Hunter explained, glancing to where Dawn and his wife were descending from the tree-house. 'But I've never heard of a newly married man remembering—until it was too late.'

'From what *I* remember, that's the voice of experience speaking,' Bunduki commented, lifting the heavy rig with no more than his usual expenditure of effort. 'You're the one we had to carry out of bed *three* days after your wedding.'

'That was *then*,' At-Vee countered, ignoring the fact that there had been more desperate and serious matters demanding all their attentions at the time his companion had mentioned. 'Now I've been married to Joar-Fane for this long, it's a very different matter. When I ask her to come to bed with me these days and she says, 'No', I'm grateful to her for being so considerate.'

'They're telling rude stories, sister,' Joar-Fane guessed, studying the two men as she and the new Mrs. Gunn were walking towards the lean-to by the corral in which the saddles could be left hanging over a wooden "burro" shaped like an upturned roof.[5]

5. *Cowhands in the American cattle-raising States always used a 'burro' if available. Should one have to leave his saddle on the ground, he placed it on its side or stood it on its head, but never laid it on its skirts, J.T.E.*

'Disgusting, isn't it, dear?' the Earth girl replied, her beautiful face alive with merriment and deep content.

'It *is*,' Joar-Fane agreed, exuding an air of pompous disapproval which Dawn had come to know was entirely false and which never failed to amuse her. 'Did I ever tell you about the last time I tried to give that lazy lump of mine a pleasant surprise?'

'No,' Dawn admitted, contriving to sound resigned. 'But I've a terrible feeling that you're going to.'

'I bathed, anointed myself all over with the sweetest smelling perfume I could make, then put on my most fetching bed gown,' the little Telonga girl continued, as if she had either failed to hear the other's last remark, or considered that it implied a desire to hear the story. However, having reached that point, she paused for a moment and darted a conspiratory glance at her companion, going on, 'And *you* know just how *fetching* one of them can be, don't you, sister?'

'I really can't *imagine* what you mean,' Dawn declared, modeling her manner upon that of a games-mistress at Roedean whose proclaimed belief that "it" was bad for one's hockey caused her to express a similar lack of knowledge. 'We "Earths" don't do such things.'

'Then where do all the little "Earths" come from?' Joar-Fane countered, thinking of certain significant sounds she had heard that morning on arriving to make breakfast and which had suggested her "sister" was not speaking the truth. 'Anyway, there I was, all ready and, even if I say it who *should*, I've never looked more seductive. So I went into the bedroom and said, "Darling, it's your wife."——.'

'Not that I'm interested,' Dawn said, with well simulated boredom, as the other girl paused for dramatic effect. 'But what did At-Vee do?'

'Jumped out of bed shouting, "Then hide me!"' Joar-Fane replied.

'Who says the Telongas don't have a sense of humour?' Dawn sighed, although she had found the story as amusing as it was intended to be even while she knew it to be untrue. 'I mean, apart from everybody.' Then, as they were now close to the two men, she went on with a smile, 'Good morning, At-Vee.'

'It was when *I* got up,' the Hunter responded.

'Which was a long time after I——!' Joar-Fane put in.

As in her husband's case, the Telonga girl was prevented from completing her statement. However, the reason was more serious than her light-hearted interruption. She noticed that Bunduki and At-Vee were not listening to her, but felt no pique as she was aware of what had caused the distraction. Barely audible, the rhythmic rumble of a drum came from far to the north. A few seconds later, although still at a considerable distance, the cadenza was exactly duplicated from another source.

'That's from Rol-Mat,' Joar-Fane estimated, mentioning the only other Telonga village to have received a visit from a member of the "Earth's" nation so far. 'But I can't make out what they're saying. Can you, dear?'

'I might if *somebody* would stop shouting in my ear,' At-Vee answered, but the timbre of his voice and the affectionate way in which he laid a big hand on and ruffled his wife's hair robbed the words of any sting.

'I never had *this* kind of trouble before he started going around with that lazy lump of yours, sister,' Joar-Fane told Dawn in mock exasperation, knowing that it had not been her speaking which had prevented her husband from reading the message that was relayed by the drummer in Rol-Mat.

Although every person on Zillikian could understand the general word-sounds sent on their respective nation's 'talking drums'—Dawn and Bunduki had been conditioned by the 'Suppliers' to be able to 'read' those of every race—only the men and women who inherited the duty of beating the percussion instruments possessed the inborn keenness of ear to detect and duplicate exactly messages at great distances. Each race's drummers could also transmit information of a confidential nature by means of secret codes known only to the initiates to their profession. However, it was distance and not secrecy which was preventing At-Vee and the other three from

154

learning what was being passed on from elsewhere by Rol-Mat's messenger.

The two couples were not kept in ignorance for long. Booming forth with great clarity, the 'talking drum' at Jey-Mat began to repeat the information. They found it to be of the greatest interest.

'From Tik-Felum of Wurka to Bunduki, *Dapan-Dankara*, at Jey-Mat. Our people have great need of your help, Fearless Master Of The Jungle. Come as swiftly as possible.'

CHAPTER THIRTEEN

WHAT YOU NEED HERE IS THE WOMAN'S TOUCH

Crouching in the concealment of a clump of bushes at a point which allowed him to draw and hold the recurved Fred Bear Super Kodiak bow at its anchor point, Bunduki made *very* sure of his aim. As his target—which could have a very great effect upon the success of the mission that had brought him to the Wurka-Telonga village—was only nine inches in height, about a third of that wide and some thirty yards away, he knew that he was going to require all his skill if he hoped to make a hit.

Even before the blond giant had visited Jey-Mat and arranged to have a request for further information passed over the 'talking drums', he had been suspicious of the summons sent by the Wurka's Senior Elder. It was either a trap, or a way of testing his newly attained status of Fearless Master Of The Jungle. He had also been aware that the way in which Tik-Felum's message had been worded did not leave him any other choice but to signal that he would accept. Although no Telonga hunter had gained sufficient merit to be given the title of *Dapan-Dankara* for several generations, tradition decreed that any man who did achieve it must be willing to travel anywhere within the nation's territory should his services be needed.

On learning the details, Bunduki had spoken with the four men from Wurka, who had not yet taken their departure due to the effects of the wedding-night's festivities. What they had told him suggested that Tik-Felum was making a test of his eligibility to be the *Dapan-Dankara*. Which, as his wife, At-Vee the Hunter, Joar-Fane, Tav-Han and the Wurka villagers, had all agreed was probably a trap. It was, the unanimous consensus of opinion had assumed, unlikely that the Senior Elder would want Bunduki to succeed in establishing his right to the title. However, they had all conceded that he could not refuse without a considerable loss of face.

As the blond giant had anticipated that he would be faced with such a situation, he had already been considering how best to deal with it. However, when he had begun to mention his intentions, he found that one aspect was not in his hands. Dawn Gunn had stated, in tones that warned she would brook no argument, her intention of accompanying him. Even if he had meant to leave her behind, he would have known that doing so would not be tolerated.

Another aspect of Bunduki's plans had been the subject of revision. It had been his intention that he, Dawn, At-Vee and Joar-Fane—whom his instincts had warned would also refuse to be left behind—would make the journey on their quaggas and *banar-gatahs*. Having conferred with one another in soft tones, the four Wurkas had offered an alternative means of transport. They had said that they would put themselves and their boat at the blond giant's disposal. Appreciating the advantages of travelling in such a fashion, he had accepted the invitation.

In spite of the Wurkas having made the suggestion, there were a few important reasons why it could not be carried out in a completely straightforward manner. From what the quartet had said, it was obvious that their participation could place their lives in jeopardy. So far, Tik-Felum was not aware of their visit to Jey-Mat. If he should learn of what he would regard as their betrayal, it would go hard for them.

Having no desire to endanger the four, who he believed would make powerful allies and competent leaders to replace the regime which was currently in control at Wurka, the blond giant had made his arrangements accordingly. Telling the others his plans, making sure that they were not overheard by anybody else, he had seen they were well received by the visitors. Appreciating that he was acting for the best, although they had hoped to play a more active part, Joar-Fane and At-Vee had raised no objections to being relegated to a minor, if important, role.

Returning to the tree-house, while the 'talking drum' was informing Tik-Felum that they would be setting off before sundown, the Earth couple had selected the equipment they intended to take along. Leaving the eight arrows with Bear Four-Blade Razorhead tips on the bow-quivers, they had placed a selection of more specialized heads which they had believed might be useful in the capacious back-quivers. In addition to the archery gear, they would be taking their knives, Bunduki's *m'kuki* and shield and the *boleadoras*. Apart from a blanket apiece, that was all they had felt would be needed. Knowing the advisability of impressing their travelling companions with their prowess as hunters, they had decided against carrying any food and intended to use their hunting skills to keep them provided.

Although Dawn and Bunduki had set out accompanied by Joar-Fane and At-Vee, leaving Tav-Han's family to take care of the tree-house in their absence, they had not stayed for long in each other's company. About a mile downstream from the lake's confluence with the river, having made certain that they were not being followed and observed, the two young couples had separated. Joar-Fane and At-Vee were to continue riding and leading the quaggas, which had been taught to tolerate them, while the other two went on by another means of transport.

Having apparently set off for their home town shortly after the meeting with the blond giant had ended, the four Wurkas had travelled only as far as a pre-arranged rendezvous before—making sure that nobody else was in the vicinity—pulling into the shore. When Dawn and Bunduki had arrived, the Earth couple had transferred with their arms and blankets to the boats and resumed the journey in that fashion. This had enabled them to travel faster than would have been possible if they had stayed mounted.

Moving on until nightfall, the party had settled on a pleasant site and made a comfortable camp. They had eaten well. In addition to the supplies carried by the Wurkas, fresh meat had been provided by the Earth couple. Dawn had felled a water chevrotain from the boat as it grazed on the bank. Then, after they had landed at sundown, Bunduki had sent an arrow into one of a flock of sandhill cranes which were flying overhead.

Before going to sleep, the girl and her husband had heard enough about conditions in Wurka to have become even more convinced that a change of policy and leadership was essential. As was invariably the habit of any faction holding similar views on gaining power, Tik-Felum and his coterie had set up effective curbs against individual liberty which suppressed all opposition. Using the most flimsy excuses to justify them, they invaded the privacy of any person they suspected of harbouring views contrary to their own and imposed fines or punishments against which there was no appeal. Not only were children encouraged to lose all regard for their parents, they were being conditioned to report any action or behaviour that might be considered undesirable by the Senior Elder and his men.

Everything they had learned was a further warning to the Earth couple that they were going into danger. Not that they had let the thought deter them. They accepted that such would in all probability frequently be the case when they had accepted the 'Supplier's' suggestion that they remained upon Zillikian.

Propelled by such highly competent oarsmen as the four Wurkas had proved to be and with the current to help, Dawn and Bunduki had been transported more than fifty miles the following day. The day after that had seen a similar distance added to the total. Throughout all that time, having kept a *very* careful watch, they had seen no other human beings. Nor, despite news of the Earth couple's departure having been dispatched by

159

the Jey-Mat's 'talking drum'—but not information of how they would be travelling—had they expected to. They had felt certain that Tik-Felum would not be expecting them to be moving so swiftly. And, even if he had anticipated an early arrival, any attempts at preventing them from reaching his village were unlikely to be made at any great distance from it. Nor had there been any great danger of being observed from another source which might have innocently betrayed them. Although the Senior Elder's summons had been relayed by the Rol-Mat's 'talking drum', their village lay some distance along a tributary of the river.

Shortly before nightfall on the second day, Dawn and Bunduki had separated from their companions. With the state of affairs that prevailed in their village, the four Wurkas had kept their intention of visiting Jey-Mat a secret from Tik-Felum's coterie. It was essential to their future well-being that their association with the Earth couple was not discovered.

Leaving the boat shortly before sundown, the girl and her husband had moved a short way on foot. They had intended to go further, but had stopped to establish friendly relations with a herd of forest elephants which had come to drink and spend the night on the banks of the river. Sleeping in safety, with the pachyderms forming an excellent and efficient guard around them, they had set off again at daybreak.

Covering the last five miles in good time, the Earth couple had found the Wurkas' village to be similar in general appearance and lay-out to Jey-Mat. It was situated on top of the long escarpment that separated the jungle proper from the ten miles wide strip of swampland which, their companions had informed them, continued to the edge of the 'Lake With Only One Shore'. Paths were cut in the face of the sheer wall, so as to give access to the citizens' boats moored on the banks of the river.

The next most obvious difference between Wurka and Jey-Mat became apparent as soon as Dawn and Bunduki were admitted through the main gates. Unlike the Jey-

Mat gates, where everybody was cheerful and friendly, the population were quiet, subdued, unsmiling and, for all that they were clearly interested in the newcomers, they made no attempt to approach and establish amiable relations.

As the Earth couple had reached the village much earlier than anticipated, they had been able to see that their arrival created not a little consternation on the part of Tik-Felum and his coterie. In fact, the five with whom Dawn and Bunduki had had most to do withdrew to their respective homes and took no part in the far from warm reception given by the Senior Elder.

The meeting had not been prolonged. Pretending to know no more than he had been told by the 'talking drums', Bunduki had sought further details of why Tik-Felum had required his assistance. He had been told that, while the villagers could deal with the usual type of crocodiles in the vicinity, over the past six months or so they had been plagued by two which were much larger, more powerful and had developed a taste for human flesh. This had caused them to take up residence close to the village and in locations which had previously been exceptionally productive fishing grounds. Nor had the attempts made by the population succeeded in removing the menace, but had cost several men their lives.

Agreeing that the situation could not be allowed to continue, Bunduki made no mention of certain other knowledge that he had received. According to the four men who had brought Dawn and him down the river, Tik-Felum had used the predators as a means of removing potential objectors to his rule. In fact, Hak-Bart— leader of the quartet—had narrowly avoided such a fate.

Much as Bunduki disliked killing animals, except for food or in defence of life, he had accepted that the crocodiles must be removed. One problem had not arisen, although he had been prepared to cope with it. When he had requested a guide, Tik-Felum had not offered the services of any member of his coterie. Instead, either because he was suspicious of the quartet's recent absence or because he knew that none of his adherents would go, the Senior Elder had assigned Hak-Bart to the task.

Wanting to impress the local population with his capability and right to the rank of *Dapan-Dankara*, the blond giant had announced his intention of starting the mission immediately. It was also his unspoken aim to bring about a successful conclusion as swiftly as possible and, from the information he had been given during the journey down the river, he was confident he could do so. Bringing to bear all of the knowledge imparted by the male members of his adoptive family on Earth and his personal experience of dealing with the *Crocodilia* while the Chief Warden of the Ambagasali Wild Life Reserve, he had been able to formulate his strategy.

Justifying Bunduki's faith in him, although puzzled as to why he had been asked to do so, Hak-Bart had carried out the instructions Bunduki had given before they had parted company. What was more, on reaching the first of the locations, the blond giant had found it to be exactly as the Wurka had described it.

In the fashion of its kind, the predator had established itself in a large pool attached to one of the myriad waterways—which formed a maze and protection against human invaders—that comprised the swamplands. On the banks had been fresh tracks and a tail mark of a width which demonstrated, even without an actual sight of the reptile, that it was a creature of exceptional size.

As Bunduki had hoped, starting out so early in the day had brought them to the vicinity of their quarry before the heat of the sun caused it to leave the water and bask on the bank. However, if an ambush was to succeed, there was one precaution which had to be taken. After the fashion of its kind, the predator had formed a symbiotic relationship with a member of another species. By a mutually advantageous arrangement, an Egyptian plover lived close to the pool and, in return for food and protection, acted as a very efficient sentry. From all accounts, it had been the bird which was responsible for the Wurka hunters' failure to stalk and kill its provider.

Leaving Dawn and Hak-Bart at a safe distance, the

blond giant had used all his considerable skill to approach the pool without disturbing the bird. Having attained his position, being unable to move closer than thirty yards because of a complete lack of cover beyond that point, he was preparing to start his task.

Satisfied with his aim, Bunduki made his loose. Relieved of restraint, the bow's limbs began to assume their normal position and, in doing so, propelled the arrow forward. Having found the three dead pike-characins,[1] provided during the night by Hak-Bart as the blond giant had instructed, the Egyptian plover was pecking out the eyes of the largest. Although the bird heard the twang of the bow's string, the blunt-headed arrow was flying too swiftly for any hope of evasive action. There was a thud and a puff of flying feathers and the threat of an alarm being given by the plover was removed.

Watching what happened from a distance, Dawn and Hak-Bart moved forward. While they exhibited stealth, each realized that the major threat to a premature disclosure of their presence no longer existed. By the time they joined him, Bunduki was nocking a second shaft, this time with a Razorhead point, to his bow's string. However, as yet, there was no sign of the quarry upon which he intended to use it.

'Do you think it's in the lagoon?' Dawn breathed, studying the glass-like surface of the dark amber water.

'I hope so,' the blond giant replied, equally quietly. 'Because I hate talking to myself.'

Having delivered his comment, the blond giant performed an impersonation of the kind of roar by which a male crocodile announced its claim to a territory. It was so close to the genuine sound that Hak-Bart stared in surprise and open admiration. However, several seconds went by and nothing happened.

1. *Pike-characin:* Boulengerella Lateristriga: *one of the* Cypriniformes, *carp, group of fish orders: Native of north-eastern South America, particularly the Amazon region, it attains a length of twenty inches and is a predator. Often lying in wait at the surface before attacking its prey, the species was a favourite quarry of the Wurka-Telonga bow-hunters. J.T.E.*

'Huh!' Dawn sniffed. 'What you need here is the woman's touch.'

With that, the girl demonstrated an equal facility for mimicry; but her grunting call was that of a female crocodile in the throes of the mating urge. Once again, the Wurka would not have known it was emitted from a human throat if he had not seen it for himself.

'There!' Hak-Bart hissed, only just managing to suppress his excitement and hold his voice to a tension-charged whisper. He pointed to the water.

Just as keen-eyed, the Earth couple had also seen the small ripple disturbing the centre of the lagoon. They knew that it was caused by the predator making use of physical adaptations for its specialized way of life. Set high upon the snout on top of the skull, its nostrils and eyes allowed it to breathe and see with little else of its body being exposed. So, although it had risen to investigate the sounds, they alone broke the surface of the water.

Using its tail in such slow sideways undulations that there was barely a motion on the surface, the predator advanced at a snail's pace across the lagoon. Measuring the distance between them with his eye, Bunduki began to take the draw on his bow. He wanted his quarry closer before he loosed the shaft, so as to make even more certain of attaining a hit. On either side of him, his wife and Hav-Bart watched with bated breath as if they had been turned to stone.

Catching his wife's eye, the blond giant gave a brief inclination of his head. Knowing what was wanted, she repeated her impersonation of a lovelorn lady crocodile in search of male company.

The nostrils and eyes sank beneath the surface!

'Damn it!' Hav-Bart ejaculated, fortunately *sotto voce*, watching a couple of air bubbles rising after all other signs of the creature had gone.

'Don't move!' Dawn hissed, duplicating her husband's thoughts and acting, without needing prompting, as he would have wished.

Freezing again into a state of complete immobility,

Hav-Bart continued to stare at the surface of the lagoon. After almost thirty seconds had gone by, he was given a further example of just how well the Earth couple understood the mentality and behaviour patterns of their prey.

Showing no more disturbance than the bubbles had in making their appearance, the nostrils of the predator broke through the glassy surface. There was barely as much as a suggestion of a ripple to betray its arrival. An instant later, almost eighteen inches behind the nose, the small protuberance of its eyes came into view. They were followed in the same effortless fashion by the whole of the head.

'So that's it!' Dawn ejaculated, in a voice so low that the words barely reached the men's ears, taking notice of the way in which there was no sign of the fourth tooth of the saurian's lower jaw. 'It's an *alligator*, not a crocodile!'

Equally aware of the most easily observable difference between species *Alligator* and the *Crocodilia*, Bunduki matched his wife's identification. Like her, he now realized that they were not dealing with the almost entirely harmless-to-mankind dwarf crocodiles[2] or 'false' gavials[3] which had been the only types of saurians they had seen in the neighbourhood of the village. Furthermore, he shared her understanding of the predator's behaviour. For all its size, which he estimated at over ten foot from nose to tail, the Mississippi alligator was puzzled and cautious. It had heard sounds resembling, but somewhat different to, those of its kind. So it was displaying care while investigating.

Watching the alligator coming slowly nearer, Bunduki

2. *Dwarf crocodile: only surviving member of the genus* Osteolaemus, *O.* Tetraspis, *inhabits streams of the West African forests and is an inoffensive creature which seldom exceeds six feet in length. J.T.E.*

3. *'False' gavial: sole specimen of the genus* Tomistoma, *T.* Schlegeli, *attains a length of more than fourteen feet, feeds exclusively on fish and is found in Borneo, Malaysia and Sumatra. It is replaced by the 'true' gavial,* Gavialis Gangeticus—*which differs in some anatomical points and grows larger, but also eats little other than fish—in the rivers and large lakes of India and Burma. J.T.E.*

completed his draw and aligned the arrow so that it would make its point of impact about twenty-four inches behind the knobs of the protruding eyes. However, he did not relax his hold on the string. Close to sixty yards still separated them and, while confident that he could make a kill at that distance, he preferred to do so from nearer to the bank. In that way, there was a better chance of retrieving the body and avoiding any suggestions that he had failed to carry out his mission.

So gradually that time seemed to be standing still, the alligator continued its wary advance towards the shore. Its head was still exposed and the outline of its massive body was discernible below the surface.

Fifty yards.

Forty!

Dawn was clenching her hands until the knuckles showed white. On the other side of the blond giant, Hav-Bart felt as if his lungs would burst. Yet he dare not suck in a breath for fear that the sound would disturb his companion's concentration, or frighten the alligator.

'*Dapan-Dankara*!' yelled a voice from not too far away, accompanying the words by banging a stick of some kind against the trunk of a tree.

Instantly, the alligator lost all of its lethargic air. Up-ending its body, so that the massive tail rose and descended on the erstwhile still surface of the lagoon with a terrific slapping sound that could have been heard for a quarter of a mile, it began to do a half-roll as a prelude to making a power dive for safety.

Swiftly as the saurian was moving, Bunduki's response had been even more rapid.

Although seething with rage at the speaker, who he suspected had created the commotion deliberately, the blond giant released the arrow as soon as the sound reached his ears. There was a solid 'whunk!' which told him that he had scored a hit. Further confirmation was supplied, by the sight of the four-bladed point protruding some six inches from the underside of the alligator's chest, before it disappeared beneath the now roily surface of the lagoon. It appeared briefly a couple of seconds later, curving upwards in a jump that seemed more suitable to a sailfish feeling a fisherman's hook than such an ungainly creature. Going down, there was a momentary flash of white from its belly as it rolled over. Although the blond giant knew that it was dead, it did not reappear and he doubted whether recovering the body would be possible.

'That was Han-Ateep's voice!' Hav-Bart growled furiously.

'There were two of them at least,' Dawn went on, anger showing plainly on her beautiful face. 'I saw them running away, but not quickly enough to do anything about it.'

'Don't worry, darling,' Bunduki replied, thinking how—in view of his wife's skill as an archer—the men responsible for the disturbance could count themselves lucky that she had not been holding her bow ready for use. 'We'll attend to them later. Let's go back to the village and tell the people they can start to use this lagoon again.'

CHAPTER FOURTEEN

HE'LL HAVE HIS PROOF

'Far be it for me to sound like a nagging wife,' Dawn Gunn said quietly, eyeing Bunduki in a disapproving manner as they walked out of the Wurka-Telonga village accompanied by several men, including the four who had brought them most of the way from Jey-Mat.

'Why not?' the blond giant interrupted. 'You always did *before* we were married.'

'I'll ignore *that*,' the girl declared, in a way which bore the unspoken addition of, "but just wait until later". 'As I said, far be it from me to sound like a nagging wife, but I do think what you're planning might be thought just a *tiny* bit injudicious.'

'I didn't know they taught you words like that at Roedean,' Bunduki commented.

'Dangerous, even,' Dawn continued, paying no apparent attention to her husband's injection. 'But that's only *my* opinion, of course.'

'When did you say you were going to start *not* nagging?' Bunduki inquired, although he agreed with his wife's comment. 'Anyway, if I can pull it off for dear old Tik-Felum, he'll have his proof in a way that should satisfy him.'

'And if you *don't* pull it off, you could be killed,' Dawn warned, then pouted. 'You haven't any thought for *me*, you brute. There's no widow's pension on Zillikian.'

For all the light manner in which they were talking, neither the girl nor her husband underestimated the danger of what he was planning to do. However, she real-

168

ized that he was taking a deliberately calculated risk and had made his decision based upon his knowledge of what it entailed. His behaviour was neither rash, nor incautious, but that which they both had agreed would best serve their needs under the circumstances.

While the return to the village should have been one of triumph, Tik-Felum had done his best to prevent it from being regarded in that light. He had, as the Earth couple had guessed, sent the members of his coterie amongst the villagers to spread the word that only visible proof of the 'crocodile's' death would be regarded as acceptable. So, with his men hovering around and taking notice of what was happening, the news that the corpse was not available for inspection produced the effect he required.

Not all of the Senior Elders' adherents were available to give him support. Deneb-Ginwe, Han-Preep, and Flant-Wiip were conspicious by their absence. Before either Dawn or Bunduki could mention the matter of the disturbance that had lost them the alligator's body, Tik-Felum had informed them that the trio were making an expedition to the coast of the 'Lake With Only One Shore'. They had left some time before, according to him, with the intention of catching some of the green sea turtles so highly prized as culinary delicacies and which would have been a fitting meal to celebrate the *Dapan-Dankara*'s mission having proved successful.

Having excused the absence of his sons and apparently had the explanation accepted, Tik-Felum had inquired into the reason for the alligator's body being missing. On hearing what had happened, but not that the Earth couple and Hav-Bart were aware of who was responsible, he had then adopted an air of such blatantly false commisseration that Dawn had found it hard to prevent herself from showing her true feelings. Nor had she felt any better disposed towards him when he had suggested that the disturbance had been the work of a river-spirit protecting the predator.

'In which case,' the Senior Elder had gone on, still speaking far louder than was necessary, so that the assembled populace could also hear. 'There are those who might say the water-spirit turned aside your arrow and the "crocodile" still lives.'

'We all saw the arrow strike and its head was sticking out of the other side of the "crocodile's" body,' Hav-Bart had protested, sharing his people's general lack of zoological knowledge and being unable to identify the saurian correctly. Oblivious of the venomous glare being directed at him by Tik-Felum, he went on equally loudly, 'It was dying as it went down and, unless the current has carried its body away, we'll find it when it comes to the surface again.'

'You say that the arrow pierced so deeply that its head came out at the other side?' the Senior Elder had asked, hoping to arouse incredulity among his audience as they were all aware of the predator's size.

'It did,' Hav-Bart had agreed, then countered swiftly, 'That is no ordinary bow and the arrows have heads on them like none I have ever seen.'

'Let anybody who thinks they aren't powerful enough to do the deed stand out and say so,' Dawn had announced, picking out the men with whom she and her husband had been in contention at Jey-Mat. 'My Lord Bunduki will soon prove whether it be true or false.'

'Come, my lady,' the blond giant had said, when nobody offered to accept his wife's challenge. 'We'll go and deal with the second "crocodile".' Instead of moving off, however, he had raised the bow so that all could see and, swinging his gaze so that it settled on first one and then the others of Tik-Felum's coterie, he continued in a carrying voice, 'But this I say, water-spirit. If you come anywhere near me, or make a sound to try and save the other "crocodile", I'll find and kill you. You have my word as the *Dapan-Dankara* for that!'

To each of the sullen crew who had helped the Senior Elder enforce his regime, it seemed that the white-haired foreigner had selected him personally for attention. Obviously the Senior Elder's story of a water-spirit had not been believed and the 'Earths' had known what had happened. There was a chilling menace in the voice and the cold blue eyes of the tremendously muscled speaker that warned he meant every word he had said. What was more, they were all aware—two at first hand—that he was capable of carrying out his threat.

Watching the effect of Bunduki's statement upon his adherents, Tik-Felum had known that he could not depend upon any of them attempting a disruption of the bid to dispose of the second 'crocodile'. They were taking the blond giant's words to heart. Remembering the difficulty he had experienced in persuading his sons and Flant-Wlip to carry out the first and infinitely safer interference, he had accepted that nothing further along those lines would be possible.

Unwilling to concede defeat, the Senior Elder had tried without success to find out what plan of campaign Bunduki was meaning to employ. He was met with such a blandly polite reply, that nothing would be decided upon until the situation was surveyed, that he was compelled to leave his curiosity unsatisfied. Nor had he been able to think up a suitable refusal when the blond giant had requested assistance, backed with a solemn promise that no harm would be allowed to come to those who were assigned to the task. Instead, albeit reluctantly, he had had to give his consent to Hav-Bart and nine other villagers accompanying the "Earths". Nor did a hope that had arisen reach fruition.

Showing a ready grasp of what was needed, Hav-Bart had selected nine companions who he was certain could be trusted. Studying them as he had stated his requirements and given instructions for what he expected from them, Bunduki had been convinced that the young Wurka had made a good choice and that he could rely upon them to do as he required.

Once clear of the village, Dawn and her husband soon forgot their levity and devoted their full attention to the business in hand. Everything they needed was available. In addition to the bows they were carrying, Hav-Bart was fetching along the blond giant's *m'kuki* and shield. It was not that the latter weapons were to be used in the work ahead, but they had all considered it inadvisable to leave such tempting articles where Tik-Felum or his adherents could lay hands on them. The rest of the Wurkas were carrying the coils of rope and *machetes*—which the large bush-knives resembled—they had been asked to supply. Apart from the girl, none of them had any idea of what lay ahead. However, such was the faith inspired by Bunduki and their eagerness to be free of the hated regime which was oppressing them that they were willing to do as he had requested without asking questions.

As a precaution against a repetition of the ploy which had come very close to losing his first objective, the blond giant had arranged for lookouts to keep watch on the village. Others were left to guard against unwanted interlopers who might have evaded the first pair of watchers. Finally, after obtaining instructions on where to find their quarry, he and the girl had continued unescorted. The remainder of their helpers were to remain in concealment and without noise until they were called.

After they had parted company with the Wurkas, the Earth couple moved in complete silence. For all the disturbance their movements caused, they might have been a pair of enormous cats on the prowl. Nor, under the circumstances, were they any less dangerous or savage than the wildest predatory creature in the jungle.

Such was the measure of competence displayed by Dawn and Bunduki that they arrived at their destination without having been detected by either their prey or its avian consort. They came to a halt, still in the concealment of the bushes which fringed the water, and looked at a lagoon much like the one in which they had encountered their previous problem. There was one major difference, but it had been anticipated. With the heat of the afternoon sun, the saurian had left the water and was basking on the sand not more than twenty feet from them. Sprawled out with its head towards the lagoon, it was unaware that they were so close. Nor was the bird, a spurwinged plover on this occasion, any more conscious of their presence. While its attention was not diverted by an easily obtainable meal, it was engrossed in carrying out

one of its symbiotic functions by picking debris from the teeth of the saurian's open jaws.

'It's another alligator,' Bunduki breathed and held his bow towards Dawn.

'If it wasn't, my lad,' the girl replied, accepting the weapon and watching her husband very carefully removing his back-quiver. 'You could forget it and use this damn thing.'

'If it wasn't and they sold life insurance on Zillikian, you'd say, "Go ahead",' the blond giant answered, laying the quiver down and freeing the *boleadora* to place on it. Still displaying excessive caution and hardly taking his eyes from the creatures on the sandbank, he discarded the bowie knife in a similar fashion. 'Now all we have to do is settle down and wait.'

Resting her husband's bow against a bush, Dawn slipped an arrow free from the bowquiver and nocked it to her string. Then she stood as silently and immobile as he did in spite of her anxiety over what lay ahead. Not a hint of her feelings showed on her beautiful face, but she sensed that Bunduki was aware of them. So she turned her head to give him what she hoped would be a smile of reassurance.

Quitting its work, the spur-winged plover took flight!

Not in panic, however, or because the girl's movement had been detected.

Instead, the bird flew unhurriedly across the lagoon and passed out of sight beyond the river. Deprived of its consort's attentions, the alligator slowly closed its powerful and awesomely equipped jaws. Wriggling its stomach against the sand, as if making its resting place softer, its eyes closed and it settled down for what the watchers hoped was a sleep.

Although Bunduki adopted a crouching posture like that of a sprinter awaiting the starter's pistol in a race that was taking place before the use of starting-blocks became fashionable, he did not move. Nor did Dawn offer to raise her bow into a position of greater readiness. However, she could feel her heart pounding like a triphammer and she had a momentary fear that the noise it was making would frighten away the alligator. Appreciating the absurdity of the thought broke the tension a little and caused her to smile.

'Damn it,' Dawn told herself silently. 'If that big lump of mine doesn't know what he's doing by now, our folks have wasted a lot of time and effort on teaching him.'

'Go on, you big ugly bastard!' Bunduki breathed, just audibly to the girl, watching the saurian open its eyes. Oblivious of her thoughts and wanting to reassure her, he went on, 'Go to sleep, damn it. I'd ask Dawn to sing you a lullaby, but *that* would scare you so deep into the swamps we'd never reach you.'

'Just you wait, my lad!' Dawn threatened in a whisper, without turning her attention from the massive, scaly predator on the sandbank. 'Wait until I get you home!'

Seconds dragged by on leaden feet, to become a minute.

Then two!

Three!

Four!

Five!

Still Bunduki watched his prey, wanting to make sure that it was fast asleep before making his move. At the end of the fifth minute, he felt that the time had come and was on the point of giving a warning nod to Dawn. Before he could do so, a fish at the far side of the lagoon sprang into the air to snap at an insect flying incautiously by. At the loud splash caused by the attack, the alligator's eyes snapped open. They closed again almost immediately, but the blond giant resigned himself to a further period of waiting.

Another four minutes crawled into oblivion.

'Oh come on, darling!' Dawn screamed, but only mentally. 'It's fast asleep. Get it!'

Sensing rather than glancing to find out that she was looking his way, Bunduki's head made a brief inclination as though he had heard his wife's entreaty. Then, giving a thunderous bellow like that of a male *Australopithecus* launching an attack, he hurtled from his place of concealment and across the sandbank.

Awakened by the commotion, the alligator seemed to

be confused and hesitated for a vital couple of seconds. Nor were the species *Alligator Mississipiensis*, or the Asiatic variety, *A. Sinensis*, as agile as a crocodile on land.

With the sand being flung up by his racing feet, the blond giant converged with the alligator. Swiftly as he sprinted, it was obvious that it could not be prevented from reaching its natural element, the water. Nor did he intend to try bringing it to a halt on dry land. Rather he was hoping to make the initial contact just before it entered the lagoon.

Watched by Dawn, who was turning her bow into the shooting position, Bunduki covered the remaining distance between himself and the alligator like a rugby player performing a tackle. Alighting on the scaly back of the wriggling saurian, as its nose was almost touching the water, he secured holds with both hands. The left enfolded the jaws in such a manner that his palm was covering the nostrils, tightened into a vice-like grip. At the same time, passing around the massive and knobbly body, the right obtained an equally secure hold of the off-side foreleg. Even as he was securing himself, drawing the saurian's close to twelve foot bulk tightly against the right side of his enormously muscled frame, they plunged head first from the sandbank. As he had anticipated, the shoreline fell away sharply beyond the resting place and they came down in a deep pool. They made a complete somersault as soon as they went under. Running forward and shouting—screaming almost—for the Wurkas to join them, Dawn saw nothing of Bunduki but the soles of his bare feet for almost a minute.

Staring in anxiety as the alligator's tail appeared briefly, to make a great arc and return beneath the surface of the amber-coloured water of the lagoon, Dawn tried to comfort herself with the thought of how its physical make-up would result in Bunduki's task—while being anything but a sinecure—being less hazardous than it appeared. For one thing, the muscles of the saurian's jaws supplied the majority of their power for closing rather than opening. So a strong man could keep the mouth shut with one hand, provided of course that he was able to obtain such a hold. Secondly, as well as being more cumbersome on land, the alligator was less adept in the water than a crocodile and not nearly so dangerous a proposition. Lastly, although the blond giant had not yet found an opportunity to avail himself of it, there was a means by which the alligator could be subdued and rendered harmless with comparative ease.

For all her knowledge, the girl was deeply perturbed as the seconds ticked away. The only sign she had of where her husband might be was given by the way in which the now muddy water boiled and swirled in concert with the struggle going on below the surface. Just as she was wondering if the alligator had dragged him off, his blond head appeared. He had time, she noticed with relief, to suck in a deep breath of air before being taken underneath again.

Panting with their exertions, Hav-Bart and some of the Wurkas arrived. As they had not been told of the blond giant's intentions, they stared in amazement on being informed by Dawn that he had deliberately tackled the 'crocodile' so as to capture it alive. Although they dwelt in terrain that had many of the *Crocodilia* as co-residents, they had never duplicated the Seminole Indians of Florida's methods of capturing the creatures.[1] So they could barely believe their eyes and ears. But they still affirmed that they would do all they could to help.

Five more times, Bunduki's head and, twice, shoulders came into view. On each occasion, he was granted an opportunity to replenish his lungs. Following every appearance, the alligator's tail would lash in fury at the surface and then the blunt, rounded, pike-like head would shoot above the water and disappear again still locked in his unrelenting grasp.

At last, the pace of the titanic struggle began to slow down. The spectators noticed with relief and delight that Bunduki was able to keep his head clear of the water

1. *No one knows who among the Seminoles was first to discover the methods by which an alligator could be captured alive by a single strong man. However, even to this day, members of that nation perform the feat. J.T.E.*

and breathe more deeply. Also, the frenzied tail lashings of the alligator were growing proportionately weaker. Finally, after at least twenty minutes of continuous efforts, they were floating still locked together as tightly as two lovers and almost motionless on the surface of the lagoon.

'Get ready!' the blond giant called, raising his head clear of the water. 'I'm going to bring him in.'

Having spoken, Bunduki and his captive sank from view. For close to a minute there was no sign of either, but Dawn calmed the Wurkas fears by explaining how he had deliberately submerged to walk along the bottom and pull the alligator after him. When he next appeared, it was obvious that he had justified his wife's faith in him. Still retaining his double holds on the jaws and foreleg, he twisted around until laying on his back at the edge of the sandbank. Having hauled the alligator on top of him, he wrapped his legs around its body in a scissor-hold.

"Wait!" Dawn hissed, as the Wurkas—for all the consternation showing on their faces at the prospect—were starting to move forward.

Obedient to the command, although they had never previously allowed a woman to dictate their actions, the men came to a halt. What they saw next would later be told by word of mouth and the 'talking drums' all through the Telonga nation. Because exactly what happened was not understood, it added tremendously to Bunduki's already high reputation and caused him to be attributed with supernatural powers.

Releasing the foreleg, the blond giant began to rub his captive's chest and belly with his right hand. At the first touch, the alligator swung its tail viciously; but as he continued with the gentle massaging motion, it relaxed.[2]

2. *History does not record who first discovered that massaging the collection of nerve centres under the alligator's throat and along the chest and belly could induce a state of trance. However, a similar knowledge with regard to crocodiles was possessed in Africa and India since long before the birth of Christ. The author cannot guess why the 'Suppliers' had not imparted the knowledge to the Telongas. J.T.E.*

Less than a minute later, it seemed to be sleeping peacefully. However, on Bunduki loosening the scissor-hold, the saurian made as if to struggle. A few more strokes of the hand brought the effort to an end and, satisfied, he nodded to his wife.

'Now!' Dawn said.

Running forward, discarding her bow and arrow in her haste, the girl was the first to touch the huge alligator. Not that the Wurkas were tardy in following her. Eager hands grasped and hauled the limp burden ashore. Not until they were doing so did the blond giant relax. Even then, he kept his hold on the jaws until they were fastened by a length of rope. Having done all he could to ensure none of his assistants would be harmed, he lay where he was to recover from the great strain and exertions of the capture, leaving them to secure the trophy.

'Now,' Hav-Bart said with satisfaction, after the alligator had been bound and sturdy splints affixed to keep the deadly tail immobile. 'Let's see Tik-Felum claim that you haven't dealt with this *one*, Bunduki!'

* * *

'*Dapan-Dankara!*' gasped the attractive, tall and slender Wurka-Telonga girl who came running into the bedroom of the house in which Dawn Gunn and her husband were spending the night. 'I need your help. Four men have taken Hav-Bart to the Place Of Punishment and will kill him unless you go to save him.'

Recognizing the visitor as Marn-Bara, the wife of their friend, the Earth couple—who had been sleeping fully clothed and who had left their bed quickly on being disturbed by her entry—lowered the knives they had kept close by in case there should be the need for weapons.

As the young Wurka had predicted, Tik-Felum had not been willing to concede that Bunduki was any more successful in dealing with the second alligator. The viewpoint was in part induced by his having been told merely that the saurian was still alive, although 'possibly' unable to cause further trouble for the villagers. Stating that he intended to go and look for himself, he had gathered the other Elders and, followed by the rest of the population, made his way to the lagoon. His reaction at discovering the mighty predator bound and helpless had not been what an outsider would have expected from the sight of such a fortunate removal of a menace to the community. Nor had his mood been changed for the better on hearing of the way in which all but his coterie had greeted the sight.

Although Hav-Bart and the other men who were involved in the capture had suggested a feast with the alligator cooked as the *piece-de-resistance,* Tik-Felum had refused. However, he had offered reasonable grounds for delaying the event. He had pointed out that the blond giant and Dawn had made a long journey and were too tired to enjoy the village's hospitality to its fullest extent. Furthermore, his sons and Flant-Wlip had not yet returned from the coast. Tasty as the alligator might be, guests of such importance could only be accorded the honour that was their due by being offered the delicious green sea turtle cooked *en casserole,* as it would have been known on Earth. Finally, the women of the village would need at least a day in which to prepare a celebration of the magnitude the *Dapan-Dankara* deserved.

Acceding to the Senior Elder's wishes, the Earth couple had said they would prefer to rest overnight and so be better able to do justice to their hosts' hospitality when all was prepared. With the point settled, leaving the butchering of the alligator to the villagers, Dawn and Bunduki had returned and were placed in a house set aside for notable visitors. Convention dictated that they occupied it, although they would have preferred to stay close to Hav-Bart. His support, they had realized, could put him in jeopardy. Tik-Felum would not lightly forget nor forgive his behaviour. However, they had felt that the danger would not commence while they were close by.

The arrivial of Marn-Bara and the fright on her beautiful face warned the Earth couple that they had made an incorrect decision.

'Take her back to her home and see she's kept safe,

darling!' Bunduki ordered, scooping up the shield and slipping his left arm though its carrying loops without sheathing the knife. 'Then come after me with your bow and the *m'kuki*.'

Appreciating the gravity of the situation, Dawn did not indulge in any of the bantering comments which would have greeted a command from her husband on less serious occasions. Instead, she sprang to where her weapons were placed.

'Take care, you big lump!' the girl called, snatching up her bow, as the blond giant plunged out of the door.

Leaving the house, Bunduki started towards the main gates of the palisade around the village. As had been the case at Jey-Mat before he had taught the hunters there the value of security, no guard was kept on it: Nor was the small door in it kept locked, but was only bolted on the inside. So he knew that he would be able to get through and, once beyond, he knew where he would have to go. Hav-Bart had told him of the Place Of Punishment and where it was located while they had been returning from hunting the first alligator.

To reach the gate, the blond giant had to pass between two houses. Moving along the alley, he found—not that he was surprised—that his coming had been anticipated and preparations had been taken to deal with him. Two men appeared as he was approaching the rear ends of the buildings. Each held a *dapur bener kris* and he recognized them as Jomus-Takn and a lesser member of Tik-Felum's coterie.

There was no time for the blond giant to congratulate himself upon his perception. He had suspected that the abduction of Hav-Bart had been carried out with the additional purpose of luring him into a trap. So, as well as intending to go to his friend's assistance, he had meant to spring it. What the plotters had not realized, because they did not use such a device, was that his shield had very special properties. They were not kept in ignorance for many seconds.

Coming from Bunduki's left, having selected that side as being safer, Jomus Takn swung a round-arm blow with his *kris*. On the right, the second man was launching a similar slice at the blond giant's head.

Neither attack made contact with human flesh!

Driven with all the weight and power of a bulky body behind it, Jomus-Takn's *kris* could not be halted although he saw that the shield was rising between it and his intended target. Nor did he think there was any need to pull back, but believed he could batter the protective device aside and reach the man behind it. When the contact was made, he learned just how wrong he had been. While the blade sliced through the hardened buffalo hide, it met and was shattered by a metal underneath that was of a far better temper than its own.

Nor did the second assailant fare any better. At the same instant as Jomus-Takn's blade was disintegrating, his *kris'* passage was stopped by the proposed victim's weapon. An arm of enormous strength held and deflected the blow.

Disengaging the bowie knife as soon as it had pushed the *kris* aside, Bunduki whipped it across in a sweep that laid the man's throat open to the bone. Then, giving Jomus-Takn no chance to recover from the shock of his weapon's destruction, the great blade came around and its clip point passed between his ribs to impale his heart.

Effectively as the blond giant was dealing with his would-be killers, he was far from out of danger. Having laid in concealment on the flat roof of the right side building's porch, yet a third of Tik-Felum's coterie had risen to watch how his companions were faring. Either he had not trusted the other two to carry out the ambush, or he merely did not believe in leaving things to the last minute. Whichever was the reason, he held his bow ready for use and was already drawing back the string ready to loose its arrow.

While the man's weapon was little more than half as powerful as Dawn's bow, at that range it could propel the long and barbed arrow with sufficient force to be lethal.

CHAPTER FIFTEEN

IT'S THE DAPAN-DANKARA!

Coming from the house followed by Marn-Bara, Dawn Gunn saw the danger to her husband and was prepared to deal with it. She had not waited to do more than snatch up the *m'kuki* before, telling the Wurka-Telonga girl to bring the two back-quivers and Bunduki's bow, setting off after him. For all that, by the time she emerged, he had reached the gap between the house and the attack was being launched. On the point of dashing forward to help him deal with the two assailants, she noticed the third man rising from his hiding place on the roof of the porch.

Although Dawn had not thought to nock an arrow to the bow, she made no attempt to rectify the omission. There would be insufficent time for her to do so and, anyway, she had another means of help more readily available. Pure instinct had caused her to take up and carry the *m'kuki* in a position suited to the purpose for which it had been designed. So she was able to put to use the training in how to throw it that she had shared with Bunduki.

How well Dawn had learned was demonstrated when, at an athletics meeting in Amabagalsi, she had used some of the knowledge to help her send a javelin for a distance equalling the record set in 1938 by the Finnish male athlete Yrjo Nikkanen.[1] Nor had her education

1. *The record was two hundred and fifty-eight feet, two and three-eighths inches. The longest measured unofficial throw was two hundred and eighty-three feet, by Arep Kibiege of Kenya in 1948.*

been confined to merely attaining a lengthy throw. In fact, her original tutors had been more concerned with instilling accuracy rather than just distance. Even before being transported to Zillikian, she had kept up her practice, and the arrival of the *m'kuki* had allowed her to bring her ability to a high level.

Letting the bow slip from her left hand, Dawn took three running strides while raising the *m'kuki* ready for casting. Taking aim as she had been taught, she whipped her right arm back and forward. Its wrist applied the twisting motion that, despite looking almost effeminate when performed by a man, imparted an added velocity and accuracy to the throw. On leaving her grasp, the stiffening ridges along the sides of the blade caused the weapon to rotate as if it was a bullet passing through the grooves along the barrel which gave a 'rifle' its name. The speed with which it was travelling caused a whistling hiss and it was soon moving almost faster than the human eye could follow.

Too swiftly, in fact, for the man on the roof to realize his peril. He was still drawing back on his bow when the *m'kuki* reached him, striking with such force that the blade plunged into his back and emerged from his chest. Giving a scream of mortal agony, he tossed his bow aside and, clutching at the shaft of the weapon that was killing him, he spun around and toppled from the roof.

Glancing back on hearing the scream, Bunduki gave a wave of gratitude with his bloody-bladed knife. Then he started to run onwards in the direction of the main gate.

'Come on!' Dawn ordered, throwing a look at Marn-Bara and bending to retrieve her bow. 'I'll collect the *m'kuki* after I've seen you safely home.'

Setting off with the other girl, Dawn slid the Randall Model 1 'All Purpose' fighting knife from its sheath. She held it ready for combat, with the eight inch long clip-

---

However, possibly for the reasons quoted in Paragraph One, Appendix Two, the international athletic authorities refused on a technicality to consider Dawn Drummond-Clayton's—as she was at the time—throw as the women's record. J.T.E.

183

pointed blade extending ahead of her thumb and forefinger. Although she was alert for any sign of danger, they arrived at Marn-Bara's house without being molested.

'Did you close the door when you came out?' Dawn whispered, noticing that it was just a little way open.

'Yes,' Marn-Bara replied, cool enough in spite of her fears for Hav-Bart's well-being to keep her voice equally quiet.

'In that case,' Dawn said, still *sotto voce* and holding out the bow. 'Take this and stay here.'

'What are you going to do?' Marn-Bara inquired, accepting the weapon.

'Take a leaf from—hey, he's my cousin-in-law now—Brad Counter's book,' Dawn replied, without realizing that she was speaking English until she was half way through the far from succinct explanation.

Making no attempt to translate the cryptic comment, the Earth girl darted forward. While visiting a ranch owned by the relatives of Bunduki's Texas-born mother, she had seen his look-alike cousin, Bradford Counter, demonstrate various aspects of a peace officer's work. In the course of his duty as a deputy sheriff in Rockabye County, Texas, he often had the need to gain swift and unexpected access to a building or room. So he had perfected effective ways of making an entrance.[2]

Despite being bare-foot, Dawn was confident that she could duplicate one of Brad's techniques. The door she was approaching stood slightly ajar and she would not need to supply enough power to spring a lock. On reaching the most appropriate distance, she launched her left leg forward and turned the foot so that its sole and not the toes made the contact. Swiftly taken as it had been, the kick propelled the door open with some force. It struck something and there was a yell which informed the girl that her precaution was worthwhile. However, she did not allow herself to be lulled into a sense of false

2. *Deputy Sheriff Bradford Counter employs the method adopted by Dawn Gunn in the author's biographical work,* THE SIXTEEN DOLLAR SHOOTER, *but used another technique in* BAD HOMBRE. *J.T.E.*

security by hearing the subsequent thud such as would be made by somebody sitting down unexpectedly on the floor. If there had been only one person lurking within, he was unlikely to have elected to stand at the hinged side of the door.

With that thought in mind, Dawn plunged across the threshold. Instead of going in erect, she crouched and, as a glance to her left proved, once again she was taking a necessary precaution. Although the room she entered was unlit, the quarter moon gave just sufficient illumination for her to see and identify the man-who was striking at her with a *dapur bener kris*-as the Senior Elder, Tik-Felum's younger son, Han-Ateep.

Unfortunately for the young man, his blow was aimed at a height which would have taken the girl across the throat if she had entered erect. As it was, the weapon passed harmlessly above her head. There was no time for Dawn to have conscious thoughts. She responded instinctively, but with the deadly precision of a highly trained knife-fighter. Twisting towards her assailant, she drove the razor-sharp blade into his stomach and his impetus took it home almost to the unlugged brass double hilt. Then, almost of its own volition, it emerged as her advance into the room drew on the sambur horn 'finger-grip' handle and liberated it. Clasping at his wound, Han-Ateep stumbled screaming through the door and collapsed at Marn-Bara's feet.

Having disposed of her attacker, Dawn did not forget that he had at least one companion present. So, advancing a few long strides across the room, she gazed about her rapidly to make sure there were no more. Satisfied on that score, she swung around to find out who the man behind the door might be and what he was up to.

Surprised, slightly dazed and with some of the breath knocked from him by being hit by the door and dumped unceremoniously on his rump, Flant-Wlip had managed to retain his hold on his *kris* when he sat down. What was more, muttering obscenities, he was already starting to rise.

The situation was such that Dawn did not dare consider thoughts of sporting behaviour. Not when she was opposed by a man taller, heavier and, possibly, stronger than herself; particularly as he was armed with a weapon almost three times the length of her own.

Darting forward, the girl saw a mixture of alarm and fear come to the man's unprepossessing face. Although he contrived to thrust himself erect before she reached him, his haste threw him off balance. Nor was he granted an opportunity to rectify the situation, or to defend himself.

Despite her antipathy towards Flant-Wlip and all that his kind stood for, Dawn could not bring herself to kill him while he was temporarily unable to fight back. Equally, she was aware that he would not hesitate to take her life if he was given the slightest chance. Furthermore, he must be incapacitated and prevented from delaying her departure after Bunduki.

With all those points in mind, the girl lashed around her knife like the strike of a diamondback rattlesnake. Its blade sliced through the skin, flesh, muscles, sinews, veins and arteries of Flant-Wlip's right forearm until it scraped the bone. Blood spurted from the wound in the wake of the withdrawing steel and the *kris* fell from a hand he would never again be able to use.

'Don't kill me!' the stricken man screamed, toppling backwards into a sitting position and cowering away from the menacing figure with its gore-smeared knife. 'The Cara-Bunte are waiting to ambush Bunduki at the Place of Punishment. Don't kill me for giving you the warning.'

* * *

Unaware of exactly what was happening to his wife, although the screams he had heard as he was passing through the main gates of the palisade had been masculine in their timbre and he knew they could not have been made by Dawn Bunduki also did not know that he was advancing into greater peril than he had anticipated. From what he could now see, he realized that things were even graver than he had expected. What was more, he was not arriving any too soon. It was clearly going to be death and not merely chastisement that was to be inflicted upon Hav-Bart. However, Marn-Bara had badly underestimated the number of Tik-Felum's coterie who were involved.

In a fair-sized clearing that was surrounded on three sides by fairly dense jungle and terminated on the fourth by the edge of the escarpment, was the Wurka-Telongas' Place Of Punishment. Out in the middle, Sraat-Challig and nine more of the Senior Elder's supporters were hard at work. Split into a group of five on either side of the bound and gagged dissident, they were straining to bend over a couple of sturdy trees which were clearly prepared for the purpose. Both had had all their foliage and branches removed and there were two ropes—the longer being pulled on by the Wurkas and the shorter equipped with a running noose—attached to the top of each.

The men were so engrossed in their task that none of them noticed the blond giant was approaching. Nor was there any reason for them to assume that he might be. They were too far from the village for the screams of Han-Ateep and other sounds to reach their ears. Furthermore, when Tik-Felum had dispatched them to deal with Hav-Bart, he had been less than frank regarding his reasons.

On calling his leading supporters together, the Senior Elder had made no reference to the news he had received shortly after nightfall. Han-Ateep and Flant-Wlip had arrived accompanied by a warrior who had announced he was a Cara-Bunte and served the War-Lord Torisaki, but he was not the pair's captive. Rather it was the other way around. As soon as they had reached the 'Lake With Only One Shore', they and Deneb-Ginwe had been taken prisoner by the crew of the war-lord's *zaruk*. On learning what had brought their captors to the region, being desirous of saving their own skins, they had offered their services in helping to trap Dawn and Bunduki of the 'Earths'. Nor had they given a moment's thought to how doing this might endanger the lives of their fellow villagers.

Having had their suggestion accepted, the treacherous

trio had guided the Cara-Buntes—who were now using the 'bull boats'—through the maze-like waterways of the swampland. Even though night had fallen by the time they arrived, Torisaki had called a halt while they were still out of sight of the village. He had declared that he wanted nothing from the Wurka-Telongas and would leave them in peace after the 'Earths' were delivered into his hands. It had been Deneb-Ginwe who had proposed where the capture might most easily take place. However, he had not cared for the next development. He was retained as a hostage while the other two were sent to make the arrangements.

Seeing an opportunity to remove both of the 'Earths' and also the leading dissident against his regime, Tik-Felum had put all his devious conniving abilities to devising a scheme which would bring it about. Having the Cara-Bunte, Han-Ateep and Flant-Wlip keep out of sight while he was giving his instructions to the other members of his coterie, the latter had not known of the trio's presence in his house.

It had taken all of the Senior Elder's powers of persuasion to obtain compliance with his suggestions. Not until he had convinced the assembled men that it could be done with complete safety would they agree to carry out the proposals he was making. Their resolve had been stiffened by the memory of the unrest and near hostility which many of the community had started to display towards them since the disposal of the two 'crocodiles' by the Dapan-Dankara. It had now been accepted that the first was dead. So they had felt that the people needed to be taught a sharp lesson. Furthermore, they agreed that their numbers would be sufficient to cope with the 'Earths' if Tik-Felum's story that Hav-Bart had gone on a hunting trip was not believed.

Giving his adherents no time to think up arguments, or raise points that might be open to question, Tik-Felum had sent them to their tasks. Only four would make the abduction, but another six were required to draw down the 'breaking trees'. That had only left Jomus-Takn with two supporters for his task. They were to wait in ambush between the guest-house and main gates to prevent the 'Earths' from interfering if an alarm should be raised.

As the Senior Elder had hoped, the abductors had relied upon the generally pacific behaviour and obedience to male orders shown by their womenfolk when removing Marn-Bara's husband. They had done no more than tell her to keep quiet before taking Hav-Bart away. However, after they had gone, she had shown something of the fresh spirit imbued among the population by the 'Earths' presence and she had gone to fetch help. Waiting in concealment, Han-Ateep and Flant-Wlip had entered the house—the Cara-Bunte having already departed to tell Torisaki of the arrangements—and Tik-Felum's summation of how Dawn and Bunduki would react to the news had, unfortunately for them, proved correct.

Knowing nothing of the Senior Elder's machinations, the men in the clearing believed that everything was going as planned. They were soon to learn differently.

While running from the village, Bunduki had heard the trumpeting of forest elephants not too far away. He had identified the particularly strident call of the big bull which led the herd Dawn and he had met on their way to the village,[3] but there was not time for him to try and summon them and see if he could enlist their aid.

Accepting that whatever action he took must be carried out alone and unaided, unless his wife was able to come on the scene swiftly enough to help him, the blond giant had already decided upon his strategy. It was based on the method in which the Masai *melombuki*,[4] Kira-Kangano, had taught him was the best way to handle the shield when meeting the charge of a lion.

Dropping and advancing his left shoulder, with the arm bent in front of it, Bunduki peered over the top of the shield's rim. This allowed the convex elliptical sur-

3. *Unlike on Earth, for some reason Bunduki had not been able to determine, the elephants of Zillikian lived in patriarchal and not matriarchal family groups. J.T.E.*

4. *For the benefit of new readers, see Footnote Six, Appendix One, for an explanation of the term,* melombuki. *J.T.E.*

face to cover all the vital areas of his body, with the exception of the top of his head. However, there was one major difference from the method he had been taught. No Masai *moran*, not even one who had attained the honoured title of *melombuki*, ever advanced to meet the lion. He waited for it to come to him.

Bearing the heavy shield with no greater apparent effort than if it weighed as light as a feather, the blond giant did not merely continue to run across the clearing. Calling upon his tremendous reserves of strength, he actually increased his pace until he was moving in a manner more suitable for sprinting in a hundred yards' race.

There was so much grunting and so many shouted accusations that one or another of the men was not pulling his weight (it being a characteristic of that kind of person that he would be terrified of the possibility that somebody else would do less than his share of work) none of the party—not even those facing in Bunduki's direction—noticed the big newcomer until he had almost reached them.

Looking over his shoulder when the sound of the running feet finally made an impression on his ears, Sraat-Challig was the first to become aware of the blond giant's arrival. At first, he thought that some form of evil spirit or unknown kind of animal was bearing down upon him at great speed. The traditional red ochre and white painted Masai heraldic device gave the shield a most eerie appearance in the half light of the clearing. Even when he realized what it was and who was behind it, he could not hold back a yell that was more than three parts' fear.

'It's the *Dapan-Dankara!*'

Letting go of the rope as he gave the warning, Sraat-Challig began to turn and his right hand went to the hilt of the *dapur bener kris* he was wearing. Behind him, also emitting shouts of alarm and consternation, the rest of his companions in both groups released their holds simultaneously. The trees snapped back to the perpendicular in a vicious whip-like motion that boded ill for anybody who was fastened between them when they were put to the function for which they had been prepared.

Before Sraat-Challig's weapon was clear of its sheath, the blond giant had reached him. Bunduki did not try to stop, nor slow his pace. Instead, letting out a thunderous bellow like that of an enraged *Mangani*, he continued his headlong and yet completely controlled dash.

Thickset and burly though the Wurka might be, his nerves were far from steady and his footing insecure. So he was ill prepared to cope with the collision. Propelled by the driving force and with the great weight of the Herculean-thewed giant's frame behind it, the shield caved in the front of his chest as if it had been an eggshell and flung him backwards. He plunged towards the four men who had been helping him to pull the rope, knocking three of them over. However, showing surprising agility in his perturbed frame of mind, the Wurka who had been next to him contrived to spring clear—but not quite far enough.

For all the good his evasion did, the man might as well have let himself become involved in the collision. Keeping moving with hardly any reduction of speed, Bunduki swung the bowie knife and disembowelled him in passing.

Hurdling his friend's recumbent body and being spurred on by a gurgle from beneath the gag, the mighty blond plunged towards the second group. Having seen the deadly effect of his tactics, only two of them had the courage to stand their ground. From the way one was producing his *kris*, he at least had not neglected to acquire the ability which in the terminology of Japanese *samaurai* warriors was called '*lai-jitsu*'.[5] While his only steadfast companion was still extracting the undulating blade from its sheath, he leapt and drove a blow at the approaching giant. Deftly interposed, the shield showed its mettle once again. While the assailing weapon was not

5. Lai-jitsu: *the fast drawing of the longer,* tachi, *of the* samaurai's daisho, *pair of swords. An explanation of how this is performed and how effective it can be in skilled hands is given in the author's biography:* OLE DEVIL AT SAN JACINTO. J.T.E.

191

shattered on this occasion, it rebounded from the un-yielding surface and caused the startled Wurka to release the hilt.

Brushing aside the amazed and suddenly terrified man as if he was merely a bothersome insect, Bunduki deliv-ered a backhand swing upwards with the bowie knife. In doing so, he demonstrated one of the advantages offered by the clip point. As sharp as and, in fact, forming an extension of the main cutting surface, the concave arc of the 'false edge' proved equally effective by slitting the second man's throat to the bone and ending his attempt to arm himself.

Even as the blond giant was about to turn and start dealing with the men who he had felled by knocking Sraat-Challig's dying body among them, he noticed something which brought him to a halt. There was a glint-ing flicker as a metallic object flashed from the bushes ahead of him. Converging with one of the fleeing Wur-kas, whatever it might be did more than merely slit his throat. Nervous reaction alone kept him running for a few more steps. His head was dangling alongside his shoulder by a strip of uncut flesh.

An instant later, another of the departing Wurkas was transfixed by an arrow. Sounds from Bunduki's rear sug-gested that the first party were also under attack from the as yet unseen assailants. Guessing what the instru-ment of decapitation must have been, he wondered who the newcomers might be. No nation with whom he had yet come into contact used a weapon similar to the kind the Karamajong and other tribes of Uganda used as a bracelet-knife.[6]

The blond giant was not kept for long before receiving the answer.

Carrying various types of weapons, most of which

6. *The Sikhs of India use much the same kind of device. Known as a 'chakra' or 'chakram', the war-quoits were carried in decreas-ing sizes over the pointed peak of the warriors' turban-helmets. They were lethal to about fifty yards, but would still inflict damage at twice that distance. In skilled hands, the Cara-Buntes' halakas were equally effective. J.T.E.*

looked to be Oriental in origin, the mysterious assailants burst into view from all around the clearing. With one exception, he decided—from what Hav-Bart had told him during the boat journey from Jey-Mat—they were a party of the seagoing Cara-Buntes.[7]

However, it was the exception which gave Bunduki his greatest shock.

Even with her hair cut shorter than on their last meeting, he recognized the tallest of the women to appear. She definitely was *not* a Cara-Bunte. Clad in her gold lamé costume and waving the ivory hilted sword he remembered so well, but with her legs and feet bare, it was Charole, the Protectress of the Quagga God.

Before Bunduki could begin to wonder how the Mun-Gatah woman had come to be with the Cara-Buntes, for he alone had managed to persuade members of two nations to work in harmony, he heard a swishing hiss coming his direction. Then, although he neither saw nor knew what it was at that moment, a throwing stick caught him on the head and he went down unconscious.

7. *Although it had been several centuries since there had been any contact between the Wurka-Telongas and the Cara-Buntes, the legends still were told about the latter. The former's hunters occasionally had seen Cara-Bunte vessels of various kind passing by in search of a way to reach the hinterland. J.T.E.*

CHAPTER SIXTEEN

TELL US HOW TO MAKE THE "THUNDER POWDER"

'Well, Bunduki of the "Earths",' said Charole, the Protectress of the Quagga God, looking down at the bound figure of the blond giant. 'So we meet again.'

'If you don't mind me saying so,' Bunduki replied. 'The pleasure is all *yours*.'

'You'd do well to consider what I mind, or I do not mind,' Charole warned, kicking the helpless prisoner far from gently in the ribs. 'I only wish that damned bitch of yours was here for me to deal with.'

'Don't worry about *that*,' the blond giant replied, thinking of certain sounds he had heard while recovering from the blow that had knocked him senseless. 'She's not too far away. And when she comes, Protectress-of-the-Quagga-God-who-failed-in-her-duty, she'll make you wish you'd gone the way of the High Priest of your accursed nation.'

'You speak well, Bunduki of the "Earths",' praised War-Lord Torisaki, pushing Charole aside as she tried to deliver another kick to the prisoner. 'Let us hope that your courage doesn't make you blind to your danger and suffering when we ask you to tell us how to make the "Thunder Powder".'

Despite a mutual eagerness on the part of the Protectress, Torisaki, and War-Lady Shushi, to set off in search of the 'Earths', they had been unable to do so for several days. Having been sent by the Emperor of Cara-Bunte to have the 'honour' of providing the large quantities of meat required for a religious festival, and knowing that any failure would be used as an excuse to depose them, the war-lord and his wife had been too cautious to offer such an opportunity. So they had considered that they must complete the task before embarking upon a private mission. If they did not, on the pretence of investigating their 'disappearance', their ruler would send a strong enough force to deal with them. There had been another benefit from attending to their duty. Its completion had, by sending the others to deliver the meat that was gathered, given them an excuse for parting company with all but the crew of their own *zaruk*. Knowing their race's inborn aptitude for conspiracy, they were aware that the fewer people involved would reduce the chance of betrayal. To attain the greatest effect from the possession of 'Thunder Powder' and 'Terrifiers', they must be kept a secret until brought into use.

There had also been benefits in the delay for Charole. It had allowed her to recuperate from the results of the two gruelling fights. With the exception of the 'Thunder Powder' and 'Terrifiers', all her property had been returned. Although she had been kept under observation, no restrictions had been placed upon her movements around the camp. Not that she had wanted to escape. She had never been on a ship, but was sufficiently intelligent to appreciate how travelling in such a manner would offer a better chance of locating the 'Earths'. It had been her belief that they would have organized lookouts among the Telongas and, even if the latter would not fight, on receiving a warning of enemies approaching the two of them would disappear into the jungle. A force arriving unexpectedly by river, which the Mun-Gatahs had never done, was more likely to catch them unawares.

At last all had been ready for the expedition. Charole had allowed herself, not without trepidation, to be transported in a 'bullboat' to the war-lord's *zaruk*. Showing a surprising compassion, Shushi had supplied her with a medication which had quelled the sea-sickness that had assailed her. After the first qualms had passed, she had enjoyed the novel sensation of travelling in such a fashion. One thing she had learned early in the journey. Useful though her sandals were when riding a horse, they offered no such advantages on the deck of the *zaruk*. So she had adopted the Cara-Buntes' way of going barefoot.

Fortune had appeared to favour the expedition. After only one day's searching along the coast, they had captured the three surprisingly co-operative Wurka-Telongas and were guided to their destination. When discussing the plan of campaign, learning that this branch of the normally pacific nation were noted for belligerence although she had seen no sign of it in the trio who had fallen into their hands, Charole had suggested that—being the only one who knew how to make them work—she should carry along the 'Terrifiers'. In this she had only been partially successful. While Torisaki had allowed her to do so, he had restricted her to only one of the devices. Bunduki had not noticed it when he first saw her, but she was carrying her 'fire box' and a bag containing the 'Terrifier' hanging across her shoulders.

For his part, the blond giant had been fortunate. Although the blow he had received knocked him unconscious, the throwing stick had been sent his way at less than full power. In fact, he had been felled by the warlord who was a master in the use of the weapon and wanted to make sure that he was taken alive. As Charole had done on the day of her capture, he had managed to avoid allowing his captors to discover he was conscious for several minutes. By the time the Protectress had come over to favour him with her attentions, his head was clear if aching and he felt that his strength had returned. He had drawn some small comfort from there having been no sign of Dawn and in seeing that, still bound hand and foot, Hav-Bart was alive.

'Why should I need courage to answer questions?' the blond giant asked, despite having a good idea of the reason.

'We wouldn't ask questions from a warrior of *your* standing without putting him to torture first and letting him display his courage,' Torisaki explained, confirming

Bunduki's suspicions. 'Would you have it any other way?'

'Even *if* I knew how to make the "Thunder Powder", you wouldn't make me tell you,' the blond giant stated. 'No matter what torture you try.'

'You don't know how to make it?' Shushi yelped, then turned an angry glare at the Mun-Gatah woman. 'Did you hear that?'

'I heard,' Charole agreed, just as indignantly. 'He's lying!'

'Are you lying, "Earth"?' the war-lord demanded.

'No,' Bunduki said, his tone so convincing that he might have been speaking the truth. 'And I've no desire to be tortured for something that I don't know. Our people have the secret of the "Thunder Powder", but no *man* knows how to make it.'

Unconsciously, the blond giant had given an explanation that the Cara-Bunte couple at least could find acceptable. Among their nation, only women took the profession of herbalist and they were willing to assume the same applied with other races.

'Does your woman know how to make it?' Shushi asked.

'No,' Bunduki lied.

'Does she?' the war-lady repeated, delivering a savage stamping kick to the centre of the captive's chest.

'No!' Bunduki said again, the word coming out in a pain-filled gasp.

'He won't admit it even if she does,' Charole stated. 'Let's catch her and ask her about it.'

'How do we do that?' Torisaki inquired.

'Make him use one of the "Hairy People's" calls to bring her here,' the Protectress suggested. 'If she hears it, she'll come.'

'That's a good idea,' the war-lord agreed and glanced around. 'Here, some of you. I want him between those trees. Start to bend them down.'

Eager hands took hold of Bunduki and hauled him to the desired position. Other members of the party grasped the ropes and began to pull. While they were doing so, Torisaki grasped the blond giant by the hair and hauled him into a sitting position, telling Shushi to liberate his hands. By the time the trees were bent sufficiently low, the war-lady had carried out her task. Her husband took one of the shorter ropes and, while she repeated the process at the other side, drew its noose tight around their captive's right wrist.

'Keep them held down, but tight as he gets up,' the war-lord commanded, as Shushi employed her *rentjong* again to sever the rest of the blond giant's bonds.

Although Deneb-Ginwe had told his captors of the trees' purpose, he had not given precise details of how they were employed. So Torisaki was making a few errors in the way he was fastening the trees. In the first place, he should not have allowed Bunduki to rise. Secondly and even more important, he ought to have made sure that the blond giant was unable to grip the wrist-ropes.

'Now, "Earth",' the war-lord said, after Bunduki had risen. 'Call for your woman to come.'

'No!' the blond giant replied.

Standing on spread apart feet, with his arms bent at shoulder height against the pressure being applied by the taut ropes around his wrists, Bunduki appreciated how his captors had made another mistake in permitting him to adopt such a posture. Not that, he told himself, it would make any great difference in the long run; but it at least gave him a fighting chance to prolong his life.

'You might as well call her,' Shushi remarked, almost as if tendering kindly and well meant advice to a friend. 'If we have to go into the village for her, we'll not leave a man, woman or child alive. And, when she sees how you've died, she'll be only too willing to talk.'

'I won't call!' Bunduki declared.

'Then die, damn you!' Torisaki bellowed. 'Release the ropes!'

Obeying their leader's command, the Cara-Buntes and Charole watched the trees—which had required five men apiece to bend—starting to return to their original positions——

They were stopped long before becoming upright!

Bracing his giant body, Bunduki threw every bit of his enormous strength into combating the strain. He was helped by the various errors that had been made while preparing him for the treatment. Usually the victim was given no chance to make ready and was subjected to a sudden snapping jerk. While he had none of that to add to his misfortunes, he was all too aware of his position. Even if his captors did not take some action to make him relax, he could only restrain the trees while his strength held out. When he weakened, they would straighten and, at the very least, he would be swung upwards and seriously injured.

* * *

'AAAH-EEE-AAAH-EEE-AAGH!'

The voice uttering the challenging roar of an *Australopithecus* might be feminine in timbre, but the sound lost little of its awesome menace because it had not been sent out by a male of the species. Coming as it did so unexpectedly, from beyond the bushes at the opposite side of the Place Of Punishment to that on which the Wurka-Telonga village was situated, it aroused considerable alarm and consternation for most of the occupants of the clearing.

Everybody except the prisoners looked around, trying to discover who—or what—was responsible for the inhuman-sounding roar. Of them all, probably only Charole and Bunduki recognized the nature of the call and knew what it must portend. However, the blond giant alone was able to guess at how his wife was intending to try and effect his rescue.

Much as Dawn Gunn's every instinct had been to dash straight out of Hav-Bart's house and warn her husband of the terrible danger that lay waiting for him, circumstances had prevented her from doing so immediately. Attracted by the commotion, men and women had appeared from the surrounding buildings and soon the whole of the grown up population was foregathered. What was more, every man was carrying something that could be used as a weapon.

One of the last to come on the scene had been Tik-

Felum. On seeing what had happened, his face had registered more alarm than grief over finding that his younger son was dead. He had seen enough to warn him that he had committed a dangerous error in tactics. All the men upon whom he was best able to rely for support were unavailable. From the comments he had overheard and the way in which many of the crowd were behaving, he had guessed that he might have need of his coterie's presence.

Sensing that the villagers were close to rising against the Senior Elder's tyrannical regime and wanting to avoid bloodshed if possible, Dawn had warned the assembled people that the Cara-Buntes were in the vicinity. However, filled with rage, grief and raw anxiety for her abducted husband's welfare, Marn-Bara had exposed the treachery of Tik-Felum and his sons. Before Dawn could intervene, giving a cry of rage, Hav-Bart's younger brother, Kal-Bart, had sprung forward to bury the blade of his *machete* in the Senior Elder's skull.

Much to Dawn's relief, the killing had not provoked an outbreak of inter-factional fighting. In fact, she considered that it had averted hostilities. There were a few men present who had agreed with Tik-Felum's policy of keeping themselves supplied through the efforts of others who were willing to work, but none felt any inclination to try and avenge him. Already aware of the majority of their fellow villagers' sentiments, most of them had assumed airs of disinterest from the beginning. The few who had showed resentment, despite appreciating that their days of officially sponsored idleness were probably coming to an end, had taken warning from the menacing attitudes of the people around them. So they had decided that discretion was called for, and they saw no reason to make a pointless display of loyalty to a man who was already dead.

Satisfied that the situation was well under control and needed no further attention on her part, although it had taken several badly needed minutes to achieve this, Dawn had announced that she was going to help her husband. Immediately, Kal-Bart and several other men had offered to accompany her. Telling them that she would reconnoitre alone first and give the call of a 'Hairy Man' if she needed assistance, she had prepared to leave.

Taking her bow from Marn-Bara, the girl had arranged to have the *m'kuki* retrieved. She had not waited for this to be done, but had asked Hav-Bart's wife to take care of it. Considering her back-quiver would be more of a hindrance than an aid to the work ahead, she had left it and Bunduki's archery equipment behind. Then, having cleaned and sheathed her knife, she had set off.

By the time Dawn had reached the edge of the clearing, Bunduki was sprawling motionless on the ground. There had been no hope of achieving anything in the circumstances, but she had drawn solace from observing that he was bound hand and foot. That implied he was not only alive, but that he had suffered no serious or incapacitating injury.

Hearing the elephants, the girl had considered that they could offer a better and more readily available source of assistance than the men of the village would be. Passing around the fringe of the clearing, she had been too preoccupied with moving as swiftly and quietly as possible to wonder how the Protectress of the Quagga God—who she too had recognized—had contrived to escape death at Bon-Gatah and arrive in the Place of Punishment. Making contact with the animals and obtaining their co-operation had consumed several valuable minutes, but she had been convinced that it was time well spent.

Nor had the girl changed her point of view on returning to the vicinity of the clearing.

That Dawn and her massive assistants had arrived without their presence being detected was not as remarkable as it might appear on the surface. For its size, a forest elephant could move with great stealth and in almost complete silence through even fairly dense undergrowth. Aware of the need to do so, the half a dozen cows and the big herd bull she was riding had approached the clearing with little noise. Their task had been made easier because all the attention of the human beings they were stalking was directed at the blond giant.

Then the girl had impersonated the *Australopithecus'* challenge!

As the last note of the eerie cry was ending, so did the elephants' silence!

Echoing the savage trumpeting of the herd bull, the pachyderms rushed through the undergrowth as if it did not exist. With their great sail-like ears spread and flapping, trunks curled upwards and tusks elevated to the horizontal, they thundered across the clearing.

Due to their homeland being insufficient in size to support a resident population of elephants and because it would have been impractical to transport living specimens in any type of vessel available to the Cara-Buntes, the huge beasts were something beyond the raiding party's ken. Although some of the rival clans had occasionally brought back tusks, trunks, hides and meat, Torisaki's warriors had never seen the animals in the flesh until that moment. However, despite the fact that their nerves had been shaken by what had sounded like the roar from one of the 'Hairy People', the discovery that the largest of the beasts was ridden by a beautiful young woman—who also appeared to be able to control the others—robbed the sight of some of its otherwise awesome effect. So, while alarmed and prepared to take reasonable precautions, they were not driven off in a state of panic as Dawn had hoped would happen.

Only Charole, having been in contact with the larger plains-dwelling sub-species of *Loxodonta Africana*, fully appreciated the deadly danger of the situation. Nor did she feel it was any the less dangerous because the elephants brought by Dawn were somewhat smaller than those with which she was acquainted. In fact, such was the extreme stress of the moment that the approaching animals seemed to be even more enormous and menacing than those she had previously encountered.

For one of the rare occasions in her life, Charole allowed fear to guide her actions. Turning, she ran towards the brink of the escarpment. By doing so, she was offering herself two possible avenues of escape. There was a steep path leading down to the place at which they had landed and where the 'bullboats' were now waiting. Or, if this should prove unattainable for any reason, she was an excellent swimmer and could dive with comparative safety into the deep water that lapped along the foot of the majority of the wall. Once aboard a 'bullboat', she was confident that she could make the *Yung-Lib* crew do her bidding. They were aware that her status had gained importance since forming an alliance with their owners.

While Torisaki lacked Charole's knowledge of elephants, he realized that Dawn would not have brought them unless convinced they could cope with his party. Their sheer size alone meant that they could prove very dangerous. Nor would the small force at his disposal be able to stop them. What was more, he suspected that the roar made by the girl was to signal for reinforcements. So, for reasons of expediency rather than humanity, he gave thought to saving his warriors from loss of life.

'Scatter into the trees!' the war-lord thundered, snatching the *lading* from its sheath. 'Get back to the "bullboats", we're leaving!'

Sharing her husband's appreciation of the peril, Shushi did not wait to be given advice. A glance over her shoulder warned that she could not follow Charole and take the shortest way to safety. So she swung and set off in what would be a semi-circular route to reach the edge of the escarpment.

In spite of having started the other members of his party on their way to safety, Torisaki did not follow them immediately. As he was to be driven off without learning the secret of the 'Thunder Powder' and doubted whether he would ever again be fortunate enough to be in a position to learn it, he intended to kill the blond giant before taking his departure. Raising the *lading* to strike, he moved forward without showing any caution.

On the point of deciding which avenue of escape offered the greatest possibilities, Charole became aware that she was carrying what might prove a means of turning the situation back into her favour. Even if it did not, she would be able to avenge herself by bringing about the deaths of one, hopefully both, of the 'Earths.' With that in mind, pausing close to the rim of the escarpment, she started to take out the 'Terrifier'.

Seing the war-lord rushing at him, Bunduki was all too aware of his peril. Dawn was unable to use her bow with any hope of success from the pitching back of the fast moving elephant. Nor was she close enough to do anything else to help. So his salvation would have to be achieved unaided. As the *lading* rose until it was behind Torisaki's head, the blond giant took a firmer grip on the wrist-ropes. Then he bounded as if performing a wrestling drop-kick. Hurling his legs forward, the soles of his feet drove into the centre of his assailant's chest.

The sheer force and unexpectedness of the attack flung the war-lord backwards in the direction of an elephant. Winded and hurt so badly that he dropped his weapon, he felt the trunk coiling around his body. The scream which burst involuntarily from him came to an abrupt end as the elephant's precision instrument tightened with brutal efficiency. Raised into the air, he was dashed down again and a huge forefoot ground his body into a bloody pulp beneath it.

Although the Cara-Buntes had scattered in obedience to their leader's orders, they were merely displaying discretion. In fact, one of the women was sufficiently cool to try and salvage something from the situation. After his capture, Bunduki's shield and knife had been examined and laid aside until they could be delivered to the 'bull-boats'. Like the others, she had been impressed by the excellent quality of the weapons and she decided to collect them before leaving.

As she saw the woman running towards the weapons, Dawn was determined to prevent them from being stolen. Bunduki was dealing with the war-lord and she had no fears for his immediate safety. What was more, she had already made arrangements for him to be helped.

Swinging her leg forward, she thrust herself clear of the swiftly-moving elephant's back. Alighting with the cat-like agility which had brought her success as a gymnast, she used the momentum she had gathered in closing with the woman.

So eager was the female warrior to acquire such desirable loot that she failed to appreciate the danger. She was bending over to take up the weapons when she received notice of the Earth girl's proximity. Rising, Dawn's right foot caught the woman in the face. Lifted erect, with her nose gushing blood, she went over backwards and her head struck the ground hard enough to knock her senseless.

Although Bunduki had saved himself from the warlord's attack and contrived to alight on his feet, the terrible strain being imposed upon his arms increased. However, he was not to suffer for much longer. Advancing and displaying the sagacity for which their species was renowned, two of the elephants applied their tremendous weight and strength to snap and bring down the trees. This gave him relief, but he was still held by the ropes around his wrists.

Glancing around as she heard the crackling of breaking wood, Dawn appreciated the gravity of Bunduki's predicament. Having carried out their function, the elephants were running on and the rest of the herd were chasing individual members of the Cara-Bunte party. There was a chance that some of the warriors who were not the subject of the animals' attentions would return and take up the attack.

Thinking fast, the girl decided what she could do for the best. Plucking her husband's knife from where it was sticking in the ground, she ran towards him. Equally aware of the peril, Bunduki put his right foot on the tree and drew the cord tight about his wrist. That allowed his wife to liberate the arm all the more quickly. Slicing through the strands, the razor sharp steel made short work of their destruction.

There was no time for either Dawn or the blond giant to speak. Nor was she able to complete the task. A fortunate gaze around informed her of what the Protectress was doing. The discovery brought pure primitive emotion. What little shred of the girl's civilized upbringing remained after the traumatic events of the evening disintegrated as her eyes met those of the woman who had twice almost caused her death.

'Charole!' Dawn screamed, and the raw animal fury in her voice made the word a savage, primeval challenge to mortal combat rather than a name.

Throwing aside her bow without a thought that she might damage it, Dawn thrust the unsharpened back of the bowie knife's blade into Bunduki's liberated hand. Then, snatching her own weapon from its sheath, she darted towards her hated enemy.

Seeing Dawn coming, Charole forgot her original intentions. All the deep and bitter hatred she felt over the way in which the 'Earths' had been responsible for the reverses in her fortunes boiled into a seething rage. She had the 'Terrifier' in her right hand and was fumbling with the lid of the 'fire box' so as to extract the means of igniting it. Discarding the device, she jerked free the carrying strap of the 'fire box' and let it fall. With both hands at liberty and an encumbrance to mobility disposed of, she started to snatch out her sword.

Running through the trees, Shushi had heard and identified her husband's scream of mortal pain. Looking around, past the cow elephant which was in hot pursuit, she swerved and flattened her back against the trunk of a large tree. What she had seen so filled her with rage that she ignored the danger to herself. Puzzled by her disappearance, the cow had its eye caught by one of the fleeing male warriors. It thundered past the hidden warlady and made him the successful subject of its attentions.

Returning to the clearing, Shushi was in a frenzy of grief and anger. For all that, she was able to decide how best to avenge her husband's death. Although the blond giant had one arm free, his other was still fastened to the top of the broken tree. So she would be able to take a more subtle vengeance than killing him immediately. His woman was running towards Charole. Her death would let him know the pangs of losing a loved one, but only for as long as it took the war-lady to give him her undivided attention.

With that thought in mind, Shushi snatched free the uppermost of her two *halakas*. No other woman in Cara-Bunte-the weapon was only employed by female warriors-could equal her skill in throwing for distance and accuracy. Never had she taken more care, nor been so determined to make a hit, as while she was preparing to deal with the 'Earth' woman.

The hole in the centre of the *halaka* was for carrying purposes only. To throw it, the user held it between her thumb and forefinger, then swung her arm in a whip-like motion horizontally from left to right.

Carrying out the procedure in a way that had become second nature to her, Shushi sent the weapon hissing towards the 'Earth' woman's running back. It was aimed to catch her behind the neck and would come close to taking her head from her shoulders when it arrived.

'Drop, Dawn!' Bunduki roared, having seen what the war-lady was up to and retaining a vivid memory of how one of the Wurka-Telongas had been killed by such a device.

Although the girl had no idea why her husband had given the warning, the urgency in his tone was such that she instantly obeyed. Nor was she a moment too soon. Spinning by above her head, the *halaka* almost brushed against her hair in passing. However, having missed, it continued its flight to Charole's horror.

On the point of dashing to meet the 'Earth' girl, the Protectress saw the deadly missile thrown and its aftermath. To her terror, the razor-edged, whirling harbinger of death was now coming straight at her. Although involuntary, her reaction was to save her life. Forgetting how close she was to the edge of the escarpment, she took a pace to the rear. Her foot came down on empty air and she toppled backwards. Just as it had narrowly missed Dawn's head, so it came close to grazing the tip of Charole's nose as it flew past. Managing to retain her hold on the sword as she plunged downwards, she also contrived to turn what started out as a helpless plunge into something just passable as a dive before she reached the river and entered it without injury.

Seeing the failure of her first *halaka*, Shushi did not offer to use the other. Instead, she rushed forward. Although she realized from what she saw that there was no hope of reaching her enemy before Dawn stood up, neither did she draw the *rentjong*. Not only could it be used most advantageously straight from the sheath, but the way in which it was produced had frequently allowed her to get the best of opponents from other nations who did not appreciate its deadly qualities.

Confirming the war-lady's summation with regard to her agility, Dawn did not stay down for long. In fact, the moment the *halaka* had passed overhead, she prepared to rise. A glance over her shoulder had warned her of just how little time was available for her to do so. Bounding up, she whirled to halt in a knife-fighter's crouch and studied the way in which Shushi was approaching.

Employing similar tactics to those which had proved successful in combats against captured Mun-Gatah, Gruziak and Amazon female warriors, the war-lady advanced with her hands held as if she did not intend to rely upon a weapon. Not until she was close enough for her system to operate effectively did she put her real purpose into effect. Darting across, her right hand closed around the extended 'bill' of the *rentjong's* 'duck's head' hilt. She commenced the move with her left leg in advance. As the blade was leaving the sheath with its cutting edge turned towards her enemy, she brought her right foot forward in a short, quick step that was calculated to add impetus to the stroke she was about to essay. The blow would be made by whipping the weapon to the right, turning her hand so that the palm was upwards and keeping the elbow close to her side. Then, on thrusting until the arm was fully extended, she would rotate her fist until its knuckles faced the ground just prior to the point penetrating the target.

On every previous occasion that Shushi had delivered

such an attack, she had emerged victorious. However, none of her former antagonists had been conversant with the most effective way in which a *rentjong* could be used. Unfortunately for her, she knew nothing of Dawn's family background.

In the course of an eventful life, Sir Armond John Drummond-Clayton had had many occasions when his continued existence had depended upon his ability to use a knife. So he had taken a great interest in all matters pertaining to the subject. While other members of his family had travelled the world studying wild animals, his journeying had also encompassed investigating the specialized ways in which the trenchant arms of various nations could be used.

Having helped in the production of her father's book[1]—which had entailed a detailed study of films showing various types of weapons in use—and being possessed of an excellent retentive memory, Dawn was aware of the *rentjong's* unique qualities. She had seen them being wielded by the designers, the Atjehs of Sumatra. Furthermore, she had learned the counter move perfected by Sir Armond. What was more, effective as the *rentjong* was, she held the finest product that the experience of expert knife-fighters and skilled craftsmen could produce.[2] One noted authority[3] had referred to

1. *Sir Armond John Drummond-Clayton's definitive work*, KNIFE FIGHTING THROUGHOUT THE WORLD, *like an equally comprehensive treatise on unarmed combat techniques written by Commander James Bond, R.N.—its preparation is referred to in his biographer, Ian Fleming's* DOCTOR NO—*were published by Her Majesty's Stationery Office. However, being classified 'Top Secret', the only copies of both works are in the possession of Britain's M.I.5 and the United States of America's Central Intelligence Agency.* J.T.E.

2. *Because of his own country's and Britain's Official Secrets Act, W.D. Randall, of Randall Made Knives, Orlando, Florida, has never been able to give Sir Armond John Drummond-Clayton the credit he deserves for his part in helping to develop the Model 1 'All Purpose' fighting knife. In fact, it was only with difficulty that the author was allowed to mention it. See Footnote 3, Appendix One.* J.T.E.

3. *Judge Roy S. Tinney, Secretary of the American Academy of Arms.* J.T.E.

the Randall Model 1 'All Purpose' fighting knife as a 're-fined and perfected "bowie".' So she was well equipped materially as well as mentally to cope with this latest threat to her life.

Acting with the same almost instinctive reflexes that had carried her through all of the evening's events, Dawn brought her knife around to meet the out-thrusting *rentjong*. At which point, Shushi learned how it felt to be taken unawares. It was a lesson from which she would never profit. She realized that her weapon was being deflected. Even as an understanding of what that meant began to sink home, it was too late to react to the peril.

Liberating her own blade, Dawn used it with swift and deadly precision!

Flickering briefly as it moved, a gash which became crimson an instant later opened across the war-lady's throat in the wake of the knife's passage. Letting the *rentjong* slip from her fingers, she sent her hands in a mindless and futile attempt to staunch the blood that was pouring from the mortal wound. Stepping swiftly aside as she completed the stroke, Dawn allowed her stricken assailant to be carried onwards by the momentum of the averted attack. Knowing that she was dying on her feet, Shushi forced herself to stumble onwards until she could fall across the lifeless body of her husband.

Still in the throes of the primeval driving force which more than anything else had kept her alive under conditions she had never known on Earth, Dawn tossed a look after the war-lady. Then she ran to the edge of the escarpment. Down below, she saw Charole being hauled into one of the 'bullboats'. Under the urgings of the Protectress, it was cast off and set into motion.

Hearing footsteps approaching, Dawn swung around ready to continue fighting. She discovered that there was no need. Having liberated himself, Bunduki was coming to join her. Before either could say a word, a hate-filled voice rose from beyond the rim of the cliff.

'The Quagga God curse you, Dawn and Bunduki of the "Earths". I'll be revenged upon you yet!'

Moving forward, the blond giant and his wife looked down at the speaker. Standing in the departing 'bull-boat', Charole was shaking a furious fist at them.

'She means it, darling,' Bunduki warned.

'Let her come back any time she likes,' Dawn replied, spitting out the words savagely. 'But if she does, *I'll* make sure she'll never have another chance to kill us!'

APPENDIX ONE

James Allenvale 'Bunduki' Gunn's tremendous physique and strength were hereditary. On his father's side, he was descended from an illegitimate son of Sir Henry Curtis who had accompanied the great white hunter, Allan Quatermain on two epic journeys of exploration in Africa.[1] His mother, Allison Dawn 'Tex' Gunn, was the granddaughter of Mark Counter, a Texan who in the mid-1800's had attained legendary status by virtue of his Herculean powers, as a cowhand, peace officer and all round fighting man.[2] Nor had his parents proved unworthy of such bloodlines. Along with Sir Armond John and Lady Hazel Drummond-Clayton, they had served in the little known but highly effective 'Group Thirteen' Special Missions Organization of British Military Intelligence all through World War II.[3]

When Bunduki's parents were murdered by Mau Mau terrorists, he had been adopted by a wealthy titled family who were related to Dawn. In their care, he had received the education which fitted him perfectly for sur-

1. *If Sir Henry Curtis's biographer, H. Rider Haggard, knew of the son, he was too tactful to mention the matter in* KING SOLOMON'S MINES *or* ALLAN QUATERMAIN. *J.T.E.*

2. *Mark Counter's history is recorded in the author's 'Floating Outfit' series of biographies. J.T.E.*

3. *Even to this day, British Military Intelligence are reluctant to comment upon, or even acknowledge the existence of 'Group Thirteen'. J.T.E.*

vival on Zillikian. Arguably the world's foremost authority on wild life and wilderness survival, his adopted father had imparted much practical knowledge. Bunduki had been taught how to follow tracks which were scarcely discernible to less keen eyes, to move in silence even through dense undergrowth, to locate hidden enemies and conceal himself from them when necessary and to climb with great agility. He had the knowledge to find or hunt for food, while his training in various forms of fighting allowed him to protect himself against predators or human foes.

In Bunduki's hands, the Randall Model 12 'Smithsonian' bowie knife—sixteen inches in overall length, weighing forty-three ounces, with an eleven inch long, two and a quarter inch wide, three-eighths of an inch thick clip point[4] blade—was an even more effective weapon than James Bowie had found the original.[5] Sir Armond Drummond-Clayton had taught him fighting techniques which were unknown in Bowie's day. In archery, he had acquired sufficient skill to duplicate most of the feats attributed to Robin Hood. From a Masai *melombuki*[6] he had learned to throw a *m'kuki*, that nation's traditional spear and handle a shield. During visits to the United States, along with his Texas-born look-

4. *'Clip' point: one where the back of the blade curves to meet the main cutting surface in a concave arc. In the case of the Randall Model 12 'Smithsonian' bowie knife, the arc's 'false', or 'top' cutting edge is five and a quarter inches in length and as sharp as the main cutting surface. J.T.E.*

5. *What happened to James Bowie's knife after his death at the conclusion of the siege at the Alamo Mission—San Antonio de Bexar, Texas—on March the 6th, 1836, is told in* THE QUEST FOR BOWIE'S BLADE. *Some authorities have claimed that Bowie's elder brother, Rezin Pleasant, was the actual designer of the knife which was made by Arkansas' master cutler, James Black. J.T.E.*

6. Melombuki: *a Masai moran—warrior—who has on four separate occasions grasped and held the tail of a hunted lion so that his companions could close in and kill it with their spears or simis—fighting knives. A man who attains the title is expected to be ready to fight anybody, or anything. J.T.E.*

alike cousin Bradford Counter,[7] he had been instructed in the arts of horse handling and lariat throwing by a pure bred Comanche Indian. To round off his knowledge of martial arts, he was equally adept at fencing with a sabre or an epee[8] and had gained great proficiency at boxing, judo, karate and plain, old fashioned rough house brawling.

7. *Details of Bradford Counter's career as a deputy sheriff are given in the author's 'Rockabye County' series of treatises on modern Texas law enforcement. J.T.E.*

8. *Generally a sabre is used for slashing when mounted, while an epee's primary purpose is thrusting and fighting on foot. J.T.E.*

APPENDIX TWO

Always something of a tomboy, Dawn Drummond-Clayton had—with her parents' full approval—duplicated the lessons in martial arts and wilderness survival that her inseparable companion, Bunduki, was receiving. Even during her formal and conventional education, which had not been neglected, she had contrived to keep up her training and did not forget what she had been taught. In addition, while attending Roedean,[1] she had taken part in every permissible form of sporting and athletic activity, excelling in them all. However, like Bunduki, she had become completely disenchanted by the blatantly one-sided political bias and hypocrisy of the international sporting bodies and authorities. So, in spite of being a world class athlete, gymnast, swimmer and fencer with either sabre or epee, she had refused to compete in their events. For all that, she had always kept herself at the peak of physical condition.

As was the case with Bunduki, much of Dawn's perfect physical health stemmed from being allowed to share in some longevity pills obtained by his adoptive

1. *Although Sir Armond John and Lady Hazel Drummond-Clayton served in 'Group Thirteen' with Miss A.P. (Amelia) Benkinsop, M.A., B. Sc. (Oxon), Honorary Member, Holloway Old Girls' Association—some details of whose career are recorded in the author's* BLONDE GENIUS, *written in collaboration with Peter Clawson—their family background did not meet the specialized qualifications for Dawn to be allowed to attend Benkinsop's Academy For The Daughters Of Gentlefolk. J.T.E.*

parents. Specimens had been given to Dr. Clark Savage, J.R.,[2] for analysis and reproduction. He had discovered that, in addition to slowing down the ageing process in human beings—granting those who took them what amounted to immortality, barring accidental death, suicide, or murder—they also gave immunity from practically every tropical disease and destroyed all such harmful internal parasites as the various nematode worms—commonly called 'hookworms'—of the genera *Necator* which might be ingested when eating the raw flesh of wild animals.[3]

So, with such qualifications, Dawn was ideally suited to survive on Zillikian and made a fitting mate for the man who had been created the *Dapan-Dankara*, the Fearless Master Of The Jungle.

---

2. *Details of Clark Savage, Jr.'s life and adventures are recorded in Kenneth Robeson's extensive series of 'DOC SAVAGE' biographies and in DOC SAVAGE, HIS APOLYPTIC LIFE by Philip José Farmer. This latter work also elaborates upon the source of the longevity pills. J.T.E.*

3. *Unfortunately Doc Savage was unable to isolate the immunity element so that it could be reproduced without the added effect of increasing the recipient's life expectancy. The latter factor, taken with the human race's ever multiplying birthrate, would have led to Earth becoming over-populated. So it was decided that the pills were unsuitable for general use and they were never released to the public. J.T.E.*

APPENDIX THREE

Dwelling upon the open plains of the planet Zillikian, the Mun-Gatah nation was so dependant upon its domesticated zebras—which bore about the same resemblance to the wild animals as, on Earth, an Arabian Thoroughbred, American Saddlebred, or English Hunter does to the tarpan, *Equus Caballus Gmelini,* or Przewalski's horse, *E.C. Przewalskii,* that are believed to have been the progenitors of all the various domesticated breeds of *E.C. Caballus*—that its entire culture was based upon the different sub-species of *Equus Quagga.* In fact, roughly translated, the nation's name means the 'Riders of the Striped Animals'.

The lowest social order ride the *grar-gatah,* which has the black and white stripes, forming a gridiron pattern on the hind quarters, in the manner of the Grant's zebra, *E.Q. Grantii.* People of the next higher grade use the *ocha-gatah,* with the orange, or cream, and black colouration of the Burchell's, *E.Q. Burchellii.* The aristocracy have the *banar-gatah,* which resembles the Grevy's, *E.Q. Grevyi,* by being larger than the other two and in having numerous narrow black stripes, but no transverse bars on the rump. A further sub-division among the classes comes from whether one rides a stallion, gelding, or mare. There are also medium and heavy draught animals known as *tuh-* and *moh-gatahs,* derived from the *grar-* and *ocha-gatahs.*

Because of their importance in the nation's religious

217

beliefs, only the six-man Council of Elders, the High Priest, the Protectress of the Quagga God, the six District Administrators and their wives are allowed to ride the rarest of the sub-species, the quagga, *E.Q. Quagga*.

Transported to the primitive planet of Zillikian by the mysterious 'Suppliers', Dawn Drummond-Clayton and James Allenvale Gunn—whose sobriquet 'Bunduki' was derived from the Swahili word meaning a hand-held firearm—were far removed from the civilized life they had known on Earth. Not only did the jungles and plains abound with all kinds of dangerous animals, the human population lived by raiding and warfare, regarding every person who did not belong to their respective nations as an enemy to be attacked on sight. So, being the only known representatives of their race, the Earth couple found that almost everybodies' hand would be turned against them. It was not a situation in which weaklings or cowards could survive. Fortunately for Dawn and Bunduki, neither of them came into such a category.

Possessed of Herculean strength, an expert in the use of knife, bow, spear and shield, Bunduki proved himself to be a warrior second to none and earned the title, Fearless Master Of The Jungle. For all that, when he was taken captive by the most implacable of their foes, only Dawn's courage and ability stood between him and a very painful death.

Just as startled as Bunduki had been at the sight of the infuriated grizzly turning upon her, Dawn duplicated his estimation of her dire straits. While her right hand was starting to pluck free a second arrow, she realized that the attacking beast would reach her before she could make use of it. What was more, despite the speed at which it was approaching, it still retained sufficient manoeuvrability to be able to counter any evasive attempt she made.

Striding out with all the speed he could muster, Bunduki converged with the grizzly. Thrusting ahead his left hand, he sank his fingers deep into and grasped the long hair on the back of the predator's neck. Giving it no chance to react to such treatment, he vaulted astride it as if making a flying mount on to a passing horse.

To Dawn, who was engrossed in trying to gauge the best moment for what in all probability would prove a pointless leap aside, it seemed as if the blond giant had suddenly materialized upon the grizzly's back out of thin air. Regardless of her surprise, she did not allow it to blind her to the fact that she was still far from out of danger. She could guess what Bunduki was hoping to do; but she was equally aware that, even if he succeeded, it would not be swiftly enough to prevent the enraged animal from reaching where she was now standing.

If you have enjoyed reading this book and other works by the same author, why not join

THE J. T. EDSON APPRECIATION SOCIETY

You will receive a signed photograph of J. T. Edson, bi-monthly Newsletters giving details of all new books and re-prints of earlier titles.

Competitions with autographed prizes to be won in every issue of the Edson Newsletter.

A chance to meet J. T. Edson.

Send S.A.E. for details and membership form to:

The Secretary,
J. T. Edson Appreciation Society,
P.O. Box 13,
MELTON MOWBRAY,
Leics.

BEGUINAGE by J. T. EDSON

To protect the life of a visiting European Crown Prince from threatened assassination, the Governor of Texas could have called up the Texas Rangers, or even the United States Army. Instead, Stanton Howard obtained the services of Ole Devil Hardin's floating outfit. Dusty Fog, Mark Counter, the Ysabel Kid and Waco had handled many dangerous people in their time but they'd never met the like of the one employed by this band of conspirators to kill the Crown Prince. Acknowledged as Europe's premier assassin, Beguinage came and went unnoticed by all except the victims. And he never failed in an assignment. The only way Dusty saw of saving the Prince was to use himself as bait for a trap—knowing that when it was sprung, either Beguinage or he would be dead . . .

0 552 10769 7   65p

THE WHIP AND THE WARLANCE by J. T. EDSON

Having thwarted one scheme to invade Canada from the USA, Belle Boyd, the Rebel Spy, and the Remittance Kid were hunting the leaders of the plot, who had escaped and were plotting another attempt. To help them, they called upon a young lady called Miss Martha Jane Canary—better known as Calamity Jane . . . Belle, Calamity and the Kid made a good team, but they knew they would need all their fighting skills when the showdown came. For they faced leLoup Garou and the Jan-Dark, the legendary warrior maid with the warlance who, it had long been promised, would come to rally all the Indian nations and drive the white man from Canada.

0 552 10964 9   65p

A SELECTED LIST OF CORGI WESTERNS
FOR YOUR READING PLEASURE

CORGI BOOKS, Cash Sales Department, P.O. Box 11, Falmouth, Cornwall. Please send cheque or postal order, no currency.

U.K. Please allow 30p for the first book, 15p for the second book and 12p for each additional book ordered to a maximum charge of £1.29.

B.F.P.O. & EIRE allow 30p for the first book, 15p for the second book plus 12p per copy for the next 7 books, thereafter 6p per book.

Overseas customers. Please allow 50p for the first book plus 15p per copy for each additional book.

NAME (black letters) _____

ADDRESS _____

(JULY 1980) _____